Hertfordshire

12/12/2011

05/01/2012

30/4/15

LET

Please renew/return this item by the last date shown.

From Area codes 01923 or 020:	From Area codes of Herts:
Renewals: 01923 471373	01438 737373
Enquiries: 01923 471333	01438 737333
Textphone: 01923 471599	01438 737599

CIRCULATING STOCK ROUTE 22

www.hertsdirect.org/librarycatalogue

Also by Louise Ure

Forcing Amaryllis

The Fault Tree

Liars Anonymous

LOUISE URE

MINOTAUR BOOKS ✿ NEW YORK

This is a work of fiction. All of the characters, organizations, and events portrayed in this novel are either products of the author's imagination or are used fictitiously.

www.minotaurbooks.com

The Library of Congress has cataloged the hardcover edition as follows:

Ure, Louise.
    Liars anonymous : a novel / by Louise Ure.
        p. cm.
    ISBN 978-0-312-37586-7
    1. Murder—Fiction. 2. Emergency road service—Fiction.
3. Arizona—Fiction. I. Title.
PS3621.R4L53 2009
813'.6—dc22

                                                2008036058

ISBN 978-0-312-61493-5 (trade paperback)

First Minotaur Books Paperback Edition: February 2010

10 9 8 7 6 5 4 3 2 1

To my sister, Lee Ure,
who always recognized my lies,
and called them a gift for fiction

ACKNOWLEDGMENTS

Once again I've been blessed to have the help of a remarkable group of friends and experts in writing this book.

I continue to owe a debt of gratitude to Judith Greber (aka Gillian Roberts) for her marvelous plotting and editing suggestions and for her friendship. I would not be writing without her. And to Brian Washington and David Arnold, whose expert advice about everything from tattoos and bodybuilding to guns and VW hubcaps made this a better book than it started out to be.

To Eldon Dallas of Arizona and Robert Levin of New Mexico, my thanks for the use of their names and so much more.

And special thanks to Dr. Jane McFarlane for her insight on the science of telematic services such as those I describe at the fictional HandsOn company. She provided the real technology. I twisted it to serve my own purposes here.

To Philip Spitzer and Lukas Ortiz at the Philip G. Spitzer Literary Agency: you two keep my heart afloat. And to Andrew Martin, Michael Homler, and the whole crew at St. Martin's Press: my thanks for your enthusiasm and belief in me.

Bruce, you are in my heart, as always.

Liars Anonymous

CHAPTER ONE

I got away with murder once, but it doesn't look like that's going to happen again. Damn. This time I didn't do it. Well, not all of it, anyway.

The incoming call showed up as an alert on my computer screen at almost midnight Friday night. I balled up the paper wrapper from the cold burrito I'd called dinner and reached for the mouse. There were more than a hundred of us on the night shift, each sequestered in separate cubicles and hunched over our screens like penitents in a confessional. The room was supercooled to keep us awake. I laughed at the irony that, although it was September, it was probably still ninety degrees outside in the Arizona desert.

According to the information on the screen, the client's name was Markson and he was driving a 2007 Cadillac Seville. The HandsOn service he'd signed up for included automatic notification to the call center if his air bag had been triggered.

"HandsOn Emergency. This is Jessie. Is there an emergency in the vehicle?"

A muffled response. Coughing. He was probably still patting back the doughy folds of air bag that had assaulted him, reeling from the sting of the high-powered blast of the nylon bag on his cheeks and chest. His face would be dusted with white powder from the explosion. His nose might be broken.

"I'm all right." More coughing. "Just got rear-ended."

"Is anyone in your car injured? Do you want me to call an ambulance?" It must have been quite a hit; rear-enders rarely set off the air bag.

There was something like a groan. Then the metal-on-metal snick of a car door shutting.

"No, I'm okay. I'll check with the other guy."

Another car door opened and shut, the sound closer this time.

"Didn't you see . . ." Markson's voice trailed off in the distance.

The map on my screen showed that the car was in Tucson. Weird. The call center was responsible for a thousand-mile section from Southern California to East Texas. Funny to get a call from just down the road.

The blinking cursor showed Darren Markson's car near Agua Caliente Wash on the east side of town. The "hot water" in the name of the arroyo was pure wishful thinking; it would only see water during the monsoon runoffs. Probably not even a paved road out there, if the map markings were right. More desert than city, really. The creosote would be taller than the Cadillac's windows.

The sound of scuffling came through my earpiece. I pushed the plastic ear bud tight to my head in concentration. Panting. A soft thud.

"I told you . . ." A deeper voice, it carried the hot, dusty smell of Mexico in the slurred bridge between the words. Almost "toll Jew."

Something slammed against nearby metal, then the sound of breaking glass.

"You lying sack of . . ." A different voice. English as a first language. Beer as a second.

Deep, fight-for-air panting. Heavy thuds of elbows or boots

against the Cadillac's solid metal door. A long exhaled breath. Then silence. A kicked pebble ricocheted off metal as someone moved away.

"Mr. Markson? Mr. Markson! Are you all right?"

The silence was louder than the voices had been.

Whatever was going on, it required the cops. I called the 911 operator in Tucson. In most cases, I'd make the connection and then let the client and 911 operator talk directly to each other, but Markson seemed to have his hands full right now.

"This is HandsOn Emergency dispatcher Jessie Dancing. One of our clients is having some trouble. He's been rear-ended out near Agua Caliente Wash, just north of Soldier Trail."

"Give me the details on the car."

"It's a white Cadillac Seville, Arizona plates, David-Edward-Nora Zero Six Six. I heard what sounded like a fight, and now I've lost contact with Mr. Markson."

"We'll send a patrol car."

I gave her my number and hung up, then flipped back to the open communications channel with Markson's car. If it was a fight, who'd started it? Markson or the guy who'd crashed into him? And I thought I'd heard three voices.

There was movement now—the susurration of fabric on fabric. And something that sounded like the glove box opening then clicking shut again.

"Mr. Markson? Are you okay?"

A grunted acknowledgment, then silence. The connection had gone dead.

I zapped an audio copy of the Markson conversation over to Mad Cow. Madeleine Cowell was her real name, but I treasured the friendship that allowed me to use the shortened honorific. She was on the concierge team tonight—the HandsOn operators that made hotel and restaurant reservations for clients—not the emergency dispatch group. *Take a listen to this*, I typed. Easy enough to walk right over to her cubicle and ask her myself, but this way I didn't have to leave my computer screen unattended.

Mad Cow's return e-mail popped into view. *Is this going to be one of the Dumb Questions?* Mad Cow and I had adapted comedian Bill Engvall's "Here's Your Sign" skits to life at HandsOn. You know the ones. "Tire go flat?" "No. The other three just swelled right up on me." The current pick for the dumbest incoming call was the guy who phoned last week and asked if I could tell him if his car was running.

Not this time. I thought this guy was in trouble, but I'm not sure. I thought it sounded like a couple of guys at a kegger, she answered.

Maybe she was right. Maybe I'd imagined the threat in those voices.

I tried to put the sounds in the most positive light. Say Markson wandered into this patch of trackless desert—got stuck in the sand—and somehow got tapped by another car that was trying to help push him out. The "I told you" and sounds of a scuffle could just be a couple of guys trying to dislodge a car from deep sand.

But I couldn't get around the third voice. The one that had said "you lying sack of" something. That made it more serious than a couple of guys straining their calf muscles and debating whose insurance was going to cover the damage.

Now that Markson's first call had been disconnected I couldn't initiate another call to his car—well, not legally. Our customers frowned on the notion that we might listen in whenever we wanted to.

His personal cell phone information was listed on the screen, too. I listened through five rings and an even-tempered voicemail greeting, then left my number for him to call back.

I turned the volume all the way up and replayed his incoming call. There was a breath of desert air and the scritch of creosote branches on metal, sounds I hadn't heard the first time around. Markson must have had the windows open. And I heard the same words as before, although Markson's voice sounded more nasal than I'd first thought. Maybe the airbag really had broken his nose.

There were at least three voices—one born in a big city in the East, one nurtured on the stony mesas of Mexico, and one coming straight from a bar. And there was definitely a fight.

I'd never had a call drop like this before. The satellite communications system we used was much more powerful than a regular cell phone, so it wasn't likely that he'd gone out of range or lost the connection. More likely, somebody inside the car had pushed the button to disconnect.

Fuck the privacy laws. I shut off the automatic recording system and pinged the car. It was still in the same spot.

I opened the phone channel to allow me to hear what was going on. Voices muttered in the distance—the cadence and consonants sounding more like Spanish than English. I couldn't tell how many voices or what they were saying. The sound of something dragged across brittle vegetation, and a rasping sound that I couldn't place. Heavy, smacking thumps of wood against something softer. A grunt of air with the effort. A scream and a groan in response.

I didn't say anything, unwilling—even though I was almost a hundred miles away—to let them know that I was a witness to the scene. A coward, hiding on the other end of a satellite phone.

The heavy thuds continued but the moaned responses stopped.

I called the cops back, but didn't tell them about listening in again on Markson's car. What good would that do anyway? It was against the law, it wasn't recorded, and I didn't have anything but a scary premonition to tell them about.

"Have your officers found the car yet?"

"They're on their way. We had a delay here with a drive-by shooting."

"Call me when you find him. Okay?"

It was almost two a.m. before I got a call back.

"This is Officer Painter."

Thank God it wasn't anybody I knew on the Tucson PD. I'd changed my name to Dancing—it was my middle name and my mother's maiden name—but there had been plenty of headlines back then that included it. Hopefully this guy wouldn't make the connection. "Did you find the Cadillac?"

"Yeah, just where you said it would be." He sounded young.

"How's Mr. Markson?"

"There's no one here."

Maybe Markson got a ride from the other driver or went to get a tow truck. But he wouldn't have needed to; I could have done that for him. HandsOn clients knew that. It's why they paid as much as my monthly food bill for the service.

"But . . . ma'am?"

This kid was making me feel decades older than my thirty-two years.

"There's blood everywhere."

CHAPTER TWO

"The car got rammed from behind, that's for sure," the officer continued, "but the blood's on the ground, not in the vehicle."

I told him about the three voices and the fight I thought I'd heard, then couldn't keep from asking, "A lot of blood?"

"It was no nosebleed. We'll have officers check the tow companies and emergency rooms. See if they've heard from him."

"Will you have somebody stop by his house, too? His wife's name is Emily." She was listed as another driver on the policy. I hadn't heard a woman's voice on the call, but I wanted to make sure she was okay.

"An officer's on his way there now."

I alerted Denny, the shift supervisor, and he had me send a copy of our data to the Tucson PD. Maybe there was something in the taped conversation or the location information that would help them find Mr. Markson.

I kept replaying the sounds and my actions until, like water on hard-packed caliche, they'd worn a thin, deep rut in my mind. Was there anything else I should have done? Should I have called out "Stop! I'm calling the cops!" over the speaker phone when I heard the beating? Would that have mattered to them at all?

Another call came in; a remote door unlock, this time from Albuquerque.

"My baby's in the car!"

She sounded like she'd been drinking, and I didn't like the notion of helping her get back behind the wheel.

"How old is your little one?" Keep her calm. Keep her talking.

"Almost eleven."

I'd have to tell Mad Cow. We may have another candidate in the Dumb Question competition.

"Are you talking about a dog?"

"A teacup poodle. Her name's Lillet, like the drink, you know?"

I knew. And I bet Mrs. Teacup Poodle Owner had more than a passing acquaintance with the beverage as well. The locked car wouldn't be a problem, but a drunk driver might be.

"Tell you what. I can get the door open right away, but it's going to take a while to recode the car before you'll be able to start it up again." So it was a lie. Sue me. "Is there a coffee shop or a deli around there somewhere? By the time you've finished a big cup of coffee, the car will be all ready to go."

I clicked the door open and heard the happy mother-and-dog reunion through the headset. She thanked me again, promising to wait at least the "required" thirty minutes before trying to start the car.

The call volume dropped off now that the bars were closed and Denny let me go home a few minutes early. I waved good-bye to Mad Cow, pantomimed "call me" so that we could make plans to get together the next day, then folded into my old pickup and cranked the windows down. Three forty-five in the morning, that shadowed netherworld between the freaks and the regulars. Too late to be out drinking, too early for normal folks to be going to work. I was alone on the road, the late summer warmth of the desert air lulling me to inattention. I coasted right through the stop sign near my house and had to circle back.

I'd signed up with Mind Your Manors house-sitting service not long after the trial ended, and this was the best house yet. A full acre of land between me and the neighbors and only five miles from the HandsOn office in Mesa; it was a fantasy-oasis of a house, with Saltillo tiles, a decent home gym, and a lap pool. Pickings were always better during the summer months: few of Arizona's snowbirds wanted to stay through the Fourth Circle of Hell that Phoenix became in July. I only had the house for another few weeks. By the middle of October, I'd be vying for the privilege of house-sitting in one of the lousy two-bedroom condos downtown.

Mind Your Manors liked me. I looked good on the application: a former nun, a nondrinker, with an allergy to pet dander. The nun part always got me the best houses, but it was no more true than the rest of the description. Sure, they could have checked out my story, but I guess I looked trustworthy. Shows what they know.

At least I had correctly answered the question on the form about whether I'd ever been convicted of a felony.

I pulled halfway around the U-shaped driveway and was greeted by the hollow-bong welcome of the copper-pipe wind chimes on the front porch. Leaving my bag on the chair inside the front door, I kicked off my shoes to enjoy the momentary chill of the earthen tiles on bare feet.

The house belonged to a couple from Minneapolis. In their late fifties, they still headed the dot-com business they'd started fifteen years ago, but they now took off four months a year to kick back and hit a little ball around Phoenix's two-hundred-plus golf courses. "We can play a different course every day we're here!" the wife had said. I lied: I told her how much fun I thought that would be. Lazy, sleep-in mornings and then free weights and an incline bench were more my speed.

Today was supposed to be my cardio day, so I did forty minutes in the lap pool, then a quick hundred sit-ups. I'd go back to the real strength training tomorrow.

After I'd cleaned up, I made a combo plate of spinach, eggs, and ground beef and took the food and a beer out to the patio. Sunrise was still an hour away, but the sky was already fringed with pink behind the Superstition Mountains to the east. I finished the dinner-cum-breakfast, pushed the chair back, and stuck my legs out straight. Like a tough piece of gristle between the teeth, I couldn't get Markson's phone call out of my head.

I was no more than a bystander here, but I was taking it personally, as if someone I was talking to on the sidewalk had tripped as they turned away. Had I distracted Markson to the point where he didn't see the danger of those other two men approaching? Hopefully the cops would find him on the road somewhere, nothing but his pride and his bumper damaged, looking to hitch a ride home.

I woke at noon to a ringing phone.

"I understand that you handled that call from Darren Markson last night," Nancy Horowitz started.

Nancy supervised the day shift at HandsOn and I had interviewed with her when I first applied for the job. Her teeth had *click-clacked* with nervous energy while she filled out the paperwork, like a sleeping rabbit dreaming of carrots. Phoenicians are too city-centric to bother with news from Tucson, so neither my name nor my face had registered with her.

"Did the police find him yet?"

"No. They talked to his wife and she says he was supposed to be on his way to a business meeting in New Mexico."

"Driving there? Does she know if he's okay?"

"I don't know."

I waited through the silence and the *clack-clack* of rabbit teeth. So far I hadn't heard a good enough reason for Nancy to call me on my day off.

"The Tucson PD asked if you could drive down to talk to them. Help explain what you saw on the screen when the call came in . . . go over the recorded conversation with them." *Clickety-click.*

Did they know about my second—illegal—call to the car? How would they? I hadn't recorded it. Nancy's voice didn't give anything away.

"When?"

"Today. I know it's your day off. . . ."

I thought I'd put Tucson behind me.

"You're supposed to contact a Detective Deke Treadwell," she continued.

Shit. Just hearing the name pulled me closer to the past than I wanted to be. He was my father's old partner and they'd spent more time together than any two heterosexual guys ought to. After five eight-hour shifts a week, they fished Pena Blanca Lake together for stripers, smallies, and wahoo, and practiced their fire-extinguishing skills every weekend barbecuing ribs and beer-soaked chicken in the backyard. Treadwell knew every detail about what had happened. And probably where to lay the blame.

"I have a root canal scheduled."

"Take Monday as a comp day," she said, clicking for punctuation. "There's one other thing."

As if Treadwell wasn't bad enough.

"Mrs. Markson wants to meet with you, too. She wants to hear the recording."

Click click click.

CHAPTER THREE

I called Mad Cow to cancel our matinee plans, then stripped down to my workout clothes. I needed to push some muscles around before heading south. It was upper body today—a push-pull split working first on the chest muscles and then on the back. Biceps then triceps and an extra set of close grip lat raises. Coming off my summer schedule, there was lots of room for improvement.

No need to take much with me: just a change of clothes in case I wound up staying overnight.

I didn't want my bosses to know I'd already taken home a copy of the Markson conversation and map markings, so I stopped at the HandsOn office on my way out of town to burn another couple of DVDs. The version I made for Mrs. Markson included the conversation with him, but I deleted the other voices and the fight beside the car. If it wound up being her husband's voice, there was no reason for her to hear the grunts of pain as he was beaten. I wondered why she hadn't asked the cops to hear their copy of the call. Maybe she thought this was all part of the HandsOn service she was paying for.

I spiked my hair and put on khakis and a long-sleeved shirt to cover the tattoos. That was another change from the old Jessica Dancing Gammage. She never would have kept a record of her pain in red and black skin art.

Traffic was mind-numbingly slow leaving Phoenix, as heavy on a Saturday afternoon as any workday rush hour. The radio announcer entered himself in the Dumb Question contest with a brayed "Hot enough for you?" I finished one of the water bottles before I even passed Sun Devil Stadium.

I'd last been in Tucson in January, almost three years ago, on the night of my thirtieth birthday. All of my family still lived there, although I hadn't seen any of them since that night. Well, none of them except the youngest of us, Bonita, and even she skirted the main topic like it was a mile wide patch of jimsonweed.

I called Treadwell when I got to the Speedway exit, and he was waiting at the front door when I pulled into the visitor lot for the Tucson Police Department headquarters on Stone.

I hadn't seen him for close to three years, but he seemed to have aged ten in that time. His hair was now more gray than brown, there were basset hound bags under his eyes, and he was toting a good thirty pounds more than I remembered. He mopped his forehead and the back of his neck with an already damp white hankie.

"I wasn't sure it was you when I heard the name. You haven't changed much. Except the hair. You're what—thirty-three now?" He wiped his hand dry before offering a shake.

"Almost." It's harder to lie when someone knows your history. Especially when the last time you saw him was at your murder trial.

"Looking pretty buff," he added, tapping my bicep with his forefinger.

"I'm working at it." I didn't mention that the bodybuilding routine had started as an imitation of the male prisoners during my eight months in jail awaiting trial.

A horny toad scooted across the sidewalk, his scales and spines rayed like a noonday sun. If dinosaurs came in teacup sizes, he would have taken Best of Breed.

"How long have you been working up in Phoenix?" Treadwell asked with a vagueness and delicacy of phrasing I wouldn't have expected of him.

"A couple of years now."

"Your father always believed you, you know."

"I know." And he still did. "I'd rather the HandsOn people not know about my life here in Tucson."

"Okay. They won't hear it from me."

Treadwell ushered me into a small interview room that held two chairs, a metal desk, a two-line phone, and an old big box computer.

I took one of the chairs, put my shoulders back, and handed him the DVD. "Do you want to use the one we e-mailed you or this one?"

"This is easier." He took the disc and slid it into the tray. "Take me through it."

I opened the data with Markson's information and the map showing where his car had been when the air bag had gone off.

"When the air bag is triggered, the car itself phones me, and I determine whether the client needs either medical or mechanical help. Then I find either the nine-one-one operator closest to that spot or a tow truck service nearby—whatever he needs—and connect the client directly to that number." I used language and syntax straight from the training manual. I couldn't afford to be Your Ex-partner's Eldest Daughter or even The Girl Who Got Away with Murder; I was a HandsOn advisor helping the police.

Treadwell jotted down the details from the screen. When he got to the wife's name, I asked, "What did Mrs. Markson say?"

"She wasn't worried at first because he was supposed to be on his way to New Mexico. Then, when the officer came by to tell her about the car, she freaked."

"Any more news on him since then?"

"Nothing."

I turned back to the recording. "That part, that's a second voice, right? With an Hispanic accent?"

"Yeah, maybe. But if he just got rear-ended, I'd expect to hear a second voice."

"What about this guy?" I turned up the volume at the point where one guy said "you lying sack" and the panting and thumping began. "That's a third voice, right?"

"I can't tell."

Should I tell him about listening in on Markson's car a second time? About the dragging, sawing, moaning noises that sounded like they came from a horror movie? These recorded sounds already made the hair on the back of my neck stand up. The ones I hadn't recorded were the stuff of nightmares.

"I thought it sounded like two guys ganging up on Markson." I didn't have much more than a gut reaction to back up my claim.

He shrugged. "I'll have Forensics listen to it."

We went through the recording three more times, and with each playing I became more inured to the sound of fists, the breaking glass, the panting, the pummeling. Maybe violence, like a chanted word, loses its meaning with repetition.

But the more I listened, the more convinced I was that Markson was either dead or dying right now.

The room felt too close, the air thick with unspoken questions. When we were done, I hotfooted it to the elevator and outdoors. Treadwell followed me out.

"Have you been to see your folks yet?"

I shook my head. "We made a deal that I wouldn't." My mother had made sure of that.

He turned away, but called back over his shoulder, "You know, I always believed you, too."

I watched him plod back into the cop shop, his shoulders

hunched against the heat or maybe feeling the weight that that belief had cost him. Deke Treadwell and my dad: the only two people who still thought I was innocent.

I had an hour to get across town to Emily Markson's house in the Catalina foothills. Not enough time to find the sandwich and cold beer I would have liked to have. And definitely too late to find a way back into the life and family I'd thrown away.

Emily Markson was probably just a couple of years older than me, but she had an air of elegance and sophistication that I could never have pulled off. A black satin robe covered her shoulders but was left open at the front to reveal a two-piece swimsuit underneath. Her hair was pulled into a tight French twist, and her lips were carnelian.

"I'm so sorry to have wasted your time," she said at the door. "I assumed the police would have told you."

"Your husband's okay?"

She didn't take off her sunglasses as she led me through the house to the backyard.

"I was frantic when the police first told me about the accident last night—worried sick until Darren called just a little while ago."

"Where is he?"

She opened a sliding glass door and ushered me out toward an acre of decking and pool. A gilded version of Tucson sat in the basin below us, as if the mythical golden city of Cibola had come to life with the setting sun. From here, you couldn't see any "going out of business" signs.

"He decided to fly to New Mexico after all. He said he left his car at the airport."

Her voice held magnolias, pulled pork, and humid nights. This was not a woman raised in the desert.

I wanted to believe her but couldn't be sure. The glasses kept me from seeing any telltale jitter of perjury in her eyes, but the nervous plucking at the robe belied her words.

"Does Detective Treadwell know?"

"I haven't talked to him directly, but I left a message. Darren only called a little while ago. He said he was between meetings." She found another piece of lint on the black satin.

"Did he have any idea who was in his car?"

She shook her head. "It must have been stolen from the airport parking lot."

Who'd want to beat up a guy in a stolen car? The car's owner, that's for sure. Or maybe the cops. I wasn't looking forward to suggesting that one to Treadwell.

"Let me get you some tea," she offered, pouring from the icy pitcher beside her.

"Thanks." Emily Markson said her husband was fine, but her fidgeting suggested otherwise. Maybe she knew who was driving the car and that was the cause of her concern. There's a fine line of distinction between anxious and nervous and both of them can make you look like a liar if you're not careful.

I leaned back and admired the view. "Have you lived here long?" The house was stuccoed to look like adobe, with sweeping vistas of the saguaro-littered hillside and the golden-bright city below.

"Only a couple of years. Darren is in real estate, and these houses were his most recent project."

"They're beautiful."

"But he has even bigger plans. That's why he set up those meetings in New Mexico."

"He's building something there?"

"No . . . I think his partners are there. I'm not sure." She paused. "We don't talk much about business." She repositioned her sunglasses a little higher on her nose.

That had been true enough in my house, too. My dad's life as a cop was full of adventures, but they were stories that gave my mother the willies, paint-by-number pictures of a night he might never come home at all. They rarely talked about his job.

"How long have you been married?"

"Almost ten years. Darren was teaching a business class at Tulane and I was a student there."

"What's his new project?"

"He found—"

"Emily?" A man's voice interrupted her answer.

"Out here! We're by the pool."

A late-thirties Adonis pulled open the sliding glass door and joined us in the backyard. His hair was blond on top but, unlike mine, it looked natural. Was this Darren Markson?

"Ms. Dancing? This is my—"

"I'll take care of this, Emily."

Morse-code gazes passed between them. He double-blinked a message and then turned to me.

"I'm Paul Willard. I live next door." He gestured to the west. "It would be helpful to hear that voice from the car. You know, just to put her mind at ease."

They must be close, if he already knew that she'd talked to her husband. But Emily wouldn't need to ease her mind at all if she knew Darren Markson was okay. Maybe the car hadn't been stolen after all. Or maybe this guy with free rein of the house was the one who wanted to hear that voice.

She halfway answered my unspoken question. "Paul's our lawyer as well as our neighbor. I called him as soon as the police came by this morning and then again when I heard from Darren."

Nice to have a lawyer on call at two o'clock in the morning. "Do you want me to leave this with you?" I held out the DVD copy I'd made.

She glanced at Willard. "Yes, but could you stay for a minute and go through it with us?" She took off her sunglasses, revealing eyes as cold as a winter night. Those eyes didn't lie. She wasn't worried; she was mad.

"There's not much more I can tell you than what you'll hear for yourself anyway. It only lasted a few seconds, and I didn't really hear anything. . . ."

She took the disc from me, holding it at arm's length with just the tips of her fingers as if it had an offensive smell. I gave up and followed her into the house with the lawyer hot on my heels.

"This is Darren's office," she said, wiping nonexistent dust from a hip-high cabinet.

It was much too pristine to be the kind of office I could work in. Two light-colored couches sat at right angles to each other, and blond wood bookcases covered two walls. The books were arranged by color. There was a sliver-thin, built-in desk with a laptop computer on it, but no sign of a folder, a loose piece of paper, or a chewed-on pencil. House as stagecraft.

"Is this your husband?" The picture had been taken in some tropical clime with palm trees, ebony-dark rocks, and a blazing blue sky. It showed Emily Markson wrapped in the arms of a man the physical opposite of the blond lawyer at her side now. He looked to be about fifty, with dark, pomaded hair and a pencil-thin mustache. His lips were barely separated, showing little corn kernels of teeth.

"Yes, on our trip to Hawaii last year."

She waved me to the desk chair and I sat down. The computer already had several windows open on the screen.

"Here, let me get rid of those." She leaned past my shoulder to click the documents closed. I didn't get much of a look at any of them, but one phrase in an e-mail caught my eye: "At the riverbed." It was signed "A" with a little dash after the letter. Maybe she'd been e-mailing friends about her car being stolen and this was one of the replies.

Once the screen was clear she handed me back the disc, returned to the couch, and hugged an olive green throw pillow to her chest.

"Ready?" I asked.

She nodded. I slipped in the disc and double-clicked on the DVD icon.

". . . *is Jessie. Is there an emergency in the vehicle?*" My recorded voice was as thin and scratchy as that of a fourteen-year-old boy.

". . . *want me to call an ambulance?*" I kept my eyes on the screen.

". . . *okay. I'll check with the other guy.*"

The recording ended just a few seconds later. I'd cut it off before the hammering of fists and the strangled breathing started. I waited a few beats, then turned to face her.

"Would you like me to play it again?"

"No. Thank you. I . . . I don't know that voice." She tilted her face up. "Do you, Paul?"

He shook his head.

I ejected the disc and placed it on the desk. "I'll be on my way, then."

She nodded and ushered me to the front of the house. As she reached for the doorknob, the sleeve of her robe pulled back, baring her arm almost to the elbow. That's when I saw the bruises.

There are supposed to be twenty-seven ways to tell if someone is lying. Whether the eyes go left or right, up or down. Body language. Speech patterns. A physical response. But a good liar knows a hundred different ways to convince you that he's telling the truth.

Emily Markson was not a good liar.

CHAPTER FOUR

I left word for Detective Treadwell, although he'd probably already picked up the phone message that Darren Markson had made it safely to New Mexico.

If that wasn't Markson's voice I'd heard on the call, whose was it? Had the car been stolen or had Markson allowed someone to borrow it? If so, it was probably someone Emily Markson knew. She said she didn't recognize the voice, but why the anger in her eyes?

And what about those bruises? Some were new, but others were already magenta and green. They ringed her wrist and continued up the inside of her arm. If Treadwell didn't already know about them, I was going to make sure he found out.

The sun was setting amid a braggart's display of orange and purple clouds over the Tucson Mountains, and the city seemed to take a breath as the air cooled to what passed for Arizona fall temperatures. I called my sister, Bonita, and explained that I was in town.

"Hey, I just booted the rest of the family out so I could pack. We have the house to ourselves."

"You leave soon?"

"Tomorrow. But no more questions till you get here."

Bonita had decided almost a year ago to join the Peace Corps, but I hadn't realized her departure date had grown so near. I stopped to pick up a bottle of champagne on the way over.

She had moved away from our parents' house when she started college and now rented a tiny, one-bedroom house on a quiet side street in the Fort Lowell neighborhood, an area more likely to have dismantled cars in the front yard than landscaping.

She met me on the front porch.

"You can hear that truck a mile away."

She was right. The exhaust sounded like a drum solo. But I knew she'd been watching from the porch since I'd called.

Bonita was eleven years younger than me, the youngest of the seven children in our family. "First there was Jessie, then three boys, then three girls" is the way my mother put it, turning me into some androgynous feral child.

The twins, Carlotta and Carmella, were pretty, but not like Bonita, and my brothers' faces were rough-hewn and craggy. The rest of us were rough drafts, and Bonita the finished novel.

My sister had done some appearance-neutering for this Peace Corps gig, with bangs cut ruler-straight and hair tied back in a loose ponytail. I pictured that blond head, in a circle with heads of coarser, darker hair, all set against the velvet green of a South American rain forest.

"Ready to go?" A heavy-duty backpack leaned against the dining room table, while a wheeled suitcase full of cords, plastic sheeting, and small vials gaped open on the couch.

"What's this?" I nudged a heavy plastic wedge in the suitcase. It was about the size of a hardcover book.

"A foot-powered generator," she said. "I'll get my exercise and power up the laptop at the same time."

I handed her the champagne.

"Let me see what's not packed up yet." She headed to the kitchen, returning a moment later with two jelly glasses and a towel. I took the wire hoop off the bottle, covered the top with the towel, and twisted until it popped.

We clinked rims. "Two years, that's a long time to be gone," I said.

"You've been gone longer."

I shook my head. "That's different."

We sipped in silence. I was thinking of the past, Bonita quite possibly of the future.

"Are you sure you want to do this?" Bonita had never been the biggest risk-taker in our brood. Hell, she probably used both birth control pills and abstinence. And she was my littlest sister. I didn't want her so far away that I couldn't take care of her the way I'd done when we were growing up. But I hadn't been of much help to her for the last couple of years; she'd probably do fine without me.

"Yeah. What else am I going to do with wanderlust and a BA in education?"

And what was I going to do with a rap sheet and a degree in philosophy? You would have thought those studies would have better prepared me to come to terms with becoming a killer, but the ethics of killing were still a muddle to me. If you take a life, does it change you? Yes, in a thousand shadowed ways. Is it worth it? Sometimes.

I'd had plenty of time in jail to crystallize my short-term creed: "Do Unto Others as They Have Done Unto Your Friends and Family." But that wouldn't help me much in a job search. I'd been stuttering along as a bartender when my friend Catherine died and I took over her quest. I hadn't planned murder as a postgraduate degree. I thought I'd settle into some teaching position in a high school—maybe get married, although there was no front-runner on the horizon. By the time I got out of jail, even bartending seemed to require more social skills than I had left.

Bonita finished her thought, not having noticed my lapse of

attention. "And after what you went through . . ." No mention of my guilt or innocence, of course. "Well, I decided that I never wanted to look back at my life and say 'I wish I had.'"

I was still trying to work through the "I wish I hadn'ts."

Bonita was kind enough not to continue the thought.

She caught me up on family news while she jammed rolled-up socks between the solar shower and shortwave radio in the suitcase. The "carbon-copy" twins, Carlotta and Carmella, were both married, one living in Flagstaff and the other in San Diego. Of the three boys—Lincoln, Martin, and John (our own assassination trifecta)—Bonita only had new news of John, who had re-upped and was now stationed at Camp Pendleton. Martin and Lincoln had turned down our father's career as a cop and had both gone into the fire department instead. Bonita said nothing had changed; they were still happily divorced (Martin) and happily married (Lincoln).

I didn't ask any questions that I didn't already know the answers to.

I told her about taking the call from Darren Markson's car and the request to play the tape for his wife.

"So that's what finally got you back to town. I didn't see anything about it in the paper." It was a nonconfrontational response. She'd been too often snake-bit by my lies to buy wholeheartedly into anything I said.

"It was probably too late for the morning papers, and it's just a stolen car. Tucson's got plenty of those."

She tucked in the flaps on a bulging carton beside her. "Martin's going to come by and get my car and these boxes, but my rent goes through the end of the month, if you want to stay for a while."

"What am I going to do in Tucson?"

"I don't know. Maybe check in with the folks?"

"You know I can't do that."

But there were a few questions about Markson I wanted to ask, and one place I wanted to visit in the daylight. I didn't even know who the victim was here. The bruised wife? Darren Markson? Some unrecognizable voice on the other end of a call for help? Emily Markson and her too-slick lawyer were hiding something and now they'd made me part of that subterfuge.

"Mind if I spend the night?"

I took Bonita to the airport the next morning, giving her my favorite talisman, a small chunk of eucalyptus heartwood carved into the shape of a quail. I didn't tell her that it had taken me that whole eight months in jail while I was waiting for the trial, scrabbling at it with my thumbnails to bring it to life. Digging . . . scraping . . . worrying at it night after night, instead of piercing my own flesh. The quail was fat and round and smooth in my hand. I gave it a farewell rub.

"Go on, take it. It's better than a St. Christopher, better than any patron saint. It protects female travelers heading south."

She tilted her head, much like the quail itself, to let me know she wasn't buying my story but still tucked the bird into the smallest pocket on her jeans.

I left her in front of the Aeroméxico counter for the first leg of her flight to Bolivia, and watched her image grow small in the rearview mirror. The patron saint of I Wish I Had.

From the airport, I looped southeast around the city, out where the streetlights and golf courses finally lost out to the Rincon Mountains and the Saguaro National Park. Just west of those foothills, I reached the location where Markson's car had been rear-ended.

I'd been right about the creosote out here. I could see the rooftops of a new housing development in the distance—the wood beams still raw—but from shoulder height down, there was nothing but sagebrush, thorny stickers, and a not-often-used dirt road.

I got out of the truck and eased the door shut behind me. I knew I was generally in the right area, but I couldn't picture Markson's car here, couldn't imagine the skritch of thorny bush against his door. Couldn't hear the desert wind I'd heard last night.

I walked farther north, toward a massive cottonwood tree that listed toward the arroyo like a dowsing rod. It stood fifty or sixty feet high, proof that this dry wash had once run full and that there remained enough water under the sand to sustain life. The tree had branched into three separate trunks down near its base, giving it a wide and low canopy of leaves like a sombrero.

Close to the shadow of the tree was a sprinkling of red glass. Markson's taillight?

I'd have to stop thinking of him as Markson, if what his wife said about the phone call was true.

I was surprised that the officer had spotted the car at all, as hidden as it would have been in the middle of the night by the brim of that leafy hat.

I expected to see crime scene tape ringing the area, decorating the branches of the cottonwood like a homicidal Christmas tree, but there was nothing. No car. No police notice. And no blood that I could see.

Lots of footprints, though. Hard-soled shoes, cowboy boots, and sneakers. The cops must have all been male; none of the prints looked small enough to be a woman's. There was one set of small, bare prints that looked almost childlike. Probably a dog or a wild cat. I couldn't read tracks for shit.

Two sets of tire marks were clear, although the dry, hard-packed sand didn't tell much of a story about them.

But it did put the lie to one theory. There was no way a car would have been stuck in this caliche-hard soil. Those voices I heard were not trying to free a car, they were fighting.

The day was already hot enough that even my five-minute sortie had given me snail trails of sweat down the side of my face.

I headed deeper into the shade of the cottonwood. Checking the ground for anthills, snakes, and tarantulas, I squatted down, then leaned back against the thickest of the three trunks. What had they been fighting about? And, whoever it was in Markson's car, where had he gone when it was over?

A hot wind rustled the branches above me and flayed green leaves drifted into my lap. I looked up. About twenty feet up there was a fork in the branch of the middle trunk. And dead center of that fork was a lighter patch of wood—bone white and cleared of foliage.

Scaling the base of the trunk was easy, but transferring to the upright middle trunk was more difficult. The dark gray bark, so deeply cracked that it looked as if it had been caressed by a tiger, crumbled as I climbed. I braced my back against one limb and my feet against another, shimmying up like a chimney-rock climber.

Once above the fork, I could see the raw wound on the top of the limb. The thick, fissured bark was gone, as were most of the surrounding leaves. In their place was a two-inch strip of newly peeled wood, bristling with shreds of something that looked like hemp or thick hair. I pulled several of the strands from the surrounding bark where they'd been caught, wrapped them in a Kleenex, and stuffed them into my pocket.

I imagined trying to throw a rope up and over that notched branch in the dark. Not an easy task on a moonless night. Those leaves on the ground may not have been the result of a desert wind. Maybe they were testament to the number of times someone swung a rope before it caught, and held, and finally did its job.

Foot by shaky foot, I climbed down the tree and reclaimed my place against the trunk. Had I heard a beating? Or was it a hanging?

My mind filled in the details. The creak of a strong fiber pulled taut. The hollow thump of pipes and boards striking flesh. Grunts from the assailants. Groans from the dying man. It fit the sounds I'd heard, but the police hadn't found any facts to prove it.

Hell, I'd always had an overactive imagination.

A twig snapped behind me, on the other side of the tree. I jumped up and peered around the trunk.

At first it was just a flash of white, then a delicate hand snaked around a branch at eye level.

I grabbed the wrist and yanked.

"*Ay! Dios!* Don't hurt me!"

She couldn't have been more than sixteen or seventeen, hair as black as a crow's wing, and eyes wide with fear. She scooted away from me on her butt.

"I won't hurt you. You just scared me." I gave her plenty of backing-up room. "What are you doing out here?" There was no sign of a car in the direction she'd come from.

"Walking . . . taking a shortcut. . . ."

"From where?"

She fluttered a hand to the southwest, an area with no immediate housing or car traffic.

"What's your name?"

"L . . . Luisa."

"I'm Jessie." I stuck out my hand. She grasped it for a tentative shake, but I tightened my hold and pulled her upright. She shuffled her feet and swatted the back of her jeans with pebble-studded hands. My guess was that her name did start with an "L," but that was where the truth had hiccupped.

Had she really just taken a shortcut? Maybe she was looking forward to the shade of this one giant tree after a half hour's walk across a brutal stretch of desert.

She was too well dressed to be a recent border crosser, with her tight jeans and clean, white Pep Boys T-shirt. Her chest was so small that Manny, Moe, and Jack evinced only smirks instead of their usual toothy grins. And the Mexico border was a full seventy-five miles away anyway; she wasn't crossing here and hiding from La Migra.

Wherever she had come from, it was a long, hot walk. Hell, even the closest bus route was a good mile and a half away.

Sweat dripped down the sides of her face, her sandals were covered with dust, and there were melon-sized wet patches under her arms. Her eyes were brimming with tears, but it wasn't clear whether that was sadness or a sign of fear. On the other hand, the thrust of her chin and the cant of her elbows definitely said defiance.

"You can't keep me here, you know."

"I'm not trying to keep you here."

She looked left and right and finally straight ahead at the tree. I followed her gaze up the central trunk to that juncture where the bark was scraped to a bone color. A single tear coursed down her face now, mixing with the sweat.

The spell was broken when a rooster tail of dust appeared over her right shoulder, from the direction of the road. One car, and coming our way. Luisa turned back toward the sound. We could both see the police car's lights above the sagebrush.

"Please. Please don't say anything."

I glanced again at the approaching car. When I turned back, she was gone.

CHAPTER FIVE

Detective Deke Treadwell pulled the cruiser to a stop next to my truck, well away from the cottonwood tree. The dust rolled toward me like a knee-high red carpet.

"You still driving a patrol car, Deke?"

"The garage was a little short of working vehicles this morning." He opened the driver's door, swiveled to the side, and placed both feet squarely on the ground before attempting to stand. Once up, he hitched his pants with both hands and shook his head.

"I should have known I'd find you here."

"Why's that?"

"You could get yourself in the middle of any mess, even as a kid. Remember when you ran away? Made it all the way to Nogales? You must have been all of twelve or thirteen."

"Eleven. And the bus driver marked my ticket with a heart-shaped cutout." Mom had just brought Bonita home from the hospital, and the twins were only two. It was my birthday, but like every other day, I was expected to take care of my brothers and sisters. Just one more day of feeling like the outsider looking in, the seventh leg on a six-legged bug, no more remarkable than any other day, but to an eleven-year-old, devastating.

Treadwell's straw cowboy hat didn't go with the dark suit. In seeming recognition of the fact, he took it off and slapped it against his leg.

"Remember how your mother always said 'We had three girls, and three boys, and Jessie'? You were always a pistol."

That alien life-form again. Prettier than my brothers. Stronger than my sisters. The first child, but a child kept at arm's length. "How did you know I'd be out here, Deke?"

"I didn't. I came out to take some pictures in daylight." He reached back inside the car for a camera. "Looks like we have a car thief on our hands, if nothing else."

But was that car thief a villain or a victim? At least the cops were still looking for him.

"Is there any news on Markson?"

"His wife says he's fine. He'll be back next week. But we still don't know who the guy in the car was, or where he's gone."

I couldn't get that voice out of my head. The man had sounded tired, resigned, slightly pissed off. *I'll check with the other guy. . . .*

"Your officer said there was blood everywhere. I don't see any." I hadn't been all the way around the tree, but if there had been a fight, it would have taken place somewhere near where the taillight had been broken.

"Probably all soaked in by now."

"Did you take a sample of it last night?"

"Give us a little credit, Jessie. Of course we did."

Good. That way they would be able to confirm that it wasn't Darren Markson's blood. And maybe they could find out who it did belong to.

"Take a look at this." I handed him the wadded-up Kleenex. "I found them in that crook in the tree—right there." I pointed and Treadwell craned his neck to follow my arm.

"Rope fibers?"

"Yeah, I think so. I think somebody threw a rope up there."

"Probably kids putting up a tire swing." He folded the tissue and tucked it into his shirt pocket.

"Only if they did it in the last twenty-four hours or so. That wood's still raw."

"I'll get somebody up there to take a look at it."

He seemed uninterested, as if a fight among car thieves didn't merit much attention from the police. There was nothing else I could do here. "See you later, Deke." I stepped toward the cars.

His voice stopped me. "Jessie? Are you staying in town for a while?"

I shook my head without turning around.

"I thought maybe you and I could go see your folks. Together, I mean."

Maybe if I was quiet long enough, the question would evaporate like the high-altitude rain that never reaches the desert floor. Maybe not.

I kept my face turned away from him.

He waited a beat. "Where are you staying?"

"At Bonita's house, off Fort Lowell." I gave him her address and my cell phone number. "It'll probably just be for tonight, though. I've got to get back to work."

"Think about it. I'll go see them with you."

I nodded, but it wasn't in agreement.

Treadwell returned to his scrutiny of the ground around the tree trunk and I moved toward the cars.

Six feet from the bumper of my truck there was a cardboard drink coaster that was cleaner looking than the rest of the litter. Right about where the mysterious Luisa had gone down. It was round. Dos Equis brand. With a handwritten note in a circular pattern around the edge. I knelt and pocketed the coaster while Treadwell had his back turned.

It may have been the kind of evidence the detective was looking for, but I was pretty sure it hadn't been there when I'd pulled up. And I didn't know if Luisa had anything to do with what I'd heard on the HandsOn call anyway.

All I knew was that someone who automatically gave a false name with no thought whatsoever was my kind of liar. And Treadwell didn't seem to know anything about that kind of woman at all.

I stopped for a six-pack on the way back to Bonita's, choosing Dos Equis, as if the purchase of the right brand might work as a talisman in unraveling the mystery of the dropped coaster. As parched as I was, I decided to save the beer till after my workout. I shouldn't have been drinking the stuff anyway; it added fat instead of muscle. Now I'd have to add more cardio to counteract it.

I looked around at the detritus that Bonita had left behind. Two bulging black garbage bags and a straight flush of empty pizza boxes in the corner. Eight cardboard boxes full of clothes and household goods that Martin would come by to pick up. Dust bunnies the size of grocery carts underneath the dining room table.

I sat down in the ugliest but most comfortable armchair I'd ever seen. As wide as a boat, with flaring arms that took up an extra three feet, it was a faded yellow fabric, with cigarette burns near the back, and a bright serape thrown over the seat cushion. Clearly, household furniture wouldn't count for much in Bonita's list of assets. Equally clearly, she wasn't getting her security deposit back.

I pulled the coaster from my back pocket and flattened it out on my thigh. It was a creamy tan, with the brand's XX marking, the face of Montezuma, and a circular pattern of Aztec art. I held it closer to read the penciled note around the edge. It was fluidly written and very light. Probably a woman's handwriting. *Juanito's 1900 F.* Nineteen hundred could be an address or a year or a price or even a time, if anybody who was part of that note had a military background. But lots of my Latino friends in high school had used twenty-four hour time, too. Juanito could be somebody's name or business. And the F? Maybe an apartment designation or part of a name. But if it was a first initial, it wasn't my Luisa. Someone she was supposed to meet?

Bonita had taken her laptop with her, so I started low tech, with the phone book. It was quite likely that Juanito was a first name, and that would be no help at all. But I checked the *J*'s just in case it was a last name. No Juanitos were listed.

The yellow pages wouldn't do me any good if I didn't know what kind of business "Juanito's" was. Maybe. Maybe. I went back to the white pages and flipped to the section that listed businesses alphabetically.

Yes. A bar called Juanito's near Ajo Street in South Tucson. The address wasn't 1900, but a bar and a beer coaster seemed to go together rather nicely. Maybe I'd found the right Juanito's. And if 1900 was a time and meant seven p.m., I still had time enough for a quick lower-body workout before I had to be there.

I pawed through Bonita's leave-behinds in search of gym equipment. Nothing solid enough or heavy enough. I finally found what I was looking for in the backyard. Two empty five-gallon plastic gas cans with handles. If I filled them about two-thirds full with sand, they'd be the perfect weight. There was an old apple crate that would work as a step and I could bungee-cord the two gas cans to a five-foot metal pole I found by the back fence to make a barbell. I checked to make sure that no neighbors had a good line of sight into the backyard, then stripped down to my underwear.

I started with squats and step-ups, adding sand to the jugs until my legs shook with fatigue after three sets of reps. Two bungee cords tied together made an ad hoc jump rope, and I alternated abdominal crunches and obliques with five minutes on the rope.

At the end, I was sweating from places I didn't know I had pores, and was as winded as if I'd run all the way to Nogales.

One more set of gas-can squats before I celebrated, holding a hose over my head and bringing blessed relief.

It was time to meet Juanito.

A smart woman in Tucson should still think twice before showing up alone in a bar at night, especially on the south side of town. I didn't want to look too approachable.

I spiked my hair with American Greaser, the only beauty product I use, and put on my favorite "keep your distance" T-shirt that said: SOME DAYS IT'S JUST NOT WORTH CHEWING THROUGH THE RESTRAINTS. The tattooed jacks around my biceps were clearly visible.

That was the first ink I got, lovingly drawn by an inmate named Lisa just before I got out of jail. She'd rigged an ink tube and needle onto the handle of an electric toothbrush, resulting in a primitive tattoo starter kit. I'd originally agreed to a more clichéd barbed-wire design, as Lisa said that was the only thing she could draw very well. But when the pain started ratcheting up, I chickened out. "Don't draw in the wire. Just make each barb look like the kind of jacks we used to play with," I told her, wiping away my tears.

"There," she'd said, dabbing at the last of the blood. "Much better than a tramp stamp or barbed wire."

I agreed.

I got to Juanito's bar half an hour early. It was white-painted brick and as small as a childless couple's home, sitting alone in the middle of a tiny dirt parking area. There were two cars and a pickup truck already in the lot. I pulled in and made a U-turn, leaving the nose of my truck pointed out.

Pushing on the wooden door, I stepped inside and waited while my eyes adjusted. The setting sun was still a good inch above the Tucson Mountains behind me, but that meant a blinding glare coming through the front windows at about shoulder height. Dust swirled through the beam, bisecting the room into shadow and light.

It was a narrow room, with a scarred wooden bar along the right wall, a handful of rickety stools, and a painted concrete floor. The customers were all at the mismatched tables along the left: one group of four card players, and two Latinos at another table who'd pushed their chairs back against the wall and sat side by side.

No sign of my Luisa. I took a stool at the bar.

"Cerveza."

The bartender, a middle-aged Hispanic man with long side-burns and full lips, tapped the Tecate spigot and raised his eye-brows in question. I nodded.

The pantomime over with, he placed a beer coaster on the bar and the full glass on top of it. "Four dollars."

I paid without complaint. The Dos Equis beer coaster was the same kind I'd picked up at the tree.

One of the wall-sitters got up to put money in the jukebox. An old-fashioned mariachi ballad, full of trumpets and strings and ululation, began to play. None of that edgy, hip-hop narcocorrido stuff here.

Gradually the room got used to my presence and conversation started up again, most of it in Spanish. I couldn't understand it all, but got the idea that one of the card players was looking for a place to stay tonight since his girlfriend had kicked him out. Another, named Marcos, had just signed on for another month with a con-struction company.

Nobody mentioned Luisa or any other woman with an *L* name.

An older Hispanic couple came in, nodded politely, and took the two stools next to me. The man ordered for the woman without asking: a sign of either a long history together or an inconsiderate date. He called her Cara, but I wasn't sure if that was an endearment or her name.

How could I find out if someone here was the *F* I was looking for? The jukebox mariachis finished another plaint of lost love.

"*¿Como está Felicia?*" the woman beside me asked of the bartender.

I choked on my beer and lost his reply in my coughing. Felicia! And if she used a nickname, it might be Licia, the word that almost came out when I asked her name. She was both the *F* name and the *L* name I was looking for, and she'd been leaving a message for someone to meet her here at the bar.

I toyed with my drink and waited, sure now that I was in the right place.

One of the card players left and two more showed up to join the table.

A few minutes after seven, the door to the storage area in the back of the bar opened and a narrow, dark head poked through.

She spotted me at the bar and turned to run. I jumped to my feet. "Felicia!"

I followed her through a narrow passageway clogged with cleaning products and liquor bottles, and out a back door that stuttered and slapped behind me.

There was no trace of her. I rounded the building at a full gallop, nearly colliding with the bartender, who'd come out the front door to watch the chase.

A car started up behind the tamarisk trees to my right, but by the time I reached the street it was already out of sight. I'd lost her.

I climbed in the truck, started it, and turned in the direction that Felicia/Luisa had gone. The bartender watched me go, a cell phone held to his ear as I pulled away.

Not knowing what kind of car I was looking for, all I could do was scan the vehicles around me for Felicia's profile. I didn't even know if she was in a car by herself.

A family in a blue pickup. An elderly black man in an equally old Cadillac. A teenager with rap music booming from a Toyota. For a moment I thought I'd spotted her in a white sedan that pulled into a Circle K on the corner, but when the driver got out, it was a long-haired boy. When dusk turned to night, I called it quits and returned to Bonita's house.

I helped myself to a cold Dos Equis on my way through the kitchen, then turned on the bug light on the back porch and perched gingerly on the rump-sprung chaise lounge. The breeze died away.

At least I knew who F was now. And where to find her.

If I'd guessed her age right, she'd be too young to be a patron at the bar. But she could sure be family. She had the same gracefully arched eyebrows and full lips as the bartender. His daughter, maybe?

But I still didn't know what she was doing at the arroyo. It had to be a good thirteen, fourteen miles from the bar. Was she there to meet someone? To leave a beer-coaster message for someone? And did she have anything at all to do with the accident or the fight on Friday night?

"What kind of trouble have you gotten yourself into, Felicia?" I asked the bottle.

CHAPTER SIX

A heavy pounding shook the front door. I put down the beer and jogged back toward the front of the house.

"You in there! Open up!"

I held my breath. No one but Treadwell knew I was here.

"Now!" the man's voice demanded. "I'm serious. I've got a gun!"

Panicked, I searched around me for a weapon. An empty pizza box wasn't going to do the job.

I tiptoed to the front door and sidled along the wall to the window. The hammering continued. I squatted down and, lifting the barest inch of dusty curtain, peeked above the sill.

Faded jeans and a worn leather belt with a tarnished silver buckle. A white T-shirt with the Tucson Fire Department logo over the left breast. And above that, the scowling face of my brother Martin.

"Jesus, Martin," I said, opening the door, "you scared the shit out of me."

"Jessie? What are you doing here?"

"Do you really have a gun? If you do, I'm not letting you in here, no matter what."

"I was supposed to pick up Bonita's stuff. When I saw the lights on . . ."

"And you were ready to do what? Shoot the squatter?"

"Naw, I didn't really—"

"Damn good thing." I turned away, leaving the door open for him. "Probably shoot your own fucking foot off."

"I just didn't expect—"

"I know." I sank into the ugly yellow chair.

Martin hadn't aged at all. Clear blue eyes, an almost-handlebar mustache, and the barest hint of crow's feet around his eyes from squinting at the summer sun.

"So, how've you been?" he said, dismissing the two-year absence and all his unreturned messages. He moved a carton of books off a dining room chair and took a seat.

"Okay. I'm probably leaving tomorrow, so if you need to take anything . . ." Monday would be the comp day I'd been promised. I had to be back in Phoenix by Tuesday evening for my shift.

"No, no, that's okay. It can wait. You just surprised me, that's all." He looked everywhere in the room except at me.

I hadn't seen Martin since the trial; there was no simple way to ease back into the banter and comfort we'd had before that time.

"I saw Paula on TV," I started.

"Yeah." He inspected Bonita's worn carpeting. "Great way to get your name on national television."

His ex-wife had taken up with an incarcerated bank robber through a church penpal program, and had helped him bust out of jail. She'd been featured prominently on an *America's Most Wanted* program last fall. That made two of Martin's family members making the news.

"It was a good picture of her." It wasn't a question but it sure could have won in the Dumb Comments category.

He looked up with the grin I remembered from his elementary school photos. "Not bad for a mug shot."

I thought about my own mug shot. Mouth held firm but straight. Eyes alight with the certitude of the righteous.

We waited while the embarrassment, the questions, the denials, and the pain settled at ankle level, like scuffed dust. After a few moments, Martin tried to start three sentences, but ultimately chose none of them, as seemingly unsure of my status in the family as my mother was. I was going to have to do this on my own.

"I'm not here about family stuff. It's for my job." I explained about HandsOn and the disappearance of the man in the Cadillac. "So I won't be here long. I won't bother anybody."

He nodded and rubbed his palms together. Washing the taint of me away? Dismissing my story as another lie? My mother's barbs must have found a place to snag. I didn't wait to find out.

"Do you want me to follow you in Bonita's car? I'll help you carry stuff . . ." I grabbed a box from the pile against the wall.

He jumped up as well. "Don't bother. I'll come back next week sometime."

He left without saying good-bye. Without touching me. As if I were a stranger he'd passed on the street. And maybe I was.

I left the house at seven the next morning, in search of a massive breakfast to make up for having drunk my dinner the night before. The pancakes had just arrived when my cell phone went off.

"Jessie? You still in town?" It was Treadwell. This couldn't be good.

"I'm at the Denny's on Speedway."

"Order me some eggs. Over easy." I glared at the phone like it had just farted.

He beat the eggs to the table by seconds, huffing into the seat opposite me with a scrape of keys and handcuffs against the laminated tabletop as the waitress plunked the plate down in front of him.

"Tell me more about this HandsOn program."

"I thought you said there wasn't any crime here."

"We've still got a car thief to find." He let the egg bleed across the plate and dunked a triangle of toast into the yolk.

I pushed my pancakes aside and looked around to signal a waitress for more coffee. No luck. There was a gaggle of them near the kitchen, but none looked my way.

"It combines three technologies—built-in sensors that give you diagnostics about the car's performance, the GPS system that gives you location and directions, and a really strong satellite phone with HandsOn advisors available at the other end."

He nodded and kept eating. When I didn't continue, he patted his lips with a paper napkin and said, "What else? Like, what do the sensors do?"

"They can tell whether you're in a crash and how bad it is. Whether you need an oil change. Why your 'check engine' light is on. . . ." I made a rolling wave with my hand to indicate the thousand other things the system could read.

"Can it tell where you've been?"

"Not unless you've asked the GPS to give you directions someplace. That'd still be in the system."

"No, we checked."

"Some rental cars have that tracking equipment installed," I added, "so they can tell if you've taken the car across state lines or into Mexico."

He shook his head. That wasn't what he was interested in.

"It should be able to tell you how fast the car was going when it was hit and whether he slammed the brakes on. Would that help?"

Treadwell returned to his eggs. "Not a lot. We can pretty much estimate the combined speed based on the damage to the car's rear end. And we found some blue paint embedded in the Caddy's bumper. It's a color Ford uses, so we already know we're looking for a blue Ford with significant front-end damage."

I stripped the lid off a thimble of half and half, added it to the cold coffee in my cup, and took a sip, thinking back to the three voices I'd heard.

"There is one other thing."

"What's that?"

"It can tell you if anybody else was in the car with him."

Treadwell sat up so fast you'd think the caffeine had reached his system, not mine.

"Weight distribution. It can tell you if there was somebody else in the car, where they were sitting, and whether they had their seat belt on."

He pursed his lips. "Well, at least we'd know whether we were looking for one car thief or two."

The money he left on the table didn't even cover the tip.

When I got back to Bonita's house I decided that the sisterly thing to do would be to clean the place up well enough that Bonita could get her cleaning deposit back. And if there wasn't any deposit to be reclaimed, at least I'd have the benefit of a clean bathtub tonight.

I poked around under the sink and opened likely boxes until I found sponges, paper towels, and a couple of all-purpose cleaning products.

I sure hoped this Felicia from the bar didn't drive a blue Ford. Maybe it belonged to Emily Markson or her ever-so-attentive lawyer-neighbor, Paul Willard. But that didn't make much sense if Markson's car had been stolen from the airport parking lot.

There might be a way to get part of the answer.

I stopped at Walgreens on my way to the South Tucson City Hall and bought a stiff, canvas arm sling and some dark lavender eye shadow, then rubbed dime-sized eye shadow dots around my throat like a necklace of finger bruises and added another smear under my left eye. Emily Markson's bruises hadn't looked much different, but hers would be tougher to get rid of.

The South Tucson City Hall still had the pale, flaky remains of a painted mural clinging to the side wall: a starlit night, an Indian chief, and what looked like a giant headless lizard. I stuck my left arm through the canvas sling and crossed the parking lot.

Three clerks were available at the counter. I chose the young, round-faced woman on the left, the one with her eyes on the countertop and a despondent slump to her shoulders.

"Can you help me, please?" The clerk glanced up, her eyes widening when she spotted the eggplant shadows on my neck. My right hand cradled my canvas-covered left elbow.

"I'm trying to find out the name of the person who owns the bar called Juanito's."

She turned to a rack of plastic shelves on her right, plucked paperwork from the third tier, and directed her reply to the countertop. "Fill in this form and you can come back tomorrow for the information. It's a ten-dollar fee for duplication and it's twenty dollars if you need it notarized."

I let my eyes well with tears. "I don't have ten dollars. And I don't need a copy anyway. Just a name."

She raised her eyes again, as if checking the shadow of a new bruise seen in her own mirror. "What is it, honey?"

"I can't make him pay until I know his name." I tried unsuccessfully to move my bandaged arm; a broken-winged mourning dove who had somehow found her way indoors.

The woman looked right and left, then leaned toward me. "He hurt you like this and you don't even know his name?"

"It was . . . he said . . . I thought he was going to be nice."

I didn't need to see her reaction. Her voice already said that she understood the intentional humiliation of a casual encounter, and the gut punch of misplaced trust.

She only hesitated a moment. "Tell me what you know, and I'll look it up right now."

I gave her the address of the bar.

"Juan Villalobos," she said, coming back from her computer search. "There are two mailing addresses: the one you gave me and this one on Silverlake." She shoved a scrap of paper across the counter.

I nodded gratefully and tucked the note into the sling. "Thank you."

"And honey?" the woman said, placing her hand over mine on the counter. "Please tell me you'll go to the police. He can't get away with this."

CHAPTER SEVEN

Back in the truck, I ripped the Velcro strip apart and took the sling off.

The bartender may not be the bar owner but at least the name could give me a place to start. And if it was the same guy, and if Felicia was his daughter, I now had two addresses for them.

I checked my watch. Just noon. Felicia had looked like a high schooler to me, so she probably wouldn't be at either address right now, but I was willing to wait until she showed up.

I called my friend Mad Cow up in Phoenix. She wasn't due into work at HandsOn until this evening.

"Hey, I got a winner last night," she said. "Maybe not a Dumb Question, but certainly a Dumb Criminal. Guy phones in, wants directions to his own house. So I ask him for the address. Says he forgot. Turns out he's one of the valet parkers at this swanky restaurant and, as long as he had the house keys along with the car keys, he thought he'd go rob the house while the owners were still dining."

"If he'd had a brain in his head, he would have just looked for the registration in the glove box. Or gone to the address book in the GPS. Most everybody plugs in their address as 'home.'"

"If he were a brain trust, he wouldn't be parking cars," she said.

"What about Mario?" I reminded her, referring to the guy she dated last summer.

"Mario's brains included several other muscle groups. Hey, are you coming in tonight? I've got a mean salsa I can bring in."

"No, I'm going to be down here in Tucson for another day." I told her about the meeting with Deke Treadwell. "You said you had a friend at the Motor Vehicle Division."

"Yeah, an old high school buddy."

"Can you find out what make and model of car a couple of people drive?"

"Sure, but the cops can do that, too. Why don't you just give the names to this detective?"

I'd already asked Deke Treadwell to believe in me one more time than I should have. If I had any curiosity about Felicia or the guy who disappeared from Markson's car, it would be better if I satisfied that urge privately.

"I'm just double-checking something. If it pans out, I'll definitely take it to the cops." I gave her the four names I was interested in.

I stopped at a Circle K for a six-pack of Diet Coke and looked up the Silverlake address on a street map.

"Hey, you gonna buy that?" the guy at the counter yelled as I refolded the map and stuck it back in the display.

"Just browsing," I said, turning toward him.

He swallowed hard and looked down. I realized that I hadn't cleaned any of the eye shadow bruises off my neck and face. I must have looked more like a fighter than an abused woman.

Back in the car, I spit on a paper napkin and wiped away as much of the purple as I could. There was nothing I could do about the tight shoulders, the steely gaze, or the pent-up anger. They'd been there so long that they were part of me now. I started the truck and headed for the Silverlake address.

It was a wide street without curbs or sidewalks, and had only a half dozen homes on the block, spread out like a jack-o'-lantern's gap-tooth smile. The lots in between the houses were bare dirt littered with glass shards, a healthy crop of McDonald's wrappers, and an abandoned toilet that sprouted a tumbleweed crown.

The Villaloboses' house was ochre-colored brick, with a bright turquoise front door and a cyclone fence that guarded a yard of dead grass. There were no cars in front of the house or in the plastic-roofed ramada at the side, and the curtains in the front window were closed.

I parked down the block, not at all circumspect in my surveillance. It was hard to be covert in a neighborhood with no retail outlets, no handy trees to hide behind, and with so few houses that the residents probably knew the names of each other's dogs.

It must have been 110 degrees in the truck, even with the windows down. Some autumn weather. After two hours, all I had to show for my effort was a sweated-through shirt and a swollen bladder.

At two o'clock, Mad Cow called back with the information I'd asked for. Felicia and Juan Villalobos had the same address and were both licensed drivers of a white 1995 Honda. Emily Markson drove a Jaguar, and her neighbor and lawyer, Paul Willard, had two cars registered in his name, neither of them a blue Ford. Of interest, though, Willard's wife, Aloma, drove a blue Taurus. Mad Cow said her driver's license photo was a stunner.

At three o'clock I gave up my post. Felicia might be coming home soon, but it couldn't be soon enough. I'd try again tonight. I threw the last empty can of Coke into the bed of the truck and was headed back to Bonita's when I hung a left without thinking.

Muscle memory, I call it—when the body does what it is used to doing, through habit or custom or ease. Like the flex and curl of weight lifting, or the hand-to-mouth gesture of a longtime smoker. It's the muscle that kicks in when you turn onto your parents' street without any intention of doing so.

I pulled to the curb a good fifty yards from the house and put the truck in park. Sat there looking at what I'd lost, although it had been here all along.

The front door opened and a tall thin woman came out. Her hair was shorter than the last time I'd seen her and it looked like she'd lost weight. She still held herself straight, but her posture eased as she picked up the hose, canted her hip to the left, and began watering the ironwood tree in the front yard.

I wondered if my mother ever thought about me at all or if she'd erased my image from her mind as easily as she'd taken my pictures out of the family album. I'd watched her grow more distant each day as the prosecution added details about my role in the death of Walter Racine. Watched as her mouth drew taut and her eyes steeled themselves against me. Watched as she approached me after the jury verdict and said, "I don't care what they said. I know you did it."

She'd pushed me against the wall outside the courtroom, blocking the view of her hurled accusations from passersby. "You are not my daughter. I'm sorry we brought you into our lives. You are an evil seed. We should have seen it when we took you in."

That was the moment that it all made sense to me. "First there was Jessie. Then we had three boys. Then three girls." Once she'd had her own children, the adopted child became less important and could be pushed away—shuffled into the role of caretaker.

Now that long-ago Easter Sunday made sense, too. We'd all been groomed and preened, hair slicked back and shoes tied, ready for church. "Let's get a picture of the family," my mother said, handing me the camera. "You take it, Jessie."

I should have known then.

"I only have six children," my mother said to me that day outside the courtroom.

I waited in the truck outside the house, watching the water soak into the ground around the ironwood, until she'd gone back inside. I started the engine and drove away.

Shoving memories of my mother's anger aside, I stopped at El Con Mall and bought a sleeveless tunic and a pair of yoga pants to replace the shirt and khakis I'd been wearing for two days. I'd already stayed longer than I expected to. But I had to be back at work tomorrow night so one more set of fresh clothes would do me. I was ready to go back to a world where no one associated my name with murder.

My cell phone rang as I trudged back across the parking lot. "Jessie, it's Nancy Horowitz." *Click click click* of rabbit teeth all the way from Phoenix.

"Hi! I'm taking that comp day you offered, but I'll be back in tomorrow night."

"Don't bother. I'm phoning to let you know that we're letting you go."

"What?" My performance reviews had been fine, and I hadn't taken a lot of days off.

"We got a call from Len Sabin in the Tucson Police Department. He was just following up on the theft of Mr. Markson's car, but he told us about your real name and your background."

I felt my cheeks redden, and it wasn't the heat.

"Jessie Dancing is my real name. I haven't lied to you about anything."

"You weren't completely honest with us, either. We aren't interested in employing someone who was accused of murder."

"Accused, maybe. But also tried and found not guilty." I tried to keep the snarl out of my voice but I didn't succeed.

"Where would you like your last paycheck sent? I've already

alerted the management of the house-sitting company you used as a reference, so I'm not sure your current address will be available much longer."

Fuck. Losing my job was one thing, but that house was the best place I'd had in two years. I wasn't even sure that what she'd done was legal—firing me for no reason and then alerting my landlord—but that investigation would have to wait.

"I'll pick it up tomorrow."

Who was this asshole Len Sabin, and why was he ruining my life?

By the time I got to Juanito's bar I had almost been able to put a positive spin on things. If I helped identify the car thief, maybe HandsOn would be grateful—maybe think twice about firing me. It was five-thirty, earlier than I'd arrived the previous night, maybe early enough that a teenager checking in with her father would still be around.

I parked around the corner, with a clear view of the back door through a tiny slice of space between a tree and a three-bay body shop. Felicia probably wouldn't recognize my truck from here and, parked behind the tree the way I was, she wouldn't be able to see my face, either.

I'd been there a half hour when the garage closed. Two of the mechanics made a beeline for Juanito's, but there were no other new arrivals.

By seven I was hot, thirsty, and bored. Out of the corner of my eye, I spotted Felicia walking out the back door of the bar. I started the truck and made a U-turn, just in time to see her buckling into the front seat of a white Honda that had been pulled up on the far side of the building.

She put her turn signal on and headed south. I followed, close enough that I could see her, far enough back that she didn't think I was tied to her bumper. The Honda traveled under I-10, then jigged left and right until I was sure of her destination. She pulled to the side of the road and parked on the dusty verge in front of her house on Silverlake.

I eased to a stop behind her and got out without shutting the door behind me. Felicia was turned away, digging something out of an oversized purse when I reached the driver's door of the Honda.

She reacted like a wildcat, battering me with her hands and purse, and slamming the door against my knees as she tried to get out of the car. I put all my weight against the door, reached in and put one hand on her shoulder.

"Calm down! I'm not going to hurt you."

"How did you find me? I don't know what you want. I don't know anything!"

I reached across her and dug the keys out of the ignition.

"I just want to know what you were doing out there in the desert yesterday. Were you there to meet someone?"

She shook her head, but there was real fear in her eyes. What was she involved with? Drug trafficking? Gangs? A car-theft ring? She was scared of somebody else a lot more than she was of me.

"Felicia, I'm trying to help you."

"You can't help me." She laced her fingers around the steering wheel so tight that her knuckles turned white.

"I'll bet the cops would like to know what you were doing out there." I hadn't planned on telling Treadwell about the girl, but the threat was the only leverage I had.

"No! Don't tell them. Please!"

She clammed up. Nothing I said made any difference. She could have been a stone. I shrugged, backed away from the door, and threw the keys back inside the car.

She picked them up off the seat, watching me with squinted eyes, until I was back in the truck.

The explosion turned my windshield to glass pebbles, and a wave of fire rolled toward me from where the Honda used to be.

"Did you see anybody else around when the car blew up?" Treadwell asked.

I shook my head. "I don't even know if she had the keys in the ignition yet."

"Then it must have been on a timer, otherwise it would have gone off when the girl first started the car back at the bar."

I had asked the first cops on the scene to call him. A familiar face, even if it was one likely to look at me unkindly, was better than a stranger.

I had been moved back a half-block from the burning car while the firemen sprayed foam around the hulking black carcass. There had been no hope for Felicia.

My mouth was dry and there was a ringing in my ears. I felt like I'd swallowed a telephone, dial tone and all. A paramedic placed a thin, foil blanket over my shoulders.

"It could have . . . we were just . . ."

I felt the proximity of death, like a coiled snake at my feet. I shivered, then bent low and vomited onto the pavement.

"Sit down right here." Treadwell guided me to the wide rear bumper of the paramedic's unit.

The front end of my truck had taken the full force of the blast. The fire department had kept the gas tank from exploding, but the hood and front fenders were charred with the black lick of flames and the pebbled windshield had collapsed.

I caught a look at my reflection in the paramedic truck's shiny paneling and laughed, a sound closer to hysteria than comedy. My eyelashes and eyebrows were singed off. Blisters had formed across the left side of my lips.

"I'm so sorry." I didn't know who I was apologizing to. To Felicia, for not seeing the danger? To Treadwell, for not giving him Felicia's name? Or to the gods, in repentance for getting involved at all?

I handed Treadwell the beer coaster, and told him about meeting Felicia by the arroyo and tracking her down at the bar. He took lots of notes.

"Stay out of this, Jessie," he said, closing his notebook.

"I hear you."

It wasn't too late to back away from this. I was only tied to Markson's car by a phone call. And that was for a job I no longer had. And who's to say that my following Felicia had anything to do with her death at all?

I used to weigh the lives I'd saved—the people I'd helped—against the life I'd taken, hoping that somehow the karmic scales would tip in my favor. I didn't think that was possible now.

The paramedics checked me out and gave me burn salve for my arms and face, but still wanted me to go to the hospital. Treadwell ushered me into the rear of the ambulance, promising to have my truck towed back to Bonita's when they cleared the scene.

"Deke," I asked before he could shut the door, "who's this Len Sabin? Why was he checking up on me in Phoenix?"

Treadwell mopped his face with a handkerchief. "He was Jim Dougherty's partner in the Walter Racine murder investigation."

In *my* murder investigation, he meant.

"I remember Dougherty. He testified against me at the trial."

"Yeah. Jimmy retired last year and Sabin's my partner now. You know, with your dad leaving and all." He paused. I hoped he wasn't going to go into all the reasons my dad quit the force. His belief in my innocence, cashing in his pension and taking a second mortgage on the house to get me that lousy lawyer, Buckley Thurber, who took the money, then told me to plead guilty anyway. Dad's depression when my mom first threatened to leave him if he continued to stand by me.

"Anyway, Sabin was real interested to hear about it when your name popped up in this investigation. It looks like he's still got a hard-on for you, Jessie."

I nodded but didn't look him in the eye.

"He cost me my job, Deke."

"I'm sorry. You know I never would have said anything to the folks in Phoenix."

"I guess your partner didn't feel the same way."

"Len's not a bad guy, Jessie. He's a good cop. But he's nobody I'd like as an enemy," Treadwell said, turning away.

Early Monday evening must not be high time for emergency room visits; I was in and out within three hours after lots of probing for nasal singeing, airway burn, and concussion. Back at Bonita's house, drained by the adrenaline high, I sat at the dining room table in silence, punctuated only by the *drip, drip, drip* of the kitchen faucet.

Bonita's neighborhood hummed with normal life—a laugh track on television, a dog barking down the block.

Those neighbors probably didn't know the patina that charred human flesh leaves clinging to the back of your throat. The shiver that won't leave your bones, even hours after the blast missed you. Maybe that's how war veterans feel coming home: welcoming the peace but still burning with the proximity of horror.

I sat there in the darkness, replaying the blast, the heat, the shattering sound, the loss.

Ah, Jesus, that poor girl. She certainly wasn't the person I talked to in Markson's car, but she seemed to be a victim of the crime that night nonetheless. I hoped I hadn't been the one to put her in jeopardy. She was afraid of something or someone, and I may have pointed them right at her.

I nudged the tower of pizza boxes in the corner with my toe, sending them sprawling across the floor.

There was a message on my cell phone from my landlords at Mind Your Manors. They didn't see a need for my services any longer. Would I please clear out and drop off the key by tomorrow?

Things were really looking up.

CHAPTER EIGHT

That night I dreamed of firewalkers—rail-thin creatures standing on glowing coals, weaving in time to a rhythm I couldn't hear. They beckoned and I came closer. One featureless creature reached out and grabbed my hand, her bony fingers cold even though they were on fire. When she turned I saw Felicia's eyes, but what had been smooth mocha skin was now blackened and hung in tatters. She opened her mouth but nothing came out.

I woke in a sweat, teeth chattering and goose bumps on my arms. It took me a moment to recognize the unfamiliar room, with Bonita's left-behind clothing still in cardboard boxes in the corner.

I pawed through the boxes, finally locating a pair of running shorts and a T-shirt that proclaimed: ROCK IS DEAD. LONG LIVE PAPER AND SCISSORS! I tugged the shirt over my head, then pushed the sleeves up over my biceps, showing off the tats.

I shut the front door quietly behind me. Dawn was only moments away.

I did a couple of stretches, using an old poster-laden telephone pole for support, then took off running north on Swan toward River Road. I had intended to jog along the Rillito River, but once

I got to the dry wash I changed my mind and continued north. It would be the same five-mile loop I'd originally planned, but this way I could pass by the Markson house.

I wondered if Darren Markson had cut his trip short and come home.

The world turned from blue-gray to wheat, then gold, as the first rays of the sun peaked over the Rincon Mountains and my shadow lengthened to a ten-foot praying mantis beside me. Although my breathing was ragged, I held my pace as the road steepened and I entered the Catalina Foothills.

This part of town was a lot more built up than it had been when I was a kid. There were condo developments within spitting distance of million-dollar homes; and Burger Kings, McDonald's, and Starbucks as prolific now as the saguaro cactus used to be. A couple of cars passed me going downhill. Business types, by the look of them.

I'd have loved to know if Felicia had some connection to Darren Markson. Or maybe she knew the guy who had stolen Markson's car. Maybe Mrs. Markson would recognize Felicia's name, not that she had any reason to see me again, or to tell me the truth if she did.

When I reached the Marksons' house I stopped at the top of the driveway, jogging in place. No lights were on; no dogs barking. If the cops had released the Cadillac back to them, it was probably in a repair shop and not the garage.

I was turning away when a movement from the side of the house caught my eye. I stepped behind the lacy curtain of a six-foot creosote bush and held my breath. Thirty feet away, Paul Willard shut the Marksons' kitchen door quietly behind himself, shrugged a white tennis sweater over his shoulders, and tiptoed across the gravel that separated his property from the Marksons'.

The jog back to Bonita's house went faster than the trip out, my mind occupied with wild speculation. Emily Markson and Paul

Willard were having an affair? No wonder he'd been the first to hear about Darren Markson's phone call. But why had Felicia been killed? Somebody was still lying.

I bought two grande coffees at Starbucks and power-walked back to the house.

A car pulled into Bonita's driveway as I was finishing the second cup. Small, tan, and unremarkable, it couldn't be anything but a rental or an unmarked cop car.

The man who got out was almost gaunt, with sucked-in cheeks and slicked-back black hair. His skin looked like it had battled acne in his teenage years and lost. I'd last seen him in the back row of the courtroom on the day the verdict was read.

"I see you got your truck towed back," he said without a greeting.

I nodded.

"Long time no see, Ms. Gammage." He offered his badge as a calling card. Detective Len Sabin. Tucson Police Department, shield number 743.

"It's Dancing now."

He went on as if he hadn't heard me. "I understand you took the call the night Darren Markson's car was stolen."

"That's right." He already knew that. Why was he here?

"Had you ever met Mr. Markson before?"

"I still haven't met him."

He clipped his badge holder back onto his belt. "And you were also at the scene of a car bombing yesterday."

I swallowed hard.

"Kind of a coincidence, don't you think?"

"Yeah. A coincidence is something you can't explain."

"Can't? Or won't?"

"What do you want, Detective?" I could feel that jail-cell chill creeping up my spine.

Sabin took a hard candy from his pocket, slowly twisted off the plastic wrapping, and popped the candy in his mouth. Butterscotch.

"I don't give up, Ms. Gammage. Ask anybody, they'll tell you. Lenny Sabin is like an elephant, they'll say. He doesn't give up and he doesn't forget."

"I was found not guilty, Detective."

He made sure there was no grime from the blast, then leaned back against the cab of my truck. "That's the funny thing about the justice system. It makes no distinction between not guilty and innocent. I do."

"Then the police department should have acted a lot faster in stopping Walter Racine."

"Is that a confession?" His cheeks sucked in and out, working the candy.

"No. It's a fact." I'd tried to tell them. If the police had listened to me then, it wouldn't have ended with two bullets in Walter Racine's head. I spun around and stormed back into the house, slamming the door.

I waited until Sabin had driven off before breathing easy. At least the guy hadn't warned me not to leave town. I showered, packed the khakis and shirt I'd worn on the way down, and picked up my truck keys before realizing that my truck was going nowhere. I didn't even know if the engine still worked, but the melted front tires and blasted-out windshield were enough to keep it off the road.

I arranged to have the truck towed to a shop for either a diagnosis or last rites.

Bonita wouldn't mind my using her VW. I grabbed the keys off the dining room table and jotted a note to Martin in case he came by and thought the car had been stolen.

Why did Len Sabin have such an anvil of a grudge against me?

Surely he'd investigated other crimes where the jury had returned a not guilty verdict. Maybe he had known Racine or they had belonged to the same golf club or something. Whatever it was, Sabin still wanted me behind bars.

There are no back roads between Tucson and Phoenix, just I-10 and a couple of frontage roads that could be dubbed Middle of Nowhere and Next to Middle of Nowhere. I was past Picacho Peak when I realized that I did, in fact, have a choice of roads before me.

I'd have to return Bonita's car at some point, but other than that, I had no reason to return to Tucson. And without a job or a home, I had no reason to stay in Phoenix, either. Maybe now was the time to make the break that I should have made two and a half years ago.

Back then it had seemed like dropping a surname and moving a hundred miles up the road was a big step in putting distance between my new life and my history. But that was an illusion—a suggestion of movement when none really exists—like the wavy promise of a mirage that disappears the closer you get.

Maybe now was the time to start fresh. A new name. No Dancing allowed. And a new place. Somewhere green and soft. Or blue and cold, although I'd feel like an alien being in either one of those environments. A dry, scaly time traveler who didn't know the secret handshake. Could I reinvent myself convincingly enough in that new world that even I could forget I was a murderer?

Killing leaves a mark on the killer as well. Not as lethal a mark, certainly, but a stain—a stench—all the same. And you wonder if others can smell what you've done. Sabin was right—not guilty was different than innocent.

I drove straight to the HandsOn office, parking purposefully in the visitor's space by the front door. Nancy Horowitz had left my check at the reception desk. I waved good-bye to the receptionist and headed to the Mansion Manqué.

There wasn't much to pack. Three years ago, I'd been a person of substance. I'd had a job—well, bartending, but at least it was regular work—I had furniture, and a real savings account. A future, for God's sake. Now all my belongings fit into two wheeled suitcases and a pillowcase full of dirty clothes, and *future* was just another tense.

I took a last look around at the good life and said good-bye.

Back in the car, I cranked the airco to frigid and debated my options. The Mind Your Manors office was in central Phoenix. I could go in any direction from there.

I cashed my paycheck at a bank branch on Van Buren and took out all but a hundred dollars of the two thousand I'd managed to set aside. Not much, but enough to live on for a couple of months. Enough gas money to get me far, far away. Maybe enough for first and last deposit on a little room somewhere overlooking a creek. In the time it had taken me to drive across town, I'd decided there were only three rules for this new life of mine: take nothing larger than a county road, eat at any place called Mom's, and turn in another direction if the sun gets in your eyes.

I headed northeast out of town, crossing the Tonto National Forest and the Mogollon Rim before arriving at Mormon Lake south of Flagstaff at nightfall. Pleased that my "smaller roads" guideline had gifted me with soaring cliffs and pine forests for a view, I was regretting the decision to wait until I found a café called Mom's. I had to settle for dinner at the gas station mini-mart and a room at the Duck Blind Inn at Mormon Lake.

The motel was squat and ash colored, with a massive neon sign towering overhead like a stern teacher. I bought a Diet Coke from the vending machine and walked to the edge of the lake. Stubby oak trees and thin, dry firs were scattered around the shoreline. Pale tufts of grass tried to wag in the evening breeze. Even with last month's monsoon rains, the lake was a shrunken, muddy pond, the water's edge receding like an old man's hairline. I took a deep breath, hunting for the pine scent I needed.

A child cried from one of the rooms on the end, "I don't want to go to bed yet!"

I wondered how little Katie was doing. Her mother, Catherine, had been dead more than three years now, washed away in an unusual October rainstorm that swept her car into the flooded arroyo like it was a twig, and then turned it upside down in the riverbed silt. There was no question of culpability; there had been other people there as witnesses. The driver behind her who had managed to brake before plunging into the torrent had done everything he could to reach Catherine, but hadn't made it in time.

If she hadn't died before going to the cops . . . if she'd lived long enough to testify against her uncle Walter . . . if I hadn't seen the danger for myself. Shit. All the *ifs* in the world wouldn't change anything. In the end, I'd had to do it alone—accuser, witness, judge, jury, and executioner all rolled into one.

I inhaled again, storing up the scent of water for the desert days ahead.

My cell phone rang as I unlocked the door to my room.

"Jessie? Where are you?"

"Mormon Lake, Deke. Taking a little R and R, since your partner got me fired."

"Get back here now."

"Why?"

"They've found a body."

My mouth hadn't caught up with my mind yet.

"And not just any body. Darren Markson," he continued.

"But he's in New Mexico. . . ."

"It doesn't look that way." Deke Treadwell, the master of understatement.

"Was he . . ." How could I put into words that vicious beating I'd heard?

Treadwell seemed to understand. "Yeah, it looks like somebody strung him up by the heels and used him for a piñata, but that's not what killed him. He was shot in the back of the head."

"Where did you find him?" Focus on the details, Jessie. That way you don't have to think about his death.

"Buried under some loose rocks out in the Saguaro National Park. A hiker's dog found him."

"East or west?" Only a cactus-lover would consider them parks, but the two massive areas made parentheses around Tucson's east and west borders.

"East."

It was pretty desolate land out there, but only a couple of miles from where his car had been found.

"How long has he been dead?" Was his really the voice I'd heard on the other end of that call? Had he died only moments later?

"We're doing the autopsy now."

I asked what Emily Markson had had to say.

"She's still insisting that she talked to him in New Mexico. When we started to ask more questions, her lawyer stepped in and shut her up."

Lawyer-lover, I wanted to say, then remembered I hadn't told Deke about either Emily Markson's bruises or her late-night visitor. And she'd told me she didn't recognize the voice on the HandsOn disc. Had that been her husband's voice?

"I still don't understand what this has to do with me. I never met the guy."

"We found a scrap of paper buried with him. With your name on it. Len Sabin's getting a warrant to pick you up."

I thought about heading north and leaving Tucson and Len Sabin behind forever. Hell, I was going to change my name and identity anyway. What difference would it make if I was hiding from myself or from the police? I threw off the guilt-warmed sheets and splayed myself across the bed. I could throw away the cell phone. Sell Bonita's car and send her the money.

I had no real reason to go back, except the desire to prove my innocence. Declared not guilty of a crime I had committed, I was not about to be railroaded into one I had not.

The sun rose in a clear sky, etching sharp shadows across the squat motel and the gray grass. There is an urgency to the shadows in Arizona, a clarion call to choose the light or the dark, to find refuge or freedom. There is no ambiguity between shadow and sunlight. Only decision. And I had decided that starting anew also meant starting clean, with no gallows hanging over me. I headed south.

Forgetting my allegiance to county roads, the drive back to Tucson took a lot less time than the trip north. I had no explanation for the note found on Markson's body, but I had a guess. Emily Markson had my name; she'd called HandsOn and requested that I come to Tucson and play the recording for her. The only thing that made sense was that while she was burying Markson's body, the note she'd written herself with my name on it had slipped into the grave with him.

The detectives had probably come to the same conclusion themselves.

Treadwell met me in the TPD parking lot, and I didn't give him a chance to say anything.

"Emily Markson wrote that note, right?"

He shook his head. "It doesn't match her handwriting."

"But who else—?"

"Come on inside, Jessie." He led me by the elbow past the ID checker behind bullet-proof glass at the front door and through the lobby. Len Sabin was waiting for us in an interview room on the third floor.

My heart stuttered when he read me my rights.

CHAPTER NINE

I told the cops about Emily Markson's bruises, about the anger on her face when she listened to the recording, and about seeing Paul Willard sneak out of her house at dawn. They took notes, but didn't seem surprised by the information.

"My only association with Darren Markson was that phone call," I insisted for the sixth time. "And the only person who knew my name was his wife." Except for the 911 operator, and the cops, and my bosses at HandsOn, that is.

"Mrs. Markson has an alibi for the evening her husband disappeared," Treadwell said.

"Who? Her lawyer?"

"We know who wrote that note," Sabin said, unwrapping another butterscotch.

"Who was it?" And why the hell wasn't that person sitting in this claustrophobic interview room instead of me?

"It matched the handwriting on that beer coaster you gave me," Treadwell said. "We think Felicia Villalobos wrote it."

"And there you were, right beside her when she was killed," Sabin added.

"I told you about that. I met her out in the desert where Markson's car was hit . . . I didn't know her from Adam. She must have written down my plate number or something . . . got my name that way." Much the same way I'd gotten her details when I called in for MVD information from Mad Cow at HandsOn.

"You don't really think Felicia had anything to do with killing Markson, do you?" I couldn't imagine the teenager shooting a man in the back of the head. On the other hand, three years ago I couldn't have imagined myself doing the same thing.

"Still, it's kinda curious," Sabin said, ignoring my question. "First Walter Racine gets killed right after you've been going on about him being a child molester and all. Then you turn up around two more dead bodies and say you have nothing to do with them, either. Come to think of it, I'd call that more than curious—more like a pattern, don't you think?" He'd twisted the candy wrapper into a tiny noose.

They let me go an hour later, finally coughing up the "don't leave town" mantra. I drove back to Bonita's house in a rage. What the hell were they thinking? I'd only come to town to help them with the recording from Markson's car anyway.

At least I had an alibi for the time his car had been hit.

But Sabin kept hinting that Markson had died much later than that, and I could easily have driven to Tucson in that time. Treadwell didn't stop him, but he didn't push me on it, either. I was betting that the autopsy results weren't in yet, and the whole thing was a game Sabin was running.

In any case, I wasn't about to sit there like a lamb and wait for them to order chops. I needed to know more about Felicia, and who she might have passed my license plate number on to. The only person I could ask was her father.

He'd already seen me in the bar, so I had to come up with some logical reason for having been there. Something that also gave me a reason to keep asking questions about his daughter. For what I had in mind, I'd need to look fairly respectable.

Bonita's boxed clothing wasn't of much help—I'd look more like a teenager's friend than an adult—so I went back to the newly rinsed-out tunic I'd worn yesterday and added a pair of pinstriped trousers that I'd last worn when I interviewed for the job at HandsOn.

Juan Villalobos probably wouldn't be at the bar today, so soon after his daughter was murdered, but I swung past the building to make sure. There was a CLOSED sign on the door, so I continued on to the Silverlake address. The earth was scorched with a ten-yard black scar where her car had blown up, and crime scene tape was still tied to four wooden stakes in the ground. I parked well away from the blast area, unlatched the gate in the cyclone fence, and hooked it again behind me.

Juan Villalobos opened the door only a moment after I knocked, his eyes dull with pain. He looked past me to the blackened front yard. He didn't say anything, but finally raised his eyebrows in question. A sad-eyed hound looking for a lost soul mate. What must it be like to imagine your daughter's death every time you open the door?

"Mr. Villalobos? I'm . . ."

"I'm sorry. I've forgotten—"

So had I. My mind was slow in coming up with a name and a story. "I'm a substitute teacher at Cholla High School. Felicia was in my English class." Cholla was the high school closest to their address. I hoped that she wasn't busing across town to another one. In that case, I'd insist that I'd been covering classes there, too.

He searched my face for a souvenir of our meeting. "You look familiar, but . . ."

"Sorry I didn't introduce myself when I saw you in the bar the other day."

"In the bar? Oh, that's right."

I don't think he made the connection to the bar at all. If he had, he would surely be worried about someone who had chased his child out the back door.

He ushered me in. It was dark with the curtains all closed, but no cooler than it was outdoors. Villalobos had either forgotten to turn on the air conditioner or he wanted his physical discomfort to match the emptiness and pain he felt inside.

The furniture was slipcovered with a light fabric, old pieces tarted up in their best finery. I sat on the edge of the couch.

"I saw the news about Felicia. I wanted to tell you how sorry we all are."

"Licia was a good girl. Everybody loved her." His eyes grew wet with the loss.

"She seemed so happy the last time I saw her."

"Happy? I hope so. She had that internship. She was doing well at Cholla. Did you know she was going to be the first person in our family to finish high school?"

I nodded. The high school would be my next stop. Maybe someone there knew what Felicia had been up to.

"We'll all miss her," I said. "Especially her boyfriend . . . um . . ."

He shook his head, but not in denial. "The Ochoa boy. I told the police that the bomb in the car would probably lead back to him. If he caused my beautiful girl to die . . ." The color drained from his face.

"Tell me about him."

"Carlos Ochoa . . . from Nogales. He's too old for Felicia, almost twenty-five. I never should have hired him."

"He works for you?"

"He used to. When I caught him stealing, I got rid of him. But he kept seeing Felicia behind my back."

An older boyfriend, especially someone your father didn't like, was the kind of person you'd meet secretly out in the desert. But she must have been pretty desperate to tell him to come to her father's bar. Maybe she'd been waiting for him outside, hoping that the father and boyfriend wouldn't run into each other.

The trip to the high school could wait. I had to find Carlos Ochoa.

It wouldn't be easy. There were lots of Ochoas in Nogales, and they were all one family. Even the first name and age wouldn't help much. There were probably a half dozen twenty-five-year-olds named Carlos.

But I had an in. An old high school friend, Beverly Drackett, had married into the Ochoa family the year after we graduated. Last I'd heard, she was living on a ranch just north of Nogales, within spitting distance of the border.

A phone call confirmed her current address and her invitation to come down for lunch. "I'm tired of talking to the kids. It would be great to catch up." We hadn't really been close enough to have much dirt to dish, but I jotted down directions to her house.

I phoned the repair shop to approve the cost of fixing the truck. New tires all the way around and a new windshield would do for now. The paint job would have to wait.

The steering wheel on Bonita's car was so hot that I wished I had oven mitts. It wasn't supposed to be this hot in September. We should have been on Simmer by now, not Deep Fry. I guided the VW to the freeway with a delicate two-finger grip that would at least cut down on the number of blisters.

I passed the three-hundred-year-old Tumacacori Mission and cemetery forty miles south of Tucson—cream and white patched-mud walls partially hidden by the surrounding mesquite trees—then was stunned back to modern times by the Rio Rico resort a few miles farther on. The resort's main building echoed the arches and shadows of the ancient church to the north, but the addition of palm trees and an impossibly green golf course gave it a Disneyland patina in this land of dun-colored hills and silver gray sagebrush.

When I spotted a highway patrol car behind me, I realized that Rio Rico would certainly be considered "out of town." Was Sabin having me followed? The patrolman swerved around me and I breathed a sigh of relief.

Beverly's turnoff was just past the resort, onto a paved, two-lane road that had opted for the pace of stop signs instead of traffic lights. It took another twenty minutes heading east through golden rolling hills before I spotted her mailbox.

She waved at me from a corral on the left side of the house. From a distance, she looked like the high schooler I'd last seen fifteen years ago. I turned the car in the direction of her wave, came to a stop, and shut off the engine.

"Gorgeous," I said, gesturing to the palomino she was grooming. His back was as tall as my shoulder and his mane glistened in the midday sun. The horse eyed me with curiosity, but once he'd established that I carried no food, he lost interest.

"That's Cochise. He's too old for riding now, but I love having him around." Beverly was still petite—soft, rounded curves and pouter pigeon breasts—but her face had become that of a disappointed adult, with a built-in scowl and the onset of gray where she parted her hair. It was like looking at those old amusement park photos where you stick your face through the oval on a cardboard dance-hall girl or gunslinger's cartoon body. You recognize part of the photo, but know somehow that the pieces don't fit.

Beverly returned the currycomb to a small tack room next to the corral and ushered me toward the house, a middle-class single-story ranch surrounded by enough acreage to call it a small kingdom. She ignored the laundry piled on the living room couch and led me through to the kitchen. I took a seat at the wooden plank table.

Beverly poured sun tea and we played the game of "what do you hear from so-and-so" for a few minutes. I lost. I'd never kept in touch with anyone from high school, but she seemed to delight in doing so. I nodded and smiled at all her passed-on news, often not even able to put a face to the name she mentioned, although her stories about Josh King, the guy I went to the senior prom with, made it sound like he was doing just fine without me.

"What about you?" she asked, after she'd shown me pictures of her children and husband, told me about her vacation to Rome two years earlier and her kids' new school, and detailed her sister's trials in adopting a child. She'd carefully avoided any questions about my incarceration and trial, although I'm sure I'd been a hot topic at the reunion that year.

I toyed with a bite of the salad she'd served for lunch, then set the fork back on the plate. "I've got my own business now. I track down missing persons. You know, people who have money coming to them, but they can't be found to collect it." You've got to say it slow and look straight at 'em. Liars look up and to the left when they're constructing a lie.

"That's so exciting." Her tone suggested that it was anything but. I think she would rather have heard about what life was like three years after having been a murder suspect. Schadenfreude, my old English Lit teacher had called it. The glee in recognizing that while you may be working at McDonald's, your classmate is flipping burgers behind bars.

I shrugged.

"How do you—?"

I interrupted her before the questions became too pointed and I had to come up with real answers about this supposed new business that would put the lie to my story.

"Anyway, that's why I'm here. I'm trying to track someone down, and I heard she was last seen with Carlos Ochoa from Nogales."

"Carlos the hothead? Or Carlos the gardener?"

"That doesn't narrow it down much, does it? He's about twenty-five, would have moved to Tucson in the last couple of years. Maybe worked at a bar up there."

"Maybe Carlos with the mustache. Let me check." She picked up a cell phone and dialed a number from memory. "*Abuela?* It's Beverly. Tomas's wife. Yes. Yes. That's the one." Her grandmother-in-law must have lots of relatives named Beverly. Or maybe lots of offspring named Tomas.

She gave the woman all the information we had on our Carlos.

"Anything else you can think of?" Beverly asked with her hand over the phone's speaker. "There are so many Ochoas around."

"He may be the kind of guy who would help himself to a cash drawer or help a few supplies go missing. And he might have been dating someone named Felicia . . . Licia." I didn't know how I was going to square those details with the notion of looking for a missing inheritor, and hoped I didn't have to.

"Why didn't you say so?" She thanked the woman on the other end of the phone and hung up. "I don't know about the cash-drawer stuff, but Carlos-with-a-Mustache is definitely dating a woman named Felicia."

"Who is he? How do you know him?"

"He's my husband's uncle's cousin. So that's . . . what? His second cousin? I've never been sure of that stuff. Anyway, he's family. And he came to dinner a couple of months ago, just going on and on about the beautiful Felicia. He wouldn't tell us who she was—said we'd meet her soon enough."

"Do you know how I can get hold of him?"

"Sure." She dug through some loose papers tucked under the telephone on the counter. "Here's his Tucson address."

I thanked her and picked up my keys.

"Jessie, don't go so soon. I was going to ask—"

I cut her off with a hug and a wave good-bye. Three years was too soon to start reminiscing about murder trials. And I don't know what I would have told her anyway.

CHAPTER TEN

It was midmorning Thursday before I made it to the address Beverly had given me. Carlos Ochoa's Tucson house, a squat, low-slung box of sand-colored concrete blocks on the east side of town, was a fixer-upper in the middle of its transformation. The building itself was at least thirty years old, and its tarred roof shingles had been torn off and littered the ground like black leaves. Gaps under the front window proved that the blotchy stucco was ornamental, not functional—pancake makeup for a house.

There was a high-pitched whirring from the backyard. I followed the sound past a drainage trail of water and through the muddy side yard.

He was turned away from me, trapezium muscles flexing and bunching on his bare back as he worked at the tile saw. Spraying water glistened in his hair. He turned when I cleared my throat.

"Can I help you?"

Close to my age, with a body both functional and ornamental.

"Carlos Ochoa?"

"That's my little brother. I'm Guillermo . . . Bill." He took off one wet work glove and offered me his hand.

"Hi. I'm trying to find Carlos."

"You've got the right place, but he isn't here right now."

I glanced at the war-zone backyard behind him. A cracked and listing baby-blue toilet, hillocks of warped linoleum tiles, and powder-dusted floes of dry wall. It looked like the house had been disemboweled.

"Do you know when he'll be back?" Maybe he'd say six hours and I could offer to wait. Maybe he'd say next year. I'd still offer to stick around.

"Don't know." He placed a newly cut square of cinnamon-colored tile gently on the ground. "He had some personal business. I haven't seen him for a couple of days."

"Does he know a woman named Felicia Villalobos? Licia?"

He shut off the machine. "Why do you want to know?"

"She's gone missing. Her father said that Carlos might know where she was."

He took two steps toward me and grabbed my arm above the elbow. "Lady, I don't know what you're up to, but the news is full of that car bomb that killed her. Now why don't we start all over again and you tell me who you really are and why you're here."

I yanked my arm back and turned to run. His hand slid from my upper arm, but managed to snag the shoulder strap to my purse. I was halfway to the car when he called out.

"Don't know how far you're going to get without these, Miss Jessie Dancing."

The clink of metal on metal.

I turned. He held my open wallet at waist level and dangled my car keys like bait.

He put the keys and purse on the concrete slab porch, and stepped over to an ice chest near the sliding glass door. He pulled out two bottles of beer, opened them with a hinge on the side of the Igloo and held one out to me.

"Come on. I'm not going to bite." He set one beer down for me, settled himself on the lip of the concrete, and moved my purse and keys to the far side, well out of my reach.

I picked up the beer, but moved back to my own corner of the porch.

"Why do you want to find Carlos?"

"I'm a friend of Felicia's father. He knew that they were spending time together, and thought . . . with the bomb and everything . . . that Carlos might be in trouble. He wanted me to check on him."

He drained a full third of the beer. "Horseshit. That's another lie. Felicia's father hates Carlos."

"Yeah, he does think Carlos is involved somehow. Aren't you worried about him?"

His thousand-yard stare carried only as far as the rickety wooden fence that bordered the yard. "Yeah, I'm worried, too. I expected him home by now."

"Did he say where he was going?"

He shook his head. "Said he had to take care of something. That's usually bad news when Carlos says it. He never really left the gang life, even if he said it was all behind him."

"Gang life in Nogales?" I pointed at the spiky shield tattoo over Ochoa's heart. *Braceros* was spelled out in medieval lettering below the shield. The Braceros were best known for drug trafficking and shaking down illegal immigrants who were trying to cross the border.

"Yeah, both of us. We thought that moving to Tucson would give us some distance. And for the most part, it did."

Much like I'd felt, getting as far away as Phoenix.

"But you think Carlos is still involved with them?" I moved behind Ochoa and bent to retrieve my purse and car keys. He didn't try to stop me.

"Maybe. We lived together when we first came to Tucson. But since he got his own place, I haven't seen him as much."

"What about him and Felicia?"

His smile was subdued. "Oh, man, that was love with a capital L. He was getting this house ready for her. Wanted to marry her someday. But the families hated it. Her father thought Carlos was too old for Felicia. My mother wants Carlos to marry Angela—the girl she'd picked out for him." He paused. "Looks like she might get her way after all."

I picked up a piece of chalk that he'd used to mark the tiles and scrawled my cell phone number on the concrete slab. "Let me know when your brother gets back."

Ochoa nodded, but kept his eyes on the back fence. He was more worried than he was willing to admit.

Idling at a red light, I replayed the conversation with Ochoa in my head. Maybe it was Carlos's voice I'd heard right after the accident with Markson's car. It had sounded young. For that matter, maybe it was Guillermo's. Either one of the Ochoas might be the one who got my name from Felicia and dropped that note in Markson's grave.

If I was going to get off the wanted poster in Sabin's office, I had to find out more about these guys. Was there some relationship between Felicia Villalobos and the Marksons? Or between the Marksons and the Ochoas? And how did that smarmy lawyer Paul Willard fit into things?

I was glad Bonita's rent was paid up for a while, but if I was going to stay in Tucson, I'd need supplies.

I stopped at a Safeway to stock up on some of the basics. Milk, eggs, coffee, and beef jerky. It was a light load, and I swung the plastic bag as I returned to the car.

My father was waiting at the VW's back door. His jaw was more saggy than chiseled now, and he'd moved on to bifocal glasses, but his eyes were still bright blue behind the magnified lenses.

"I was wondering who'd be driving Bonita's car."

"Dad." I wanted so badly to wrap my arms around him, but didn't know how he'd react. We'd left a lot unsaid at our last meeting, that day he'd chosen to sever his ties with me in order to preserve his marriage.

"Oh, honey." He opened his arms wide and I moved into them. "God, it's been so long," he said into my hair. He pushed me back at arm's length and sidestepped the last two and a half years. "You look great. What are you doing back in town? Is everything okay?"

I explained about HandsOn, Markson's call, and Len Sabin's crusade.

"I'll call Deke. He'll know what to do."

"I've already seen him. He's doing what he can, Dad." I could hopscotch past a two-year absence as well.

He watched silently while I unlocked the car, put the groceries on the passenger seat, and rolled down the window to cool off the inside.

"I know you didn't kill anybody, Jessie. You couldn't."

My dad's personal Pledge of Allegiance. I loved him for it, even if some of the faith was misguided. And what he didn't know definitely would have hurt him.

I wrapped my arms around him, still innocent in his eyes.

I should say it now. Tell him that all his support, all the money he'd put up that that first lawyer frittered away, all the fights he'd started, were a waste. That I was guilty as charged.

I couldn't do it.

"The jury says I didn't."

"That's good enough for me. Come have dinner with us, Jes. Come see your mom."

"Can't. I made a promise."

"It was a stupid promise."

I remembered my mother's snarled accusation outside the courtroom. "I only have six children!"

"It scared her, Jessie, that's all. Thinking that the county attorney might be right. I'm sure she understands now. Come home. Have dinner with us."

I shook my head. To my mother, my father's sin had been to believe in me. What had the last three years been like for him? Did he have to muzzle himself not to defend me in conversation? Or had he, too, settled into a smaller, safer life without me?

"Go home. Tell her I'm in town. Then we'll see where it goes from there."

He offered his arms once more. I hugged him tight, feeling the pain that three years as Believer In Chief had cost him.

CHAPTER ELEVEN

I dropped off the groceries at Bonita's and left a message on Martin's voicemail that I'd be staying for a while. Interesting that he hadn't told my parents I was in town. The first year I'd been gone, Martin would leave phone messages every few months with greetings, news, and updates. When I didn't respond, the calls grew less frequent, finally petering out about a year ago. I guess Martin finally agreed that there were only six kids in the family now.

I'd need a job soon, not for immediate living expenses, but for money to get out of town. A new life, somewhere far away from memories of Walter Racine. And equally far away from a cop named Sabin who saw me as the villain in both old and new crimes.

In the meantime, I needed to know more about the Marksons, the Villalobos, the Ochoas, and Paul Willard. I'd start with the lawyer, because I already trusted him the least.

Twenty cents a minute bought me computer time at Kinko's, and a Google search didn't take much longer than that. Willard had grown up in Phoenix and become a partner with his firm's Tucson branch six years ago. They handled all kinds of legal work, but it looked like their bread and butter was estate management and corporate representation. I wondered if he handled Markson's real estate business as well as his personal legal work, and whether any of the Ochoa operations were clients of his.

I did the same kind of search on Markson. Nobody had changed the corporate Web site yet; it still featured a photo of a black-haired, thin-lipped Darren Markson with the tagline "A Markson house is a Mark of Distinction!" There was a sidebar about his firm donating funds and personnel to build day-care centers in several low-income housing areas around the city. All in all, he looked like a saint.

I didn't know enough about the patriarchs of the Ochoa clan to do a comprehensive search of their businesses. They probably owned half of the sweatshop-like maquiladoras across the border and almost all of the fruit and vegetable importing from the northern Mexico states, but they rarely had their name in the company business. They'd more likely be named something like "Frutas de Sonora" or "O&R Manufacturing."

A Google search for Guillermo or Carlos Ochoa gave me far too many options. I'd do better if I found people who knew Felicia and could tell me more about her relationship to Carlos.

I logged off and paid for my time. Rolling down the windows on the VW again, I waited for the furnace air inside to dissipate before getting in the car. I'd been sidetracked by the discovery of Carlos Ochoa, so I hadn't talked to anybody at Cholla High School. Now was as good a time as any to change that.

I didn't know if any kids would still be around this late in the afternoon, but I might be able to catch one of the teachers.

The school was a linked set of hexagonal structures around a green quad. There were no spaces left in the visitor lot, so I cruised over to the student parking on the east side. Hell, the VW looked more at home there anyway.

The front doors of the building were propped open and I followed the hallway to the principal's office. Two women about my age were leaning across the linoleum-topped counter discussing recipes.

"I'm with the *Examiner*," I lied. "We'd like to do a follow-up story on Felicia Villalobos, the young woman who was killed in that car blast this week. Is there anyone here who could help me?"

"I was her homeroom teacher," the young woman on my side of the counter said, extending a hand. "Sally Martin."

"Jessie." Thankful that she hadn't asked for ID, I pulled a small spiral notebook from my purse. "Were you close to her? Is there anything you can tell me about her?"

"She was a great kid. More mature than many teenagers. She was doing well."

"Did she belong to any clubs or organizations?"

"I think she was in the journalism club," the woman behind the counter said.

She reached to her left to grab a yearbook, then paged through the book until she came to Felicia's junior class picture. Felicia looked happier in the photo than she had at the arroyo.

"That's right," the blond homeroom teacher said. "And she was following our public safety program."

"What's that?"

"We're a magnet school. There are special classes to get the kids ready for legal and law-enforcement careers."

"She wanted to be a cop?" I made a note with a question mark behind it.

"No, a lawyer."

I made another note. Felicia may not have been just the first high school graduate in her family; it sounded like she was on the road to even more than that. How did she get involved in something that scared her so badly?

". . . like to see it?" She was mid-sentence and I hadn't heard any of it. "It's really state-of-the-art."

I had no idea what I was agreeing to, but turned to accompany

Sally Martin down the hall. The linoleum floor had a waxy sheen and our steps sent echoes ahead of us like explorers in a cave.

"Here," she said, opening a door and flipping on the light.

It was a courtroom, as real as any I'd ever seen, right there in the middle of a high school. The judge's bench was raised, and the prosecution and defense tables lined up in supplication at its feet. I walked down the aisle, ran my fingers over the defense table, and approached the bench.

"Go ahead and take the judge's chair," Martin said. "The kids say they feel different when they're asked to take the role of judge or jury in one of our mock trials."

I walked behind the witness box and sat down in the judge's chair, spinning around like I was trying it out before buying it.

"Felicia did a great job last semester on a mock trial. She wanted to specialize in immigration law."

My mouth was dry and I felt light-headed. I hadn't been in a courtroom since my own verdict was read, and this room was bringing all the bad parts of that memory back. The photos of Walter Racine's dead body next to the car—his leg sticking out like a bent match and one eye still open, surprised by the gaping wound in his forehead. His wife Elizabeth's testimony about how I'd hounded the police to bring charges against her husband. I stared at the defendant's chair in front of me.

"Can I get some water?" I croaked.

"Sure. It's just around the corner."

She led me back to the hall and a drinking fountain.

"Sorry. Don't know what happened in there. Must be a touch of heatstroke."

"Sure," she said, but I knew she didn't believe it.

The secretary was still in the office when we got back.

"I forgot to ask, are there any students that Felicia was especially close to?"

Sally Martin reached for the yearbook, flipping past the individual photos to the club and activity section. "I've forgotten her name . . . what is it . . . Susan? Sandy? She was in the journalism club last year, too, and they were always sitting together. Stacy, that's it. Here she is." She tapped the face of a tall, thin blonde with charcoaled eyes.

"May I borrow this?" I used a Kleenex to mop the remaining sweat off my forehead before picking up the book.

"Sure. Anything you need. Just bring it back when you can."

The secretary's voice caught me at the door. "When do you think this story will run? I'd like to cut out a copy for our display in the hallway."

I'd seen the display cabinet on the way in. Right now it held sports trophies and a papier-mâché horse's head to represent their mascot, the Charger. A sad obituary about the death of a budding lawyer would change the tone perceptibly.

"As soon as I can make it do her justice."

I stopped at the garage to pay the bill for the truck repairs, and they offered to follow me home. I gave the guy a ride back once I'd parked the VW.

Felicia's journalism club friend was Stacy Kronwetter. A call to information confirmed only one number with that last name in Tucson. I phoned, hoping that the *Examiner* reporter ruse would work twice.

"Stacy? I'm writing a piece about Felicia for the paper. Do you think we could meet for a little while and talk about her?"

Stacy was less wary about meeting an adult she didn't know than I would have been at her age. Maybe it was the journalism connection that sparked her interest. Hopefully, it wasn't something she did on a regular basis after an Internet or telephone contact.

"But I've got to get to work," she said.

"Where's that?"

"The sunglasses kiosk at the Tucson Mall. I could take a break around seven."

We agreed to meet at the smoothie place next door. I recognized the thin face and heavy eye shadow when she came in. Seventeen going on thirty.

"Can I get you something?" I already had a peach juice and wheat germ concoction in front of me.

"Just water."

She'd be down to a hundred pounds by the end of the semester at this rate. I got her a large bottle of water.

"I'd like to know more about Felicia," I said when I sat back down. "The police are looking at her friendship with Carlos. Do you think he had anything to do with getting her killed?"

She unscrewed the cap and took a sip. "I don't know. Carlos is a great guy, but he has some lousy friends."

"Like who?"

She eyed my notebook with suspicion. I closed it and put it back in my bag.

"Ricky Lamas. Bob Eleven. Reuben something-or-other. It starts with an S."

I committed the names to memory, not wanting to scare her off with a notation.

"Do they go to Cholla?"

"No. They're friends of his from Nogales. But a couple of times they came to parties up here."

Maybe they were part of Carlos's gang past.

"Are they about his age?"

She nodded. "Yeah. They said they went to school together. And they were sure old enough to buy beer."

"Tell me more about Felicia. Did she like hanging around with these guys? What was she like with them?"

"She hated it. Carlos was so different when they were around—all like 'hey, *cabrón*' and 'in your face,' and like that. He was lots nicer when it was just him."

"Did Felicia ever seem scared of them?"

"Not Licia. She was all like, 'I can take care of this.' She was going to be a lawyer, you know?"

"What are you going to be?"

The fluorescent lights overhead caught the gleam of her glitter eye shadow and she grinned. "A reporter. Just like you."

The sun was down and I needed to go down with it. Roll around with the sweat and the stink until I couldn't remember my name.

I'd been too long alone, and today was looking more lonesome than most. Lying about who I was all day long—to teachers, to teenagers, to good-looking Hispanic guys, to my father. Just another cover story for a life, not even the life I wished I'd lived. I'd dated a guy once who couldn't tell the truth if he was paid to do so. But his lies were crafted to make himself look more respectable, more interesting. "That your car?" someone would ask. "Nah, it's a loaner. My Porsche is in the shop getting all tricked out."

My lies, born out of self-preservation, were meant to create a barrier between myself and the world—a hard-edged shadow line of separation. That separation had become even more defining when I found out about my adoption. My whole life had already been a lie.

I stopped at a bar with a flashing neon arrow promising icy-cold beer. Miranda Lambert's "Crazy Ex-Girlfriend" was playing on the jukebox. "To a hammer everything looks like a nail," she snarled.

I knew how she felt. Back in Phoenix I had been able to keep the guilt-shakes away. I'd never wondered what each day might have brought Walter Racine, if he'd lived. I hadn't hungered to find out who my birth parents were. Here in Tucson, the shakes were back in force. What did I stand for? What could I count on? Who was I?

Tonight, for just a moment, I wanted to lose myself, punish myself past the point of redemption, and forget all about being Jessica Dancing Gammage—whoever that was.

I sat down next to a cowboy at the bar. He was whippet thin, with deep-set eyes and a black Stetson that curled unevenly on the sides. No wedding ring, but there was a lighter place on his finger where one had recently been. He looked younger than me, and didn't seem to mind that.

"You ride?" I asked, pointing at his midsection.

"Only for money." He tipped the salad plate–sized belt buckle up to the light until I could see the design. Silver hills in the background and a bucking horse in gold in the center. "Second Place, Texas Rodeo 2006," it read.

"Bareback or saddle?"

His lips curled in understanding. "You sound like you ride for money, too. Are you a pro? A cop?"

I shook my head. "Just a girl looking for a good time."

He stacked his change on the bar and tapped it in a rhythm that didn't match the song coming through the speakers. "Is there a husband out there somewhere who's going to start banging on the door just when things get interesting?"

"Nobody," I promised him.

"Then let's go."

He paid for my beer, downed the rest of whatever was in his shot glass, and took me by the hand. We didn't have far to go; there was a U-shaped motel next door that promised air-conditioning and free cable for only $19.95 a night.

I waited outside while he got a key. He kissed me on the cheek and guided me toward a room on the far end of the U with a hand on my ass.

"I guess today's my lucky day," he said, flattening me against the inside of the door. "By the way, my name's—"

"Shh." I held my finger against his lips. "Get a condom, cowboy. And no names."

I didn't stay to see what was on cable. Aching, sore, and a little bruised around the mouth, I put my clothes back on in the dark and left the cowboy snoring.

It was only midnight, but my blood was singing. I knew I wouldn't be able to get to sleep and I was hungry. I cranked the windows down and headed east, stopping to buy a giant chicken burrito at a takeout place on Grant.

I'd thought my route across town was aimless until I realized that I was only a couple of blocks from Carlos Ochoa's house. I slowed and turned onto his street.

It was a quiet neighborhood; a dog nuzzled a garbage can on the corner but nothing else moved in the street. I saw a blue glow behind some bedroom curtains and someone whistled, probably for that errant dog.

I stopped in front of Ochoa's house. Nothing going on. And why should there be? The house was a shell; Guillermo certainly wouldn't be staying there.

For no good reason except eternal hope, I walked around to the backyard. The tile saw had been removed, maybe taken back to the place he'd rented it from. My feet left dainty canyons in wet mud as I approached the concrete slab of porch.

Damn. I should have expected it. He'd washed my chalked phone number away.

CHAPTER TWELVE

Deke Treadwell woke me at ten o'clock the next day with heavy pounding on the front door.

"Jessie! Get up!"

I patted down my cockatoo hair and pulled on the clothes from last night, smelling the mingled musk of cowboy sweat and semen as I dressed.

I was cranky. "What is it?" I said through the screen door.

"I need help with some information we got back from HandsOn."

"Ask them. I don't work there anymore." I turned back toward the kitchen and the empty coffeepot.

Deke opened the screen and invited himself in. "Here, I brought you this." He handed me an industrial-sized cup of coffee. "Thought you might need it."

"Thanks, but . . ." How did he know I'd need coffee in the middle of the morning? Had he seen me pick up the cowboy in the bar?

"I came by late last night, saw the V-dub in the driveway but couldn't get an answer from you."

"I got the truck back." I didn't like the notion of Deke or anybody else in the Tucson Police Department checking up on me.

I detoured to the ugly yellow chair in the living room and Deke took a seat at the dining room table.

"Here's the data we got back from HandsOn," he said, leaning across the empty space between us with a stapled sheaf of papers.

I flipped from the graph on the first page that showed the velocity and braking speed, past the car diagnostics, to the weight distribution and tire pressure chart in the back.

"What do you want to know?"

"That page, the one you're on . . . what does that mean?"

I scanned the graph and the chart below it.

"It means that his tires were properly inflated for the load he was carrying."

"Is that all?"

"He had something else in the car."

"Where do you see that?"

"Look here." I grabbed a pencil off the dining room table and circled two numbers. "This one's Markson. A hundred and eighty pounds. And there's no weight in the front passenger seat."

"So?"

"But right here," I continued, "is something weighing fifty or sixty pounds in the backseat."

"His luggage, maybe? We didn't find any in the trunk."

"Only if he puts a seat belt around that suitcase." I circled the line on the chart that proved it.

There were lots of things that Markson could have had in the backseat—luggage, paint or tile samples for his houses, a heavy briefcase. Groceries or office supplies. But I would have put most of those things in the trunk, safe from prying eyes, if nothing else.

And why belt them in? Maybe they were fragile and he didn't want them rolling around. Ceramic tiles? Bottles?

I would have loved to ask his wife if he carried heavy stuff in his briefcase. Hopefully that would be Treadwell's next stop. He was still shaking his head when he left.

I drained the coffee he'd brought and made the call I should have made yesterday.

"Raisa? Can I come by today? I may need help again."

Raisa Fortas was the Pima County public defender who'd been assigned to my case three years ago, after I'd fired my father's choice of lawyer. She stood only four-foot ten, had a pronounced mustache, and chain-smoked Karelia Slims from the Ukraine. She also breathed fire in a courtroom, cowing both county attorneys and the juries with what she called "babushka guilt": "You think Jewish or Catholic mothers can guilt-trip you? You've never heard it in Russian."

She'd never asked if I'd killed Walter Racine. Instead, she showed me the evidence and the witness list that the prosecution had prepared and said, "Which of these is going to be a problem for me?" We'd gone through the list item by item. The phone calls I'd made to Children's Services and the cops about Walter Racine? That could help the prosecution prove motive, but nothing else. They'd done a cursory investigation and said Walter Racine was not a child molester. Did she have to worry about them coming up with the gun? Not a problem.

She told me to come downtown at noon and we could get together for lunch. I squeezed the truck into a space in a public lot off Stone and met her in front of her office. She was lighting the tip of one thin cigarette from the glowing ember of another. She made it look like a magic act.

"Madame Public Defender," I said with a smile. She held her arms wide, a lit cigarette in each hand, the handle of her cane hooked over her forearm, and offered herself for a hug. When she stepped back from my embrace, I saw the anger in her eyes.

"Is something wrong?"

She shrugged. "I really needed this smoke. Just got a lesser charge for this sweet little Mexican girl whose baby died while she was trying to cross. But she should never even have been prosecuted."

"They said she killed her baby?"

"Yeah, because they couldn't catch the damn coyotes who brought them over. It makes me so damn mad." She picked a piece of loose tobacco off her tongue.

"She wouldn't give them up?" The coyotes are "human jackals" who take money from immigrants who want to cross the border, then often leave them locked in sweltering trucks or alone without water in the desert.

"She didn't know any names. Or, if she did, she was worried about what they'd do to her family in Mexico."

"What happened to the baby?"

"She got caught in a tug of war between the mother and one of the coyotes." She took a long drag off the cigarette. "Like a rag doll, the poor thing."

The horror of what that mother must be going through, I thought. In trying to save her daughter's life, she'd killed her.

Raisa linked her arm through mine and guided me down the street to a hole-in-the-wall sandwich shop. "What's up with you? Are you in trouble again?"

"I'm not sure." I told her about my new life in Phoenix, about hearing Markson's car accident and the beating, and about Len Sabin's interest.

"You should have shut up the minute they had you in that interview room."

"I know. But until Sabin read me my rights, I still thought I was helping them."

"Horse pucky. You should stop helping them and start helping yourself. And they should have known that you were represented by counsel." She draped a paper napkin over her knee and picked up the pastrami sandwich she'd ordered.

"Still? Even when they're talking about a different murder?"

"Even more important then. You tell them to call me next time."

I promised I would. It was probably just a courtesy on Raisa's part. She couldn't represent me until I was charged with a crime and then asked for a public defender. Or maybe there was some carryover if she'd represented me once before. I didn't know, but was grateful for the backup nonetheless.

She leaned on me on the way back to the County Legal Services Building, her limp a bit more exaggerated than I'd remembered, her hair a bit grayer than it had been. But I'd changed, too, since that time, both inside and out.

"Watch out for Len Sabin," she said when we parted. "I've had a couple of cases against him since your trial. He still thinks of you as the one who got away."

Raisa's warning was still ringing in my ears when I turned into the driveway at Bonita's house. I considered backing up and pulling away when I spotted Sabin in the webbed chair on the front porch.

He got up and sauntered toward the truck.

"Ms. Gammage," he said around the candy in his mouth, and ignoring my desire for a new life with a new name.

"What a surprise, Detective." I got out of the truck but kept my distance.

"Just thought I'd let you know that we've confirmed Markson's time of death."

"Then you know I had nothing to do with it."

"On the contrary. The injuries he got in that beating Friday night had a lot of time to bruise up. He may not have been shot until much later, maybe even the next day."

What? He thought I somehow arranged to be on the receiving

end of Markson's phone call on purpose? And then came to town to kill him? Not even the most prosecution-friendly judge or jury in the state would believe that.

"Saturday," he went on. "When you were in town. Hanging around the place we found his car. And then right there when somebody else gets blown up with a car bomb."

"You remember my attorney's name, don't you, Detective? Raisa Fortas? Contact her if you have any other questions for me."

I brushed past him and unlocked the front door, but didn't stop shaking until I heard his car pull away.

Where had Markson been between the time I heard that beating on Friday and when he was shot? He hadn't been in a hospital, although he would surely have needed one. And if they were going to kill him anyway, why had they waited until the next day to do it?

Maybe someone had been holding him for ransom. That would explain Emily Markson's not calling the police immediately when she heard from her husband on Saturday morning. If she'd really heard from him at all. Had it been a call from the kidnappers instead of a call from New Mexico?

Unless . . . maybe I'd heard somebody else get beat up that night and Markson was in on it. Just because his body had bruises and injuries doesn't mean that was the beating I heard.

Deke Treadwell said they had taken blood samples out in the desert the night they found the car. He had no reason to tell me the results of those tests, unless you counted friendship as an excuse.

"Deke?" I said into the phone.

"Now don't start in on me about Len Sabin, Jessie; he's just got a bug up—"

"It's not that, although I wish you could call him off. Remember those blood samples you guys took the night you found Markson's car? Was it his blood?"

He waited long enough to tell me that friendship didn't weigh quite as much as professionalism, then finally coughed up the answer.

"Yeah, it was his."

So much for the Markson-as-villain theory. I may not have been there for the whole opera of his death, but I sure heard Act One.

"And somebody else's," he added.

I took advantage of a free introductory day at a local gym to work out my frustration, pushing myself to do both upper- and lower-body workouts since I didn't know when I'd get another chance to get my hands on real equipment again. It was much more civilized than sand-filled gas jugs, although I cringed when I heard Stabbing Westward's "Save Yourself" crashing through the sound system. That was too close to the truth. I managed a hundred pounds on the incline bench press and did extra sets of leg extensions and leg curls, just for the pain of it.

Back in the truck, I was draining one of the gym's free bottles of cold water when I glanced in the rearview mirror, my attention caught by the vertical hop of the car behind me.

It was a classic low rider—a Cutlass from the late seventies by the look of it—with an airbrushed black pearl finish. It must have had a hell of a hydraulic system, as the driver made it hop like a jack-in-the-box as we waited for the light to change.

Four guys in the car, all slunk down like they were in easy chairs. Three of them had bandanas folded like caps over their heads and tied in back.

We made it another six blocks before a light stopped us again. This time the low rider pulled alongside me. Gold spoke wheels and whitewall tires.

The guy in the front passenger seat turned and stared at me. Latino. A teenager. No emotion but steely resolve in his eyes. I wasn't about to get in any mad-dogging contest with him so I turned away, but not before I saw his bare hand come up above the window frame, fashion itself into the shape of a gun, and finger-shoot me in the head.

"Pow," he mouthed as his hand jerked with the imagined recoil.

CHAPTER THIRTEEN

"Are you still looking for Carlos?" the voice asked.

"Who is this?" There weren't many people who had my cell phone number.

"Guillermo Ochoa. We met yesterday at Carlos's house."

I wasn't likely to forget him. "I thought you'd washed my number away."

There was a smile in his response. "Not before I committed it to memory. . . . So you came by the house again?"

Jesus, I'd just entered myself in the Dumb Question contest. I might as well have been wearing a "bimbo" sign.

"Have you heard from your brother yet?"

There was a long pause, then, "No. I was hoping you had something new on your end."

"Not really." Where should I start? With HandsOn? Or my murder trial? Felicia's beer coaster? Or the identification of Markson's body?

"Can we get together?" he asked. "Maybe if we swap stories . . . I'm getting worried about Carlos."

I wanted to swap more than stories with him. We agreed to

meet for dinner at Mariscos Chihuahua. I was tempted to ask for a couple of hours to go get my hair done, get a make up lesson, buy new clothes and get my teeth whitened, but agreed on seven o'clock.

I pawed through the clothes in my suitcase until I came up with a halter top and jeans that made me look five pounds thinner and five years younger. Those, plus a substantial application of American Greaser to spike my hair, would have to do. I pulled the shirt tight at my waist. You couldn't see the body of the dragon tattoo that sat right at my tailbone—just the scaly tail that crawled up my spine. That ink had hurt a hell of a lot more than my jailhouse jacks, but I was used to pain by then.

I didn't know if I could trust Guillermo, but he was my only potential source of information about Carlos, and Carlos was my best link to Felicia's death. That, of course, could track back to Markson's death and Len Sabin's reason to come after me.

I'd pump this guy for as much information as I could get.

The first few minutes at the restaurant were awkward—me sucking down a creamy *horchata*, him stripping the wet label from a bottle of beer he'd ordered before I got there.

"Do you prefer Guillermo or Bill?" was my most incisive question.

"Guillermo. Bill's just the English version, not my real name." He said he worked for an equipment rental place. "Generators, loaders, just about any tool. That wet saw at Carlos's place was one of ours."

I told him about HandsOn and getting the call from Markson after his car had been hit. I omitted any reference to my life in Tucson before that.

When the waitress came by again, Guillermo asked for the fiery shrimp *endiablados*. I ordered fish Culichi style, hoping that the creamy green sauce wouldn't be as hot.

"Why do you think Felicia went out there?" I asked after telling him about my first run-in with the teenager.

"It was a special place for her and Carlos. He was doing the framing on some new houses going up out there after her father fired him from the bar, and she'd meet him at the arroyo when she could get away. I think it's where they really fell in love."

"You think that beer coaster was meant for Carlos?" I'd told him about the note written on the edge of it.

He nodded. "I'm sure of it. But if she wanted him to come to the bar, it must have meant that her father was keeping close tabs on her. I can't imagine any other reason she'd risk having her father see Carlos." He paused. "It also means that he's been gone a lot longer than I thought. I was supposed to help him on the house starting on Wednesday. When he hadn't shown up by Thursday, the day I met you, I was getting worried. But now it looks like he might have been missing since last Sunday when you found Felicia at the arroyo."

"Tell me about Carlos. What's he like?" I picked at the french fries that were glistening with sauce from the fish.

"I'm the big brother, but it doesn't always feel that way. Sometimes Carlos does all the protecting."

He took a long swig of beer.

"We didn't move to Nogales until I was twelve. Carlos was six. Before that, we lived in this little piss-water town in Chihuahua. Our biggest adventure was going down to the arroyo, pretending to be conquistadores or banditos, flailing around with cholla cactus branches like they were whips. One day, we'd followed a branch of that dry creek bed for hours, and we'd wandered away from anything we recognized and got lost. Night got cold. I got a fire going. Picked some of the barrel cactus buds. . . ."

I waited while he peeled another beer label.

"They call that Desperation Fruit, you know that? The barrel cactus? Sometimes it's the only thing available to eat in the winter, and man, we were hungry. Anyway, our parents didn't find us until the next morning. I kept Carlos distracted by telling him stories—happy endings, you know? No ghost stories—until they came to get us."

He pushed his plate away, nothing but shrimp tails left.

"Just a few years later, it was Carlos telling me stories with happy endings. We'd moved to Nogales and life was rougher there. Carlos got tough fast. Pretty soon he was the one with all the answers."

I pictured the sharp peaks surrounding Nogales like the walls of a coliseum around the gladiators. And just like that arena, the fighting was done at street level—by gangs, scam artists, pimps, and coyotes.

He shook his head at the memory.

"Six years younger than me—skinny as a rail and carrying this big, splintery stick around—and all the time telling me that things would be okay, that he'd protect me."

I began to see why Felicia had loved him.

"Where do you think he is?"

He shrugged. "Nobody in the family has heard from him. I'm going down to Nogales tomorrow. See if the Braceros know anything."

"Want some company?"

His mouth tightened. I knew he wasn't looking forward to confronting the gang he'd tried to leave behind.

"No, you shouldn't—"

"I want to."

And I knew just what to bring as a party favor.

My father taught all seven of us kids to shoot. He'd say, "If I'm going to keep guns around the house, I want you to know what to do with them. And what not to do." My mother, who already disliked the fact that he was a police officer, did not take well to these desert target practice sessions.

I'd done fine with the Glock like the one my dad carried every day, but less well with the sniper rifle. I didn't need a two-foot barrel and sight to find those hubcaps I was aiming at anyway.

After my dad's big pistol, Catherine's little snub-nosed .38 had felt like something a Barbie doll would shoot. .

Ted Dresden, the prosecutor in my murder trial, had told the jury that Walter Racine had been killed with a .38, and that his niece Catherine had had one and could have given it to me before her death. He was right about all of that. What he couldn't prove was that her .38 was the murder weapon, and that I was the one who'd used it.

That was because he couldn't find it.

I could. And I needed it now.

I waited until after midnight, when the moon had set and I had a better chance of not being seen. I plugged a Charanga Cakewalk CD into the player, opened the windows, and headed east. The plodding-horse rhythm of "Belleza" made me feel like I was making the trek by mule. No moonlit shadows. The saguaros stood as dark and still as an army of surprised soldiers in surrender.

I parked in the lot and took the steep dirt path that led down to lower Tanque Verde Falls. There was water running in the creek bed—shallow and slow, none of the monsoon flooding and crashing waterfalls that had given it life in August. Halfway down the trail I spotted the three dark red boulders in a pile that were my signpost. I squatted beside the bottom one and dug with the garden trowel I'd brought from Bonita's house. ·

It had been three years since I'd last been here and the dirt was hard-packed and dry with the smallest tuft of thorny grass covering my prize—my shame.

After only ten minutes of digging I felt a corner of the freezer bag I'd left behind. The contours of the gun were clear, even the little triangular piece of hard rubber missing from the grip. The three .38 rounds I hadn't needed that day rolled around the bottom of the bag like pebbles.

I knew how stupid it was to dig up evidence for Sabin. What if he found the gun on me and could prove that he'd been right all along?

Hell, he already knew he was right. And he knew he couldn't nail me for a crime I'd already been tried for.

Fuck him.

CHAPTER FOURTEEN

Guillermo picked me up at Bonita's house at noon. The old Camaro he drove was dented and primer gray, but the engine hummed like a turbine.

It took a little more than an hour to traverse the empty stretch of road between Tucson and Nogales. Plenty of time for me to sneak sidelong glances at his face, at that right eyebrow bisected by a thick scar that almost reached his eyelid. He stared forward, his mouth taut with worry.

"With a family as big as the Ochoas," I said when we passed the exit for my friend Beverly Ochoa's house, "I thought you'd have an army of people out looking for Carlos."

"They're all asking around. They're looking. We're going to try some of the places they haven't been yet."

"The Braceros?"

"That's part of it."

"How'd you two wind up in the gang?"

He pushed his hair back with his fingers. "It's a long story. The short version is that we were safer with them than against them.

They have a lot of power in Nogales and the cops don't have the money or the manpower to control it."

We drove through the checkpoint at the border and showed our passports to the Mexican officer at the booth. There's not much scrutiny when you head south; no one cares about terrorism or illegal immigrants going in that direction.

"I thought when you came north it was to the Arizona half of Nogales." The two cities straddled the U.S.-Mexico border, but were more fraternal twins than identical. Even the vegetation lost hope on the Mexico side.

"My family got papers and moved across when I was in my teens, but our first house was on the Mexican side so we'll start there."

"What about the Braceros?"

"They'll be there, too. The drinks are cheaper."

We stopped at a red ALTO sign a block down. The tinny thrum of a mariachi's cheap guitar leaked through an open door.

"How many times do you suppose that guy's had to play 'Cielito Linda'?" he asked, locking the car. "It must be like reading the same bedtime story to your kids every night."

Some of those old songs were still my favorites. "When's the last time you heard 'El Niño Perdido'?" That plaintive trumpet solo was as sad as the lost child it represented.

"Too long." He opened his wallet and took out a photo of a young man with wild, dark hair. His mouth was turned down on the left side, looking weighted by the thick mustache.

"That's Carlos?"

"Yep. Keep an eye out for him or his car, Okay?"

"What does he drive?"

"A Ford Escape, maybe three, four years old."

"What color?"

"Blue."

Aw, shit. That matched the paint on Markson's bumper.

. . .

We drove through Nogales, south to the neighborhood where the Ochoas had first lived, leaving the tourist areas behind. Sturdy houses perched like lookouts on the rocky hills, and small shacks with tiny ramadas crowded the flatland. A *carnecería* graced one corner, with skirt steaks and chorizo hung on hooks in the window. A small *taquería* anchored the right side of the intersection.

"There were six of us living here," Guillermo said, pointing at a concrete block building the size of a lean-to. He knocked on the door but there was no answer. "Let's try the *taquería*."

We walked across the intersection, took seats at a rickety wooden table, and ordered two *horchatas*.

Guillermo introduced himself to the old man behind the counter.

"Juan Pantera," the old man said in reply. "I know your name, but never met anyone in your family. I took this place over from my cousin just a couple of years ago."

Guillermo placed Carlos's photo on the table. "Have you seen him in the neighborhood recently? Maybe with some of the Braceros?"

Pantera opened a bottle of Tecate for himself and joined us at the table. He was Yodalike, with a bent spine and a cobweb of straggly white hair. His hands were oversized on long, thin arms, and moved in slow wiping motions across the clean tabletop.

He nodded. "He was here this week. Maybe Wednesday? I gave him a plate of food."

"He had no money?" Guillermo asked.

"No money. No identification. He said he'd been mugged."

"Was he badly hurt?"

"Bad enough. His eye was the color of a sunset."

Guillermo's eyes dimmed with the knowledge of his brother's pain. "Did he say where he was going from here?"

"He left with two Braceros—*bastardos*." Pantera spat toward the doorway.

"Do you know these men?"

"One of them. Ricky Lamas. He's like all the rest—*criminales, traficantes*." Pantera moved back behind the bar.

I'd heard Lamas's name before. "Felicia's friend said she met him with Carlos in Tucson."

"I guess Carlos didn't get as far away from the gangs as I thought he had."

"Where to now?"

"The Braceros' clubhouse."

The "clubhouse" turned out to be a noisy, dark bar called El Gallo Rojo, on a narrow street that paralleled the main drag, Callé Obregon.

Music blared from this bar, too, but not the old mariachi ballads we'd heard earlier. This was the trumpet-snare polka style of narco-corridos, the songs that take traditional Mexican music and twist it into a paean to drug traffickers.

"*Me apodan El Sinvergüenza . . .*" the voice sang in tribute to a man who robs and kills without shame. I understood the killing part, but not the shamelessness of it. It's nothing to celebrate.

I had expected the Braceros to be in leather jackets. Net snoods over long hair or bandanas in gang colors, folded over foreheads. None of that here. This wasn't the street side of the Braceros; it was management.

There were ten or fifteen Latino men, some sitting and drinking, some standing at the bar. Two of them looked like bodyguards, one at each entrance, with a hand tucked deep inside a jacket.

Talk stopped when we came in and somebody turned down the music.

They were older than I'd expected, too—midtwenties, early thirties. Cowboy hats and bright-colored shirts, and their cell phones either on the table in front of them or clipped to their belts.

"*Hola, hermano*," one seated man said. "Long time no see."

"Chaco," Guillermo said with a nod. "I'm looking for my brother."

Chaco must have been the leader here, although only body language would have told you so. He wasn't the oldest, strongest, or nastiest-looking of the crowd.

"You can't even say hello to your *compañeros* first? Ask how we are?" There was a dark, pumpkinseed tattoo under his left eye.

Guillermo took two steps closer to the table, but ignored the question. "I want Carlos. Where is he?"

A sinewy little guy next to Chaco whose soul-patch beard had grown into a long tangled dreadlock put his hand under the table. His forearm was marked with a three-inch XI tattoo. This must be the famous Bob Eleven that Stacey Kronwetter had mentioned.

I put my hands to my sides, glancing behind me to make sure I was still more than an arm's length away from the bodyguard at the door.

"What do you want with that pussy? Is his mama calling him? Oh, Carlos! It's time for dinner!"

Guillermo lunged, upturning the table and twisting a handful of Chaco's shirt at the neck. The kid with the XI tattoo wrenched Guillermo's head back and jittered a knife against his bared neck. The bodyguards held their positions, but had their guns drawn and aimed at Guillermo's heart.

I reached slowly under my shirt and slid the little snubnose from my waistband. The gun was steady, just inches from Chaco's head. "*Basta!* Let him go."

Surprise registered on Chaco's face, but he nodded to the bodyguards and the guy with the knife. Guillermo got up, dusted himself off, and took the gun from me. He gestured to the three men between us and the door. They cleared a path and we backed out of the room.

"I want Carlos," he repeated at the door. "Nothing else."

"Hurry," I said, looking back in expectation of a dozen armed men on our tail. My hand was still frozen into a shooter's grip, unwilling to admit that I wasn't holding the gun anymore.

"No rush," Guillermo said, handing the LadySmith back to me. "They know where to find me."

Stuffing the gun back into my waistband, I almost tripped over the dark car in front of me.

"Careful," Guillermo said with a smile. "Wouldn't want to scratch Chaco's new ride." He raked a key from the front door all the way to the Cadillac's taillight.

We drove north, back through the center of the city. Three blocks shy of the border, my heart finally slowed to a normal rhythm.

"Stop here," I said.

"Where are we going?"

"Come with me. We need a dose of old Mexico." I pulled Guillermo through the door and into a dark restaurant on the corner, bypassing the maître d' and stopping a mariachi with a gourd-shaped guitar.

"Do you know 'El Niño Perdido'?"

The man smiled and held out his hand. I gave him a ten and he waved one of his trumpeters off into the next room. A moment later, I heard the lonesome notes of the "lost child" coming from the distant trumpet. The nearby musicians repeated the phrase, calling the lost child home.

"I wish it was that easy," Guillermo said.

CHAPTER FIFTEEN

The strains of that trumpet still echoed in my head on Sunday morning.

I missed my friend Catherine like she was a country I could no longer visit. We'd met in college, swimming mile after mile in adjacent lanes at the university pool at dawn, the water—that most precious of commodities in the desert—cradling us, wrapping us, pushing against us as we swam. Then we'd move into lazy backstrokes, taking turns to tell our stories, our dreams. I stood beside her when she married Glen. I wept when I first held her baby girl.

It was beside another pool just three years ago that Catherine first told me about the abuse. Her marriage to Glen had disintegrated earlier in the year, leaving Catherine rudderless.

"For years, I tried to tell myself it was all innocent, that Uncle Walter didn't know what he was doing and how it hurt me."

"Are you saying your uncle abused you?" Catherine had only mentioned her aunt and uncle in passing, as the people who had raised her when her parents were killed. Good people. Churchgoers.

She nodded. "It started when I was six. Katie's going to be six soon."

How could I have known Catherine all these years and not known this? My stomach ached with the knowledge that she had kept the horror to herself for so long.

"You've got to go to the cops."

Catherine shook her head.

"What does your aunt say? Does she know what a danger he is?"

"She never believed me. No one did."

"I believe you."

We'd go to the cops and to Children's Services, I said. I didn't know if they could charge Racine for molesting Catherine; it had been so long ago. At a bare minimum we could get their attention. They could put him on a watch list so that it didn't happen again. Force the family to get him treatment.

None of that had happened by the time Catherine died.

Three weeks later, after I'd seen little Katie in Walter Racine's arms, I did what Catherine would have wanted me to do.

I needed sunshine and caffeine to shake off the memories of my last days with Catherine. I did a quick workout in the backyard, then sat on the porch with a *café con leche*.

I was not ashamed of killing Racine, but doing it while Katie was there didn't rest as easily on my conscience.

I'd gone to great pains to make sure I had an alibi. Signing up for that continuing education course in Phoenix. Making the supposedly boneheaded move of parking at a fire hydrant once I got there, and leaving my car in the police impound all weekend. Hitchhiking back to Tucson where I borrowed my brother's car while he was out of town.

It was all the easier because it was Halloween. I'd worn a mask and a ghostly sheet over white jeans and a T-shirt. I didn't stand out from any other trick-or-treater on the street, even though I'd had to wait almost a half hour for Racine's car to pull into the driveway.

I hadn't known Katie was with him that night. She was tucked into the backseat when I approached the car. I made him kneel and

I shot him twice in the back of the head. I was turning away when I saw the little girl, her eyes wide with fear.

She didn't recognize me behind the mask and costume.

"It's okay, honey. You stay put. I'm going to lock the door so you'll be safe. And I'll call someone to come get you," I'd said.

"Are you an angel?"

"Sort of."

I called the cops from a pay phone two miles away. The prosecutor, Ted Dresden, had tried to use that 911 tape against me at trial, but they couldn't make a clear voice match so it didn't do much damage.

The last time I'd seen Katie was in the courtroom. Under delicate questioning by Dresden, she'd still insisted that a guardian angel had come to help her when her great-uncle had been killed.

Katie would be almost nine now. Her father, Glen Chandliss, had moved to Colorado after the divorce and hadn't interfered when Catherine's aunt Elizabeth said she'd raise Katie. I wondered if she still lived out by Davis Monthan Airforce Base. It was midmorning on a weekend—they might still be home.

I stashed the little .38 in a bucket under the kitchen sink and piled rags and cleaning products on top of it. I didn't want to be driving around with a gun today if Sabin was anywhere nearby.

Although I'd changed a lot in the last three years—the spiked blond hair, the tattoos, the muscles—I didn't want either Katie or her great-aunt to recognize me today. I remembered all too clearly Elizabeth's rage at me from the witness box. I put on running shorts, a baseball cap, and oversized sunglasses as a minimal disguise.

When I reached their neighborhood, I parked around the corner and jogged past the house. There was a five-foot stucco wall around the front yard; I couldn't see much unless I got close to the property line and peeked in. I saw nothing on the first pass, so I continued down to the end of the block and circled back.

I jogged in place, this time hearing girlish laughter from the front yard. There was an inch-wide gap between the wooden gate and the wall, giving me a thin slice of the courtyard. I took off the sunglasses and pretended to clean the lenses on the hem of my T-shirt.

Two girls were drawing a complex maze of pathways on the sidewalk with colored chalk. One child, a blonde, was clearly the director of the drama, the other a passive but willing game player. The quiet girl looked up at the gate, and I saw Catherine's eyes, recreated here before me in the body of a skinny, almost-nine-year-old girl. I started to cry.

"Are you okay?" Katie asked, approaching the gate. She put her face right up against the gap. "Do you want a glass of water?"

"I'm okay." I sniffled and wiped my nose with the back of my hand.

"Why are you crying?"

"Don't talk to strangers!" the other girl called, dropping the chalk and taking Katie by the arm, then stage-whispering behind her hand, "It's not polite to ask people why they're crying."

"Lizzie!" Katie whined, drawing out each syllable.

"You can ask," I said. "I was crying because you remind me of my friend, Catherine."

"That was my mother's name," Katie said.

I nodded. "It's a beautiful name."

Guillermo's call caught me at a red light.

"They found Carlos's car."

"Where? Is there any sign of him?"

"All I've got is a message that says they found the car at Greyhound Park."

"I'll meet you there." I hung up, not giving him a chance to contradict me. It was a straight shot down Golf Links Road to the dog track on the south side of town. Twenty minutes later, I was there.

A loudspeaker boomed across the half-empty parking lot and cheers erupted from the tiered stadium to the west. Empty cardboard boxes and grimy, loose papers swirled and eddied across the asphalt.

I circled the eastern edge of the parking lot twice before I saw the tow truck and the South Tucson police car tucked behind a Dumpster on the other side.

What made them notice the car in the first place? Was it parked in an illegal space? Had it crashed into something? Maybe Guillermo had filed a missing person's report and some sharp-eyed cop had spotted the license plate.

I didn't have to get any closer to see the damage. The front and back bumpers were crumpled like blue wrapping paper and both headlights were broken out. One light dangled almost to the ground like some monster's eye in a horror film, but it was clear that the damage hadn't been caused by the Dumpster. I didn't know how old the dents in the back were, but the front-end damage matched the collision Markson had described.

Guillermo pulled up alongside my car, got out, and approached the South Tucson cops.

"Tell them to call Detective Treadwell," I said before he got too far away. "This may have been the car that hit Darren Markson that night."

Guillermo grimaced and turned back toward the two policemen. One of the officers leaned into Carlos's car and pulled a child's car seat from where it lay on the floor of the back seat. I joined them next to the Dumpster.

"What would he have been doing with that?" I asked.

Guillermo shook his head. "I don't know. It wasn't hooked in or anything. Just laying there."

"My God." There was a bloody handprint on the plastic seat, just below the soft yellow duck-patterned fabric.

It took Treadwell almost an hour to get there, and when he did he was quick to draw the same conclusion I had.

"Get this car towed to Forensics," he said. "And have them dust the child's car seat for prints right away."

He turned to Guillermo. "Is your brother friends with anyone who would need an infant or toddler's seat?"

Guillermo shook his head. "Not that I can think of. But there's lots of kids in the family."

The crowd roared from the stadium. It was either a close race or a big winner.

"We'll check the paint—see if it matches what we found on Markson's—" Treadwell was interrupted by the arrival of Len Sabin, bringing his sedan to a brake-destroying stop just a few feet from my back bumper. Sabin hitched up his pants and joined the group, turning his back to me and facing Treadwell.

"What are these two doing here?"

"They're the ones who called us in. No sign of the car's owner, but it looks like this could be the vehicle involved in the attack on Darren Markson."

"That wouldn't surprise me," Sabin said, somehow suggesting that anything I was involved in must be nefarious.

I ignored him and turned toward Treadwell. "Did Emily Markson say anything about her husband having a child's seat in the car?" A twenty-pound seat, plus the thirty or thirty-five pounds of a toddler, could have been the weight of that seat-belted something I'd seen on the HandsOn printout.

Treadwell said no, but made a note in a spiral-bound notebook.

If there had been a child in Markson's car, who was it? And where was he now?

The police dismissed us and roped off the area around Carlos's car. I leaned into Guillermo's window as he clicked his seat belt into position. "Follow me back to my place."

He started the car, the radio coming to life with the engine. An Amos Lee song was playing, the sad resignation in his voice asking, "What in the world has come over you? What in heaven's name have you done?"

"Ah, Carlos." He sighed, and his eyes filled with tears.

Guillermo parked behind my truck in Bonita's driveway and followed me inside, his eyes taking in the shabby, impermanent condition of the living room.

"Are you moving in or out?"

"Neither." I explained about my sister's departure to South America.

I opened two beers and we tap-danced around the fear in the air for a few minutes.

"What do you think happened to Carlos?" I finally asked.

He hung his head. "I don't know. But it doesn't look good."

I perched on the edge of the yellow chair and put my arm around his shoulders. He moved back against my body, muscles knotted by either training or tension. "Tell me about the last time you saw him."

He told his story to the floor, as if I wasn't even there. "He came by the rental yard to ask me to come work on his house. But he was really antsy, spacing out in the middle of the conversation, all wild-eyed, like somebody was sneaking up on him."

"Was he back on drugs?" Drugs and the Braceros would be a

bad mix. And could be reason enough for someone to have gone after Felicia.

"Just a little blow. Nothing like we'd been doing before."

"Did he say anything? Was anything bothering him?"

"He was always talking about Felicia—how she was going to come live with him. He said he wanted to go back to school, maybe get into the construction business. He'd get quiet sometimes, but I didn't get the idea anything was bothering him." He hunched his shoulders, dislodging my hand.

I couldn't let it go unspoken anymore. "Do you think Carlos is the victim here—or the killer?"

Guillermo bristled at the thought, then sighed.

"Maybe both."

I heard the throaty roar of a big V8 outside, bragging on its horsepower and torque. I pulled the curtain to the side.

It was the black low rider again, this time the song blasting from the windows was about the hazards of smuggling: "They take the load to the border but they won't be paid. They'll only get stopped at the checkpoint." The four bandanaed bobbleheads in the car nodded and swayed to the beat. The guy in the front passenger seat stared at Guillermo's car, then finger-shot me the way he had at the intersection on Friday.

"Braceros. Did they follow us back here from Greyhound Park?" I asked Guillermo over my shoulder.

"Maybe. If they're holding Carlos then they probably would have had a watch on where they dumped his car, too." He tossed his empty bottle into a cardboard box in the corner, unphased by the appearance of the gangstas in the street. "They probably followed me from the house. I told you they know where I live."

"Should we tell the cops?" I may have done jail time, but that didn't mean that I was blasé about armed felons hanging around my house. In some ways, I was still a regular citizen.

"Tell them what? That the Braceros have moved their influence north to Tucson? They already know that. And I don't come from a background that's particularly comfortable running to the cops with information."

Just like Raisa Fortas's young Latina client who wouldn't give up the names of the coyotes who helped her cross the border.

"Are the Braceros still bringing in illegals?"

He rolled his eyes at my naiveté.

"Anything to do with kids?" There had to be some reason that Carlos's car had a child seat in it.

He grabbed my hand. "C'mon. Let's get out of here."

"I'm serious. The Braceros bring across illegals. Carlos was hooked up with them again. And now there's this bloody handprint on a child's car seat." This was a whole different kind of sin against children than I'd faced with Walter Racine, but it made my skin crawl just thinking about it. Kidnapping for ransom? Illegal adoptions? The child slave trade? Pedophile rings?

Guillermo took my face in his hands. "Listen to me. We don't know anything yet. We don't know where that car seat came from. We don't know who last drove Carlos's car. We don't know if it had anything to do with Markson's death or Felicia getting blown up. We don't know if it has anything to do with children at all."

"And we don't know where Carlos is," I finished for him.

"I'll find him." The screen door slapped shut behind him.

CHAPTER SIXTEEN

Three separate mysteries and I didn't know enough about any of them. Who had killed Darren Markson? Who had blown up Felicia Villalobos? And what had happened to Carlos Ochoa?

I didn't have the resources or capability of the police force, but that didn't mean I couldn't ask questions.

One of the directions I'd been sidetracked from was learning more about Felicia. Okay, she was doing well in school. She wanted to be a lawyer. She had a lover she had to hide from her father. I wondered if there was any more family around. Any siblings? And what had happened to her mother? I called Juan Villalobos.

"I'm the teacher who came by the other day. We're planning a memorial newsletter about Felicia and I wanted to make sure we had all the details right."

"Uh-huh." His voice still sounded dull and slow with the pain.

"Did Felicia have any brothers or sisters?"

"Two sisters. They're with their mother in Chihuahua. Her *abuela* has cancer, and they're all staying to take care of her."

"Of course . . ."

"I couldn't take care of all three girls myself. The little ones are only seven and nine. They're going to come join me and Felicia when—" He hiccupped a half-sob.

"I understand."

"Felicia, she was almost an adult. Such a good girl."

"Thank you, Mr. Villalobos. We'll be in touch when—"

"Oh, Miss . . . um . . . could you return some books for me?"

Books? Had his grief focused on the tiniest things—those that he thought he could handle without splintering under the weight? Don't deal with the funeral arrangements. Stay arm's length away from thinking about the blast that tore your little girl apart. Don't look at the scorched earth in front of the house. But make sure you return Felicia's overdue library books? My own version of focus-on-the-stuff-you-can-deal-with was to put pennies and nickels in rolls. Somehow, those paper tubes gave me a sense of order and peace in an uncontrollable world.

"Of course, how can I help you?"

"She had some office binders here, you know, for her internship. Some project she was working on for her sponsor. They may want it back."

That's right. Somebody (Her father? That homeroom teacher?) had said something about Felicia having an internship. "I'd be happy to deliver it for you. Who's her sponsor?"

"I don't have a person's name, just the company. It's a law firm. Willard, Levin and Pratt."

Holy shit.

"Detective Treadwell," he answered.

"Deke, Felicia Villalobos was doing an internship at Paul Willard's law office."

To his credit, Treadwell didn't ask who was calling, but it did take him a second to catch up.

"She was?"

"Yep. Remember, she was in prelaw classes at Cholla? And she wanted to be a lawyer? Well, guess what? She wound up doing work for the guy who's fucking Darren Markson's widow."

"Language, Jessie. Language."

I had to smile. Deke Treadwell would never think of me as an adult.

"What are you going to do about it? There's your link between Darren Markson and Felicia Villalobos, right there."

"I'm going to ask Willard about it. Maybe it's just a coincidence."

I thought it was much more than that, but had to remind myself that I'd used that same argument with Detective Sabin, urging him to understand that my proximity to both Markson's and Felicia's death was just bad luck. "Can I be there?"

"No."

"Will you tell me what he says?"

"No. Thanks for digging this up, Jessie. If there's anything to it, you'll hear about it one way or another. But stay out of this."

"Why? Len Sabin thinks I'm already up to my neck in it."

"Then don't prove him right."

He hung up without saying good-bye.

Who could help me find out more about Willard's law firm? Another lawyer, that's who. I called Raisa.

"Serves me right for giving a client my home phone number," she said. "I used to have Sunday nights to myself."

There was no background noise on the call. No TV, no music or laughter, no banging pots and pans. I wasn't sure I'd interrupted much of anything. Not risking annoying her, I put my curiosity on hold for twelve hours.

"Can I buy you breakfast before work in the morning?"

. . .

We met in the Blue Willow parking lot at seven and were the fourth group in, even though they were just opening the doors. A thin woman with a ponytail and a peaceful smile showed us to a corner table in the sunny, brick-floored patio. Birdsong and the sound of a fountain greeted us, but no other diners were close by. I asked for the tofu scramble and fresh salsa. After decrying her cholesterol level, Raisa ordered the massive avocado and jack cheese omelette.

"What can you tell me about Willard, Levin and Pratt?" I asked after the food arrived.

"They're major-league pricks. They pay well. They want your soul. They never settle out of court." She buttered a piece of toast and took a bite.

"Are they really jerks or just tough negotiators?"

She put down her fork. "They were defending this pharmaceutical company against damages for a side effect from its drug to treat Parkinson's disease. This guy, a normal family man, had only gambled once or twice a year, maybe on office pools or at a local casino. But right after he started taking this drug for his Parkinson's, he turned into this compulsive gambler. Couldn't walk away, even when he knew it was time to quit. He lost everything—his house, savings, everything he owned. Anyway, WL and P wanted to nip it in the bud before it became a class-action suit, so they brought in all these experts, and dug into the guy's life. Came up with every other time that this guy had ever gambled—even if it was just church raffles—and showed that he made really lousy bets. They said he was such a bad gambler that he would have wound up losing his savings anyway. The jury bought it. The guy committed suicide the next day."

"Because he lost the case?"

"No. His wife said somebody had left him notes about his family being better off with him dead. That he'd ruined them with his bankruptcy and this was the only way to fix it."

"Was there any proof it was WL and P?"

She shook her head and took another bite of the eggs. "Nothing they can prove. But I overheard Marcus Pratt in the hallway the next day joking about suicide being the next side effect they'd be accused of. He got a big kick out of it."

"Do you know anything about the other principals? Levin? Or Willard?"

"Levin comes from a family of German Jews that emigrated to Sonora, Mexico, almost a century ago, but I've never worked with him. And Willard doesn't do criminal cases so I haven't been up against him in a courtroom, but he sure knows how to turn on the charm at the ABA meetings."

I told her about Willard's connection to Felicia Villalobos and to the wife of the murdered man I'd overheard at HandsOn that Friday night.

"I would have thought he was too savvy to get involved with a client's wife. Just goes to show, nobody's immune to love."

"Have you ever met Willard's wife?"

"She's a former Miss Mexico City, or something like that. Gorgeous. And she's supposed to have a temper."

"Is Willard the kind of guy who would oversee a high school intern directly?"

"Probably not. None of the principals would, really. Felicia was probably doing some filing or transcription for one of the secretaries."

"But she would have been around the office." That proximity was enough for me. Markson-to-Willard-to-Felicia was less than six degrees of separation.

Raisa surreptitiously rubbed her hip and thigh.

"Leg acting up?" She'd been born a few years too early for the arrival of the polio vaccine to the Ukraine.

"Just a bit." She scootched her legs to the side and levered herself up.

I paid the bill and helped her into her car. She attached the seat belt and stopped to light a cigarette before starting the car.

"You're not getting involved in this investigation, right, Jessie? We don't need one more reason for Len Sabin to think you're in the middle of this."

"I won't get involved at all," I lied.

Lying came easier these days, I thought, resting between five-minute punishments with the bungee-cord jump rope. It was the prosecutor, Ted Dresden, who had first dubbed me the Queen of Liars Anonymous. His case had been thorough, his evidence damning.

His witnesses testified that I had threatened Racine. He could prove that I knew where Catherine's gun was, and that I knew how to shoot it. He had my fingerprints on Walter Racine's car from when I leaned in the window to console Katie.

Worst of all, the cops on the witness stand said Walter Racine was innocent; he'd done nothing to Catherine or her daughter. Horseshit. I had seen him in the playground with Katie just the week before I killed him. His hands had lingered too long when he straightened her tights, hadn't they? And his eyes had been too glassy and wistful as he watched her pump higher on the swing. It wasn't proof, but after Catherine's chilling tale of her childhood, it was enough for me.

Dresden's summary to the jury left me red-faced with shame, but still not enough to confess. "She's lied to you about everything," he said. "About believing that the system would take care of Walter Racine . . . about not returning to Catherine's home for the gun . . . about not taking the law into her own hands. If there was a twelve-step program for liars like there is for alcoholics and gamblers, Jessica Gammage would be its queen and founder and president. And now she wants you to become liars, too. Lying to yourself about who killed Walter Racine. There is no reasonable doubt here, ladies and gentlemen. There's not even the shadow of a doubt. There is nothing here but Jessica Gammage's lies."

I denied it, of course. Not the part about trying to stop Racine, but the part about pulling the trigger.

And those lies got easier to tell every day. Unlike other twelve-step programs, mine didn't include repentance or atonement. No Thirty Days Honest tokens, no promises to quit.

I guess the jury hadn't believed Dresden after all. Or maybe they did, but decided that Walter Racine deserved to die. None of the jurors looked me in the eye after the verdict was read. No secret winks, no chatty farewells. We each turned away, complicit somehow in the lies that still rang through the air—all of us secretly proud killers of Walter Racine.

The ringing phone brought me out of my wallowed memories.

"Jessie?" my dad asked. "Are you free for dinner? Your mother would like to see you."

CHAPTER SEVENTEEN

The mailbox at my parents' house sported a new coat of black paint and the thorny ironwood in the front yard was green with fresh leaves, none of which had dared to fall to the ground. Someone had raked the gravel driveway into concentric waves, like a small rocky tide hitting the shore of the front porch.

My truck was a shipwreck in the middle of this geometry.

I scrunched up to the front door, leaving foot-shaped indentations I was sure my mother would rake away the instant I was gone.

Unwilling to assume that I was still part of the family, I knocked and waited at the closed door. My father's insistence upon my innocence three years ago had been the reason for my mother's ultimatum: *Choose your adopted daughter or your wife. You can't have both.*

He chose silence and a continued life with the woman he loved. I'd hated him for it then—I'd hated them all—but I understood it, too. It was my mother's own personal defense policy: wall it off, separate yourself, and don't let others touch you.

"Come in, honey," my father said, swinging the screen door open toward me.

I kissed him on the cheek and moved past him into the living room. Nothing seemed to have changed in the almost three years I'd been gone. The long sofa with the curled, dark wood arms still sat at a perfect third-leg-of-the-triangle position to the corner. A short stack of newspapers was precisely aligned next to the leather reading chair. Two days of papers, max. *More than two days and it's not news anymore,* my mother used to say.

Maybe the philodendron had added another foot or so of waxy green leaves, but even that new growth had been pruned and trained into a Doric column of green. I'd had to polish those wide fronds with a dab of mayonnaise every Saturday as a kid. I wondered who did it now.

The TV was on, with a local news anchor talking about the potential bankruptcies of medical centers in the city because of having to treat illegal immigrants when they fell victim to dehydration, violence, or sunstroke as they crossed the border. The volume seemed a little louder than my parents used to listen to it. The first sign of their aging? Or had my own ears changed? Maybe I had spent too much time alone in small quiet rooms to appreciate it.

Nothing seemed changed, and yet I was seeing it all through new eyes. Had that dining table really been big enough to hold all nine of us? My usual chair had been on the boys' side of the table, plunked down between Martin and Lincoln to arbitrate fights during the meal. It had never felt crowded.

There were only three place settings there tonight, one at each end of the long rectangle and another in an eleven o'clock position to the head of the table. It was two against one, no matter how you looked at it.

"Jessica." I turned.

My mother stood erect as a general, her gray eyes wide but unsympathetic. She held her mouth closed and straight, her arms at her sides. She was wearing a crucifix I hadn't seen before, thin gold with a red stone at the center. There were a few more crow's-feet at the edges of her eyes, but the Arizona sun could do that to you. So could steeling yourself against the jibes and blandishments of neighbors and in-laws. So could hardening your heart and sending your adopted daughter away.

"You've changed your hair." She said it without reaching toward me. No compliment. No opinion. Just a statement of fact, with her arms pinned to her sides like they were stapled there.

"Yeah, I've changed." She didn't ask how.

"It's not much of a dinner," she said. "How do you like your eggs?"

As if I were a stranger, someone she had never cooked eggs for before. Someone whose table manners she hadn't corrected at every meal for almost twenty years. My heart shattered.

I guess I'd always known, way down deep where the soul takes root, that she would never forgive me. But I never expected her to forget me.

I followed her into the kitchen, handed her the carton of eggs and leaned against the refrigerator door as she worked. She cracked one egg—*tap, tap, TAP*—two soft and one hard, separated the white from the yolk, then poured the white into a ring she'd placed in the hot pan. She waited a moment for the albumen to settle, then added the yolk, dead center in the ring. "If you put the whole egg in at the same time, it can turn out lopsided," she'd explained when I was a child. I didn't fry my eggs that way anymore, preferring to let things lie where they chose. Sometimes, like truth, even burying them under a distracting sauce.

She portioned refried beans and eggs onto three plates, then added a rolled flour tortilla and a small dish of hot, fragrant salsa. A do-it-yourself huevos rancheros kit, served the only way she was capable of doing it, with the food walled off, separate and not touching.

I carried the loaded plates into the dining room, waiting for my mother to indicate each person's place. It was the first time I could remember sitting at that table when I hadn't been the one to place the silverware. "The knife protects the spoon," she'd taught me early on. "Put its blade to the left. You can never tell when the fork will try an attack."

Mother gestured to the seat next to my father—six feet and two-and-three-quarter years away from where she pulled out a chair for herself at the other end.

My father nattered on during the meal. No news of Bonita yet, he said, although the Peace Corps had sent a message that she'd arrived safely in Bolivia. Martin was studying for the chief's exam—Hadn't it been especially hot this year? The water bill was through the roof.

I nodded and smiled in response, adding nothing about my own life, but waiting for someone to ask nonetheless.

No one did.

I guess my mother hadn't changed her mind after all—still keeping her family safe from killer daughters and off-center eggs.

My father walked me to the door. "Give her a little time, Jess."

Another three years? A lifetime?

I was flipping through radio stations for something happier than the Dixie Chicks when the first motorcycle cut in front of me. I slammed on the brakes and the steering wheel jigged a little to the right before I could correct it. Another two bikes roared up to my left and then two more behind me. The baby brothers of the Braceros tribe again, with blue bandanas on their heads, and wiry arms draped over the ape-hanger handlebars.

"*Hola, chica!*" the one on my left called. He puckered and air-kissed when I looked over. I dropped the transmission into neutral and revved the engine, unnerving the guys in front of me enough that they sped up and gave me a little room.

I was still in a residential neighborhood. No traffic coming my way and no pedestrians on the street. It was going to take more than a revved engine to get these guys off my tail.

Grant Road was just ahead. I swung around the corner to the right as the light changed to red, floored the gas, and pulled into the fire station across the street with my brakes squealing.

"You can't park there," a young fireman said, coming out of the public access area on the right side of the building.

A covey of motorcycles turned in behind me, blocking my exit. I got out of the truck and tugged my T-shirt back into place. Glancing back at the young Latinos, I shrugged—*whatcha gonna do?*—then turned to the firefighter.

"Is Martin Gammage on duty tonight?"

Martin refilled my coffee cup and sat back down.

"Sorry to pull you away from your TV show," I said.

"Nothing but reruns. So how did it go at dinner?"

"Dad told you about my coming over?" Maybe it was a good sign if the family was talking about me again.

He shook his head. "I drove by on my way to work and saw your truck parked in the driveway."

I guess there were still only six kids in the family.

"It was okay. Mom's not ready to make any changes, but it was nice seeing her again." Yeah, Martin, it's a barrel of laughs to watch your mother unhook you from the only anchor you've known for thirty years as easily as if she was untying an apron.

He must have seen the sadness behind my response. He changed the topic right away.

"What's with that gang of motorcycles that followed you in?"

I explained about the connection between Markson and Felicia, and following that trail to Carlos and the Braceros.

"We've had to deal with some of their victims," Martin said.

"What kind of victims?"

"Illegals they've left in the desert. Men they've killed in drug deals. There was a crack house off Prince Road that exploded, killing all six people inside, including a baby. Putting that fire out was no cakewalk."

"So the cops know about them and don't do anything?" Just like they'd done with Walter Racine. I'd never believed it when they said he was innocent.

"They do what they can. I've got a friend on the Gang Task Force who says this group is getting more dangerous every day."

If their prominence in both Tucson and Nogales was any indication, I agreed with his assessment. I waited until I was sure the motorcycles were gone, then gave my brother a hug good-bye.

"You going to be around for a while?" he asked.

"I don't know." Len Sabin might have something to say about that. And, as much as I might want to get away, I had nowhere else to go.

I fired up the truck and put it in reverse.

"Take care of yourself, Jessie."

I had to. Nobody else was lining up for the job.

Bonita's house would have been too quiet, with too much empty space to fill up with grievances and reflections. I needed noise—an excuse not to talk or think. I headed east, back to the bar where I'd found the cowboy.

It was quieter on a Monday night, just two tables of drinkers. A loquacious old man with whiskers in his ears held court at the bar.

"What can I get you?" the bartender asked. He had black hair curling just over his collar and a soft voice to go with it.

"Something that will take me a million light years away from Tucson."

He smiled. "Coming right up."

He returned with a martini glass full of something pink and slushy, a drink that in my former bartending life I would only have offered to blondes who ended their names with an *i*. "Guaranteed to cure what ails you."

"Thanks." I took a sip. Bitter and sweet at the same time. Kind of like dinner with my mother. "It may take more than one of these."

He mopped an already clean spot on the bar in front of me. "You were in here the other night, right?"

"Uh-huh."

He glanced both directions to make sure the other drinkers were taken care of, then ran his finger across my lip. "I've got another cure for the blues. Can you hang on a half hour until I get off?"

I could and did.

He was reaching for my belt buckle before we even made it to the door of the truck. I put the key in the lock, swatting away the hand at my waist. "Let me get this open."

"I'll tell what I want to get open." He reached into the front of my jeans.

"Hold on. Let's get inside first."

"Yeah, let me get inside." He spun me around and plastered me to the cab of the truck like wallpaper. His breath was a combination of mint and sewer.

Had it come to this? That losing myself to mindless, fetid groping was better than the silence inside my head?

"You know what? This wasn't such a good idea."

"Uh-uh. No fair going back now." He unzipped my pants and pushed my jeans and underwear down past my hips.

I was pinned to the door, and hampered by not being able to kick with my pants down. I gave him a shove that sent him sprawling.

"I said no."

I opened the truck door and reached for the tire iron under the driver's seat.

He sprang up, grabbed my left arm, and pulled. "I'll show you what happens to a cock tease."

I didn't fight the tug, but kept spinning past him. I smashed the metal bar down on his forearm and he dropped to his knees.

"And I'll show you what happens to a rapist."

I got in the truck and laid rubber taking off.

CHAPTER EIGHTEEN

It was after two a.m. when I finally made it back to Bonita's house. My nerves were as tight as barbed wire and my hands still shook from the confrontation with the bartender. What the fuck was I doing?

My dad used to keep a red metal air tank in the garage to inflate the dozens of basketballs and bicycle tires that a family of seven kids required. I'd been surprised that first time I filled it up with air at the gas station. It weighed no more full than empty. Was that what I was doing now? Trying to fill the emptiness in me with something as weightless and insubstantial as air?

I had already put the truck in Park before I noticed the slice of light coming from the partially open front door.

No one on the street. No cars or motorcycles that I hadn't seen before. And no sound from inside.

Of course, the gun was in the kitchen instead of in my hand. I pulled out the tire iron again. It would give me enough protection until I could get inside.

Tiptoeing along the side of the house and across the patio, I ducked below the windows and avoided the patches of full moonlight that made the scrubby dry grass look frost rimed.

The light from inside was brighter now—probably the bedroom lamp or the overhead light in the hallway—but I still couldn't see anything through the glass pane on the kitchen door.

I drew a deep breath and stopped to dial 911 on my cell phone, but clipped the phone back on my waistband before pushing the Send button. Slowly, slowly, I turned the key in the lock. A single loud click.

I opened the door and stepped in, but immediately tripped on a mop that had been left leaning against the table. Down on all fours, I scrambled to the cupboard that held the gun.

Nothing. The cabinet door was already open, the contents of the cleaning bucket strewn like piñata candies across the kitchen floor.

Tire iron in hand, I moved swiftly through the rest of the house. Bonita's boxed belongings had been upended on the floor of the bedroom and the mattress was sliced into puffy ribbons. A bottle of ammonia had been emptied on the bed. In the bathroom, the medicine cabinet had been ripped off its hinges and someone had left a stinking pile of human shit in the middle of the floor.

The front door itself was undamaged, but the jamb had been pried away from the wall. And that ugly yellow chair had taken its last breath. It lay shattered in a dozen bulky mustard colored pieces like a jigsaw puzzle created by a madman.

The gun was gone.

Of course, I knew who had done it. Confident that I wouldn't be home, the Braceros had made sure that I paid a price for having dodged them.

I opened the windows in the bedroom, refolded Bonita's clothes, and put them back in the cardboard boxes, tucking the flaps securely under each other to keep the tops closed.

I lugged the mattress out to the truck and hefted it into the back, then lovingly placed the splintered remains of the yellow chair, the dining room table, and three shattered chairs on top.

I could have called the cops, told them about the gang following me, and the theft of the gun, but why give Sabin the satisfaction of knowing he was right? He'd wanted that gun three years ago. I had no doubt that he'd find some way to use it against me now, even if it didn't involve Racine's murder.

My anger fueled the cleanup. I carried, I cleaned, I cried—not in weakness, but in frustration. I'd made an enemy of this Latino gang, but the good guys who were supposed to be protecting me were just as likely to come after me. Damn. Swiping wildly at the word *puta* that had been spray-painted across the living room wall had succeeded only in smearing the red letters into a bloodred scrawl. Now it could have been translated as "whooooore."

The bathroom took more courage. Covering my nose and mouth with my T-shirt, I shoveled the shit into a plastic garbage bag and tossed it into the front yard. Could've used that jug of ammonia right about now.

I added the bag of shit to the load in the bed of the truck and reversed out of the driveway. I'd be waiting at the dump at dawn when they opened.

The Braceros were telling me to get out of town. I wasn't sure what I had done to piss them off. Interrupting their drinking festivities in Nogales? Asking about Felicia and Carlos? Dodging their motorcycle advances last night? Whatever it was, they were warning me off.

And I'd been telling myself to move on, too. There was no hope of a reconciliation with my family, I had no more business to be done here in Tucson, and Len Sabin was too interested in me for all the wrong reasons.

But now I was pissed.

I stopped on the way back from the dump for a big breakfast burrito and was waiting at the Wal-Mart outlet when it opened.

I was down to a box spring and one dining room chair at Bonita's house. If I was going to be staying for a while, I'd need a few more creature comforts.

I prowled the aisles, gathering the bare necessities. Bonita's furniture had been Downscale Dorm Room. My decorations would be Early Biker Chick. I got a pea-green beanbag chair, a foam pad to replace the sliced mattress, a set of two TV trays for tables, and a bathmat, so that I wouldn't think about what had been on the tile floor. New cleaning supplies, including ammonia, two gallons of white paint, and new locks for both doors. Within an hour my shopping cart and my credit card were both loaded.

Back at the house, I turned on both the swamp box cooler and an electric fan to keep the air moving and went to work. The new coat of paint looked so good in the living room that I continued on into the bedroom, but the quart of ammonia was barely enough to make me feel that the kitchen and bathroom had been cleaned of the Braceros' presence.

After I'd replaced the locks, rehung the bathroom door and medicine cabinet, and spread a new set of sheets across the foam pad, it began to feel like home. I flopped down on the beanbag chair, opened a beer, and grabbed the phone.

"Department of Corrections? I'd like to be added to the visitor list for one of your inmates. Paula Gammage—I think she's using the name Paula Chatham now." I took a long swig of Genuine Draft. "Perryville facility, that's right." I gave them all the informa-tion they needed to clear me for the approved list.

"Visiting hours are Saturday and Sunday, from nine to three-thirty," the corrections officer said.

"I'd like to be on the list for Saturday, please."

It would be nice to catch up with my ex-sister-in-law of *America's Most Wanted* fame. She was the only criminal I knew, except for me. Oh sure, there were all those folks I'd been incarcerated with at the county jail while I was waiting for my trial, but I wasn't sure which of them I could trust. In matters of crime, it's always best to stick with family.

The next day was October first. I phoned Bonita's landlord and arranged to pay another month's rent on the place. I didn't mention the new locks and new coat of paint. Any goodwill the repairs would have generated would have been offset by the damage to the furniture, anyway.

Arizona doesn't pay much attention to seasonal change except that October signals a drop back into theeighties for the first time since Easter. I worked out with my homemade gym equipment in the backyard, seeing the bartender's sneering face and hearing the roar of the Braceros' motorcycles with each curl. Anger—at them for their bullying and machismo, and at myself for letting it happen— ran through me as I pumped the sand-filled containers again and again. I'd been dipped in rage for three years now, the coating getting thicker and thicker with each injustice, each disappointment, each bit of control seeping away.

Guillermo called three times, but I didn't pick up. His last message said he'd come by after work. I didn't want to be here. Getting involved with him and his missing brother had caused both the Braceros and Detective Sabin to come after me. I didn't want to get any more ensnared than I already was in a situation that was blossoming craziness.

At sunset, I got in the truck, rolled the windows down, and left to find some dinner, settling for cottage cheese and two packages of sliced turkey from the grocery store. Time to get back to my build-muscle-not-fat diet. Time to reduce the cardio and increase the weight lifting. Time to get strong. Be prepared. Time to take charge again.

It was too early to go home; Guillermo might still be looking for me. I drove west through Gates Pass, the city lights a star-studded reflection in my rearview mirror. Descending to the valley floor on the other side, I spotted the plastic flowers and white cross that mark the site of a death on the roadside. Had someone fallen asleep and driven off the edge? Had he walked along the roadside, deaf to the sound of a truck approaching him from behind? Whatever happened, someone had bothered to remember him, to place a sad, plastic reminder of his existence where others could catch it in their headlights and for just a moment, wonder who had left this world, and who he had left behind.

I hadn't seen a Day of the Dead altar at my parents' house, but it was probably too early for my mother to have assembled it yet. It wouldn't be lit until November, although she was undoubtedly mentally selecting the memorabilia, the sugar skulls, the candles that she'd need. The first day of November was to remember lost children and infants. The second day was for adults.

I was eight when she first let me help with an altar. She settled a gardenia in a shallow glass bowl in front of a flinty-eyed picture of her mother. A clutch of daisies became the bed for her sister's gold hoop earring. It was the first year she marked my aunt Helen's death.

I added the braided blue collar my old cocker spaniel had worn and a sprig from the potted fern out front he'd liked to pee on. My mother pushed them to the back of the table, keeping the apron of the altar to showcase her own pain.

Maybe she'd put a picture of Bonita on the altar this year. Not that she was dead, but being gone a worrisome distance away was just as bad. That deserved prayer and remembrance, too. I doubt that my mother had ever included any reminders of me.

On Friday I called Deke Treadwell and told him I was heading back to Phoenix for the weekend, to wrap up the loose ends of my life.

"How can we reach you if we need to?"

"You have my cell phone number."

"I mean, where can we find you? Where will you be staying?"

That was a little too much supervision for my taste. They may have thought I was somehow involved with Markson's and Felicia's deaths, but so far I wasn't charged with anything. Treadwell would have to settle for vague.

"I don't know yet. I'll find something cheap once I get up there."

I was on the road by seven the next morning, in order to be at the prison when visiting hours started.

Traffic was light and I made it all the way to Chandler before I needed a refill on my coffee. Then it was a straight shot through Phoenix and another twenty miles west to reach the prison.

The Perryville complex, the largest female-inmate prison in the Arizona system, spilled over both sides of the road, but the part I was going to was the giant octagonal razor-wired section on the east. I pulled into the parking lot and followed the signs for arriving visitors.

The waiting room was packed with parents, children, and spouses, all craning to see the next inmate admitted to the visitors' room. One ruddy-cheeked father counseled his six-year-old daughter on the finer points of prison protocol. "Remember to tell Mommy how much we miss her and how beautiful she looks." The little girl nodded solemnly.

It took twenty minutes for Paula to come through the door and I hardly recognized her when she did. Much like my own jailhouse metamorphosis, Paula had become tauter, stronger. She was no longer the soft-spoken blonde who had swapped recipes and diet advice with me.

She was only twenty-seven now, but it looked like she'd added a decade's worth of tough and smart in the three years since I'd seen her.

We got permission to go out to the exercise yard and took seats at an unoccupied picnic table.

"Sorry I wasn't around for your trial," I said. Paula had struck a plea deal about halfway through her trial, which made perfect sense given the evidence lined up against her. It would have been hard to stick to a not guilty plea when the *America's Most Wanted* cameras found you in bed with the escapee, wearing the top to his orange prison scrubs as a nightie.

She smiled. "Nor I yours."

"How's it going in here?"

She shrugged. "There's a good Bible study group. And I got on that team of inmate firefighters—we were working all summer on the wildland fires."

I'd read about their efforts to help staunch the giant fires that had raged across Arizona, blackening fifteen thousand acres of land and turning what was already hot dry earth to ashes. They used a Marine cadence when they marched: "Standing tall and looking good. Ought to be in Hollywood."

"Martin would be proud of you." When they were married, Paula had been the perfect firefighter's wife, but hadn't taken an interest in the field herself. What she had taken an interest in was redeeming prison penpals from their evil ways.

"What about Dixie?" I asked. Sam "Dixie" Chatham was her current husband and the bank robber she'd risked her freedom to bust out of jail.

"We write a lot. I'll be out in sixteen months"—she rapped her knuckles on the table—"but he's got another six years. I'll be waiting for him."

I waved away a fat-bodied bee that thought we should have picnic supplies in front of us and looked around for a shadier spot to sit. Every place with more than a square inch of shade had already been claimed.

"I hope it works out." That was a lie, but I knew how important lies could be to you on the inside. Sometimes even something that slippery was enough to get you through the day.

"Paula, I need to get a gun."

I let it sit there, just as bold and stupid and crass a request as it was.

"Oh Jessie"—she started shaking her head—"you aren't in some kind of trouble again, are you?" Counseling me as if I were the prisoner and she the right-thinking do-gooder stopping by on an autumn morning with reading material, advice, and a sense of superiority.

"Maybe. But it's not of my doing. The gun's for protection."

"How am I supposed to help you get a gun?" she whispered, gesturing to the other inmates, the razor wire, and the guards stationed at the corners of the yard.

"You and Dixie, you know people."

"Yeah, and they're all in prison."

"There's got to be somebody on the outside. Who did Dixie deal with?"

She waited so long that I didn't think she'd answer me, then said, "Go see Herman Prosky. He sells turquoise—onyx—in Quartzite."

I knew the town. It was about 110 miles west from where I was now, across some of the most desolate land God had ever squatted over. "But the big gem show is in February. Will he be around?" Anybody with a lick of sense would have left Quartzite by April and not come back until December.

"He runs the hamburger stand in the off-season. Tell him 'Paula remembers Ajo.'"

"What does that mean?"

"That's where I bought the guns off him for Dixie's breakout." During her trial, Paula had never given up the name of the guy who sold her the guns. He owed her for that, and maybe I could be the way he paid her back.

I brushed off the seat of my pants as I stood up. "Thanks, Paula."

"I'll be praying for you."

CHAPTER NINETEEN

It took less than an hour and a half to get to Quartzite. Not even the highway patrol wanted to spend time on that road, so I was safe speeding. Sure, it was the multilane highway between Phoenix and Los Angeles, but it was also the hottest, ugliest stretch of road in the state. Featureless flat desert rolled away in all directions. No vegetation higher than your knees, and even that was parched and gray.

I didn't have a temperature gauge in the truck but my bare arm out the window confirmed that October temperatures had not yet arrived in La Paz County. God's country, my ass.

In winter, the little town of Quartzite swells from its usual population of two thousand to over a quarter of a million, playing host to one of the largest RV-based snowbird communities in the world, and holding nationally known gem and mineral shows. By July it is a hellish ghost town.

I cruised up and down the main strip twice, then chose the most disreputable-looking hamburger stand of the three that were available.

A gaunt, stray dog panted in the shade of a Dumpster and a Gila monster warmed itself on a flat stone next to the front door. Its bands of black and pearl scales looked like something on offer at the gem show. I pulled open the warped screen door and crossed the three feet from the entrance to the counter. A double helix of fly-studded paper twirled overhead.

"Herman Prosky around?" I asked the heavyset man who was scraping the grill.

"Who's asking?" He didn't look up from his task.

"Paula Chatham asked me to stop by and say hi. Says she remembers Ajo."

"Ajo?" He finally looked me in the eye. "That doesn't mean nothing to me but 'garlic.'"

"Well, literally, yeah, I can see what you mean." *Ajo* did mean "garlic" in Spanish. "Paula said you might be able to help me out with something."

He put down the spatula and approached the counter, wiping greasy hands on an already spotted apron. "You a cop?"

I shook my head. "Farthest thing from it."

He detoured around me on the way to the front door, locked the screen, and turned the sign around to read BACK IN 15 MINUTES. I followed him through the kitchen and out the back door.

His used-to-be-mobile home sat dead center on a square concrete pad behind the burger joint. If it had been a fried egg, my mother would have applauded the placement. He held the door open for me and I preceded him up two steps and into the trailer. It smelled the way Herman looked—old, unwashed, and greasy.

"Whadda ya need?" he asked, closing the door behind him. The smell grew stronger.

"I'm looking for a gun."

"Really? I thought you were here for a Tootsie Roll pop." He snorted, then opened the tiny refrigerator and pulled out a beer without offering me one. "So, what'll it be?"

"Something small."

Prosky sat down at the built-in U-shaped dining table and yanked up the seat cushion on the rear bench. Digging out a rolled towel, he unfurled it on the table.

"Ya got yer Colt, yer Ruger if you like .45s. This is the best bargain today." He pointed at a short-barreled revolver with a white plastic grip that looked about as durable as cotton candy. "An RG .22. I can let you have it for a hunnert and seventy-five."

He didn't see any spark of interest in my eyes, so he dug deeper into the bench seat and came out with another towel, this one wrapping a longer shape. "How about a rifle? I'll give you a better price on this Ruger Mini-14 than you could get at Wal-Mart."

"What's that?" I asked, spying a familiar shape in a fold of cloth under the rifle.

"Oh, this little thing?"

It was a twin to the LadySmith I'd used to kill Walter Racine, but this one had deep red, burled wood instead of the hard, black rubber grip that one had. It looked like Prosky was holding a beating heart in his hand. I had to have it.

"How much?"

He named a figure that was triple the retail price, but I wasn't in the market for retail. I got him to knock it down fifty bucks and throw in a box of bullets and a little switchblade with a five-inch double-edged sticker and called it quits.

It was already almost three o'clock and the sun was doing its worst. I bought a bag of ice and two big bottles of water for the trip back home. More than a hundred degrees and sunset was still four hours away.

I dunked a handkerchief in the melting ice and wrung it out loosely, leaving in the small chips of ice that had gathered in the folds. I sighed as I wrapped it around my neck.

I'd be back in Tucson by dark.

The setting sun turned the sky from persimmon to bruise. My mind spun with the tires. I still had so many unanswered questions. Who had buried a note with my name in Markson's grave? If the note was in Felicia's handwriting, then Markson might have been alive as much as two days after the attack. Where had he been? And if he was already dead, why hadn't they buried him?

Treadwell should know by now whether the paint on Carlos's car matched Markson's. But where was Carlos and why did he have a child's seat in his car?

Emily Markson's role in this wasn't clear, either. She'd lied to the cops about her husband being in New Mexico on the night of the attack and she was fooling around with her lawyer-neighbor. That, plus the bruises on her arms and the cryptic e-mail I'd seen signed "A" about meeting someone at the arroyo, left too many gaps in her story, too.

And what about that creepy Paul Willard, hooked into this both by his affair and by Felicia's internship? I could understand if he wanted to get Markson out of the way, but what did Felicia and her boyfriend have to do with that?

It was only eight o'clock by the time I got back to Tucson. Not too late to check in with my friendly local cop.

Deke Treadwell's house was only a mile from my parents' place, tucked into one of the side streets behind the Arizona Inn. I pulled up at the curb and shut off the engine. In case the neighborhood wasn't as safe as it looked, I locked the new LadySmith in the toolbox in the back of the pickup.

All the lights in the house were on, although I couldn't hear any noise from inside. I passed the squat, fat palm tree by the front porch and was greeted by the smell of pot roast.

"Jessica? Is that you? My, you've changed."

Mary Louise, Deke's wife, hadn't changed at all. Her hair was still iron-filing gray, in tight curls like a poodle's around her face. Her arms were open in welcome.

"Come in! Come in! It's been such a long time since we've seen you."

I guess Deke hadn't been passing along the news of my arrival in Tucson any more than my brother Martin had.

"Hi, Mrs. Treadwell. I hope I'm not interrupting dinner."

"Nonsense. We have plenty. Come along." She swept me through the tidy living room—plastic coverings on the armrests, plastic ficus in the corner—and into the kitchen.

"I thought you were up in Phoenix," Deke said, putting down his fork.

"I got back earlier than I expected." He gestured me to sit, and I pulled out the chair next to him at the small round table. Mary Louise put a plate loaded with carrots, potatoes, parsnips, and fork-tender beef in front of me. So much for my promised diet.

"Biscuits, Jessica?" she prompted.

I'd come by to pump Deke for information, but that could wait. I wasn't about to turn down any of Mary Louise's cooking. I had fond memories of evenings spent here eating macaroni and cheese and mustardy potato salad, but what I most loved her for were the deliveries of chocolate-chip cookies and lemon bars to me in jail. The sweet treats rarely made it past the guards, but just the thought that she had come by with them made my days easier.

We talked the silly superficialities of weather and whereabouts until our plates were empty and cleared away. "Why don't you two go sit in the living room and I'll clean up," Mary Louise said, sensing our unspoken need.

We ignored the living room and headed for the aluminum glider on the back porch. Deke took up three-quarters of it and I let his feet set the rocking pace.

"What did you find out about Carlos's car?" I asked after a moment of silence.

"Jessie, don't put me in the middle of this—"

"You're already in the middle of it, and so am I. I don't want to be flying blind if there's something I ought to know."

He sighed and rocked another three times. "The paint on Ochoa's car matches what we found on Markson's Cadillac. He was involved in the rear-end collision."

"Do you know if Carlos was driving?"

"His prints are all over the car, but there are others, too."

"Maybe Guillermo should listen to the HandsOn call. He'd recognize his brother's voice. Maybe he'd know the third guy, too." I looked sideways at him. "There really were three, right?"

"Yeah, the forensic team says it's three voices. Maybe—"

"What about the child seat?" I interrupted.

"There's no reason that Carlos needed one and no proof that he ever bought one. But Darren Markson bought a car seat just like the one we found and put it on his company credit card a month ago."

"What did his wife say?"

Deke kept rocking. "More of nothing. She had no idea . . . He never mentioned it . . . They didn't need one . . . Maybe he bought it as a gift for an employee."

"Well, maybe he did. But why would he have had it in his car on the way to a business meeting in New Mexico?" Until I heard a better answer, I was assuming that the sixty-pound weight that HandsOn had recorded in the back was a child's seat. A child's seat with someone sitting in it. Who was that child and where was he?

"Any more news on Felicia's internship? What did the guys at the law firm say?"

"Willard says he knew about the internship but never had any dealings with her. She seemed to work in Levin's group, but even there it was just filing and stuff."

I still wasn't willing to shrug aside her internship as "just a coincidence." I had only glanced at the Willard, Levin and Pratt documents that Mr. Villalobos had given me. But if Felicia was just doing filing, why did she have the law office documents at home at all? They deserved a closer look.

"Jesus, Deke. This is getting scary. Darren Markson is found dead more than two days after I talk to him. Felicia gets blown up right after I meet her. And now there may be a child involved? What are you guys doing about it?" I rocked our glider faster and it protested with a high-pitched dry squeak.

"Leave it alone, Jessie. We're working the case."

"Did you check Markson's other phone calls through the Hands-On system? Maybe one of the earlier calls—"

"Give it a rest, Jessie." He stood up and walked to the leafy mulberry in the center of the backyard. "Emily Markson's lawyer is trying to restrict our use of the HandsOn information. Says that all that data is owned by the Marksons, not HandsOn, and any use of the information would be like forcing the Marksons to testify against themselves."

"But you got a subpoena that night, right?"

Silence. Deke kicked at the tree trunk.

"You didn't?"

He shook his head. "We got the nine-one-one information from your call, then contacted HandsOn and asked you to come down. Your bosses probably shouldn't have released the information without a subpoena or approval from the Marksons."

"You were looking for a man who was in danger. Isn't there something about exigent circumstances?"

"Nothing exigent in calling you the next day, I guess." He stripped a small branch of its leaves and littered them on the dry grass. "Anyway, a judge is looking into it now."

"And Emily Markson is trying to keep you from getting the information."

"Yep."

What was she hiding? The HandsOn information couldn't implicate her—she said she was home at the time of the attack. And it couldn't implicate her husband; he was dead. Unless they were both involved in something they didn't want the cops to know about.

It looked like I had already passed along the HandsOn information illegally, so I might as well keep going. I told Deke about listening in to Markson's car a second time on that call.

"That scenario matches somebody stringing him up from his feet and beating the shit out of him," he said.

"Is that what his body looked like?"

He nodded. "There were rope burns around his ankles and he'd taken a beating before he was killed. Broken arm, cheekbone. Broken ribs. The bruises had had enough time to show up, anyway. But he would have lived if somebody hadn't put a bullet in his head."

I was back to my original hypothesis that Markson had been held for ransom. But now I had more questions. Where was the child who had been in the backseat? And why didn't Emily Markson want us to find out?

CHAPTER TWENTY

Sunday was always a good day for resolutions, and on this Sunday I resolved, once again, to get back to my workout schedule, to find a way to expend my energy in something other than rage. I found another gym on the east side of town offering free introductory sessions, so I took myself, caffeineless, over for punishment.

A kickboxing class and a solid hour of weights got my blood moving again after that lethal pot roast, and worked out some of my aggression.

I couldn't ask Darren Markson and Felicia Villalobos what had happened. Carlos Ochoa could probably help, but I couldn't find him to ask, and the Braceros only seemed to be peripherally involved because of Carlos's participation with them. If Emily Markson and Paul Willard were putting up a fight to keep the HandsOn data confidential, they wouldn't be of any use, either.

The weak link here might be Aloma Willard, Paul's beauty contest–winning wife. If she didn't know about her husband's affair, I could use that as leverage against him. I had to find a way to get her talking.

All I knew about Aloma Willard was that she drove a blue Taurus, she was beautiful, and she was from Mexico City. That may be all I needed to get started.

A quick log-on at Kinko's confirmed that Aloma Willard (née Sauza) had won the Miss Mexico City crown ten years ago. The photo they used on the Web site, if it was anywhere near current, was a knockout. Lustrous hair, the kind of big eyes you only see on velvet paintings, and clavicle definition that was sharp enough to cut paper. She'd made it to third runner-up in the national pageant.

I used another fifteen minutes of Kinko's computer time to mock up fake business cards while I was there.

Not willing to chance that Paul Willard would be around the house on a Sunday, I put off my plans to meet his wife until the next day. That left me enough time to go over Felicia's notebook from the law office.

I settled into the new beanbag chair with an iced coffee and Felicia's black three-ring binder.

It wasn't an official document from Willard, Levin and Pratt, just a notebook Felicia had used to gather all the background, names, and numbers she'd need for her internship. The first tabbed section included a phone list, an organization chart, and a floor plan for the law firm. Their offices were in an old converted adobe house, so the layout wasn't very complicated. There was a star next to the name Serena McDowell, the assistant and secretary to the partner Robert Levin. Felicia hadn't paid any particular attention to Willard's name on any of the lists, although his office and Serena McDowell's desk space looked like they'd both been carved out of the same space, maybe a previous dining room.

The next section included PR releases and newspaper clippings about the law firm, and a copy of a speech one of the lawyers had given about immigration law. The newspaper clippings were nothing special: announcements of promotions and partnerships, and a photo of the partners at a groundbreaking ceremony.

The third tab of the book, however, held the contracts for Darren Markson's firm to build and manage six day-care centers, four in the city and two more on the Arizona side of Nogales. I didn't understand a lot of the legal language that WL&P had included, but it looked like the cities were paying for the land and Markson's development company was paying to build and manage the centers. I couldn't see how he'd make a lot of money that way, but maybe it was his way of tithing.

I flipped back to the newspaper photo in the previous section. Yep, the groundbreaking ceremony was for the first of the day-care centers, including a complete recreation facility for kids from the newly built low-income housing area near the airport. Interesting that the law firm was represented there as well as their client. A short, smiling Darren Markson was the guy with his foot on the shovel, but his lawyer, Paul Willard, was right there beside him. And the caption said that the dark-haired man with the ox-bow hairline on his right was Levin, the *L* part of WL&P.

I jotted down the addresses for the other five facilities.

If Felicia had access to the Markson contracts, and Paul Willard represented Markson at the law firm, maybe she'd had more business dealings with Willard than he'd told the police. And if she hadn't worked directly with him, what was she doing with Markson's contracts?

On Monday, I waited until ten o'clock to call the Willard house, to make sure that the lawyer would have already left for work. I wanted to give Aloma Willard enough notice of my visit to give me some legitimacy, but not enough time that she could thoroughly check out my credentials.

"Aloma Sauza?" I asked when she answered the phone.

"My last name is Willard now."

"Of course. But your public still thinks of you as Aloma Sauza, Miss Mexico City."

When she didn't hang up, I knew I had her. "I'm with *Round Up* magazine. We don't just focus on current celebrity lifestyles. Our readers want to know what's happened to all their favorites . . . how the rest of your life has turned out."

"My life?"

"Of course! Our readers want to know what other fabulous things you've been up to since you won your crown."

"Like a 'where are they now' story, right?"

"That's it. Anyway, one of our reporters is in Tucson today and would like to come by for a short interview, if that's okay. I know it's not much notice, but we're on a deadline. Do you have some time available this morning? Maybe at eleven?"

She agreed.

I arrived at the house just a few minutes before eleven. My old pickup was pretty distinctive, especially with its now blackened hood. I couldn't take a chance that her neighbor, Emily Markson, would remember it from my first visit so I parked around the corner and hoofed it to the Willards' front door.

Aloma Willard wore thirty-something well. Her skin looked like it would taste of cinnamon, and her ankles were those of a racehorse.

"My name's Laura Dunn," I said, offering one of my newly minted *Round Up* business cards. She ushered me in.

The house, like her voice, held nothing of her Mexican heritage. A rose-patterned couch in cream and pink faced the wall of windows looking over the city, and a baby grand piano graced the far wall.

"Do you play?" I asked.

She narrowed her eyes. "Yes," she said slowly, "that was my talent in the competition."

Uh-oh. A little more research into her glory days would have stood me in good stead. "Of course it was. I meant do you *still* play?"

"A little."

We took seats on opposite ends of that garden bed of a couch and I flipped my notebook open to an empty page. It took thirty minutes of reminiscing about her pageant days before I could bring her around to current day topics.

"I understand that your husband is a lawyer."

"Yes, he's a senior partner in his firm."

"I imagine that gives you the opportunity for lots of good works in the community. Charity balls, special projects."

"That hasn't changed since my pageant days. I still take charitable work seriously. But now, of course, I'm representing both Mexico and the United States."

"Can you give me some examples?" I drew a series of squares on the small page, as if getting ready to record a long list.

She poured us both glasses of sparkling water before replying. "Well, we support the arts, of course. The symphony, the opera."

I made small notes.

When she couldn't come up with any other charitable ventures, I prodded her. "What about your husband's business? Is there anything there that our readers would like to know about? Any charitable works or projects that you and he are proud of?"

"Well, the day-care centers, of course. Paul is—I mean Paul and I are—in partnership with a few others to build day-care centers here in southern Arizona where they're most needed for new immigrants and struggling families."

"That's a coincidence. I met someone at a Career Day presentation I did at Cholla High School who told me about a project like that. Felicia Villalobos, I think her name was. Do you know her?"

"She works at Paul's office. A sweet kid—on some kind of work-study program, I think. I met her at one of their office parties. Paul has really taken her under his wing." She patted a rosy cushion into place under her arm as if it, too, belonged under a wing.

She didn't seem to be aware of Felicia's death, or of Paul Willard's denial of having worked closely with her. If the police really were following up on the coincidence of Felicia's internship with the law firm, they hadn't gotten to Willard's wife yet.

We chatted about other celebrity issues: fashion, favorite restaurants, and world peace. There was no need to use her husband's philandering as leverage to get her to talk. She'd just confirmed his involvement not only with Felicia but also with the day-care centers.

"Don't you want new pictures for the story?" she asked as I made my way back to the front door.

"I'll bring the photographer next time," I promised, although the only new photo I wanted was a mug shot of her and her husband, if they were knee-deep in Markson's death. I didn't know how this day-care stuff fit in, but if both Willard and Markson had been involved with it, and Felicia kept a copy of the contract at home, then that was more than just coincidence, and had all the earmarks of a scam.

Unless, of course, the day-care centers were part of Felicia's commitment to improving the lives of newly arrived immigrants, a goal that fit her desire to be an immigration lawyer. Maybe she heard about the project at work and thought it was a good idea. Damn. How could something look both so angelic and so evil at the same time?

I was idling at a red light when my cell phone went off.

"Can you meet me right now?" Guillermo was almost out of breath with the question.

"What is it?"

"I got a call from one of the Braceros. He says he's seen Carlos and he wants to meet at a bar in South Tucson." He named a bar and a street corner.

"I'll meet you in the parking lot."

I peeled out when the light turned green, then turned on the blinker and pulled into a sandy turnout on Swan Road, where I retrieved the gun from the locked box in the back of the truck.

"What does that mean?" I pointed at a neon sign that said EL ESPE-JISMO, across the front window of the tiny building.

"Mirage," Guillermo said.

The first four letters of the word were shorting out, sending a Morse code neon message out across the parking lot. I bet the regulars called it something more like the Gizmo.

"And here I thought mirages were supposed to be seductively attractive images." The building was made of cadaver-gray concrete blocks, pinged by enough bullet holes to make a connect-the-dots drawing. Rusty wrought-iron bars guarded windows so dirty that you couldn't even tell if the bar was open.

"Who's this guy we're meeting?"

"Jorge. I don't know him well; he joined up after I left the gang. But his aunt is my mother's best friend, and he heard we were looking for Carlos."

"Why didn't he come by your place?" I wasn't sure why Guillermo had called me for backup. It sounded like the guy was practically family.

"He says he can't be seen with me. That's why he picked this place."

He got that part right. Nothing but empty lots and self-storage warehouses for a half mile around. At the end of the street was a small bodega with three tired plastic pennants that looked like they were signaling surrender in the hot wind.

Guillermo pushed open the metal door and I followed him inside. The silence was disturbed only by the clink of glasses being reshelved and the sound of water running in a deep sink.

There was only one customer, a square-jawed Latino with bad acne, sitting at a cigarette-scarred table in the far corner. He was one of the younger variety of Bracero, maybe sixteen or seventeen, wearing a dingy wifebeater, and baggy black pants riding low on his hips. Guillermo went straight to him.

"*Hermano,*" he said, executing a complex, four-beat handshake that ended in a position that looked like arm wrestling.

Guillermo pulled out a chair for himself and nodded for me to take a seat at the next table. I did, keeping my back to the corner and my eyes on the door.

"You've seen Carlos?" he asked when Jorge didn't volunteer any information.

"What'll it be?" the bartender interrupted, approaching the table with a short stack of tiny paper napkins. He was a grizzled white man, wearing a twin of the shirt Jorge had on.

"Two beers," Guillermo said. I shook my head at the bartender's invitation to make it three. He didn't ask for the kid's ID.

Jorge waited until the beers were delivered and the bartender was back across the room flipping through the paper.

"I haven't seen him. But I heard."

"What?" Guillermo looked like he was ready to grab the kid by his scrawny T-shirt and shake him. "You said you'd seen him!"

"He wanted out, is what I heard. He was trying to fuck up the deal."

"What deal? Where is he?"

The kid lowered his voice, as if a host of eavesdroppers had descended upon the room. "I don't know anything about it. But I heard they were keeping him on the east side of town. Someplace they called the Red Tile House. He's in the garage."

"How come you're telling me all this, *vato*? Did Chaco tell you to come find me?"

"No man, I swear. I hear they've fucked Carlos up good. And

I . . . he was good to me. Helped me along at the beginning. I owe him."

"But you don't owe him enough to stand up for him, huh?" Guillermo's fists were clenched.

"I'm telling you, man. I only just heard about it. I was in Nogales when you and the *chica* came in. I heard you asking about Carlos. That's why I called." The kid was flop-sweat-nervous, but I didn't know if he was afraid of Guillermo's temper or the Braceros' retribution.

I heard two motorcycles approaching and walked quickly to the front window, my hand already on the gun in my purse. They were big bikes, all right, but not Braceros. Just two old white guys looking for the freeway entrance. I looked back at Guillermo and shook my head. The kid breathed a sigh of relief.

Guillermo threw some bills on the table. "Get yourself another beer."

I joined him at the front door. He turned back to the kid and tapped his fist twice on his heart. "Thank you, man." A gladiator's salute.

CHAPTER TWENTY-ONE

"The Red Tile place?" I asked once we were back in the parking lot.

"I'm not sure. Chaco's uncle used to have a place on the east side of Tucson where we'd hang out when we came up from Nogales. God, I don't know, it's been ten years. I think it had a red-tile roof."

"Can you find it again?"

"Maybe. But if Carlos is there, we'd have a better shot of taking him at night."

The Braceros probably knew both our cars. That wouldn't be so important in the dark, but if we were going to be cruising up and down their street in broad daylight, it might be a good idea to get another one.

We drove back to Bonita's and picked up my sister's VW. I drove, so that Guillermo could let his eyes wander across undeveloped, sagebrush-strewn lots and down dead-end streets. We circled the same blocks a dozen times before he found a neighborhood that looked familiar.

"Around here somewhere," he said. "That dry Tanque Verde

riverbed was north of the house. And it was on a short, narrow street. No sidewalks."

Things had probably changed dramatically since he was last here. New houses were springing up like locoweed. Streets were wider and straighter now, in anticipation of a flock of new snow-birds moving south. But the view was still disheartening. Spray-painted gravel, brown grass, and thorns. A sea of one-story houses in dun colors, all bowed down by the sun and heat to the point where they seemed too weary to even get to their knees, let alone attempt a second floor.

"What's that?" I pointed to a small house at the back of a narrow lot. I'd almost missed it between the chain-link fences on either side. The tile looked more faded terra-cotta than red, but it was the U-shaped tile they'd used on houses built in the first half of the last century. I let the engine idle.

"That's it. Let's circle the block and see if getting to the garage is easier that way."

I made a left and then a left again, stopping where I thought we'd be aligned with the property on the next block. There was an empty lot, then a chain-link fence. Beyond that, a tarpaper roof lit-tered with needles from the neighbor's tamarisk tree.

"That could be the garage."

Guillermo agreed. "And we won't have to go past the house if we come this way."

I marked our spot on a city map I found in the VW's glove box, and we returned to Bonita's house. We had at least six hours to kill before it would be dark enough to attempt our rescue.

"We ought to call the cops," I said. "Tell them what you heard. Let them go check out the house."

Guillermo shook his head. "Not until I know what Carlos is in the middle of. If it's something the cops can pick him up for . . ." His voice drifted off. He still didn't know if his little brother was the victim or the villain here.

Guillermo paced another lap from the front door to the back. "They may have had him for as much as a week and a half. I don't know what we're going to find—what kind of shape he's going to be in."

"You've got to be prepared for anything," I said, mentally piling up the first-aid kit from my truck, a flashlight, the gun, maybe a sheet if we needed to create a makeshift gurney to carry Carlos back across the lot to the car. "Do you have a gun?"

He shook his head. "I gave that up with my other life."

I pawed through the boxes in Bonita's bedroom until I came up with a baseball bat. "Will this do? Or do you prefer a tire iron?"

He hefted the bat. "This'll do fine. Plus a length of chain, if you have it. And some bolt cutters."

I nodded. I'd always stocked my vehicles with the kind of stuff that would get my brothers out of whatever minor scrape they'd gotten into growing up. Need a tow? Call Jessie. Run out of gas? Call Jessie. Lost the key to the toolshed? Call Jessie. It was an old habit that was hard to break. I got the chain and the cutters from the truck.

Guillermo was on the phone when I came back in, giving someone Bonita's address. "Can you be here by nine? And bring Little Joe with you."

"Little Joe?"

"If that house is where they're keeping Carlos, it's going to take more than just the two of us to get him out. I'm calling in reinforcements."

The reinforcements arrived with the darkness, in the shape of Guillermo's cousins—Esteban, Miguel, and Joe. Miguel was the youngest—about eighteen—and the quietest. He squatted in a corner of the living room cleaning his fingernails with a saw-toothed switchblade. Esteban and Joe brought guns.

Little Joe was anything but little. He was ripped, with better muscle definition across the lats and delts than I had seen since the last Mr. Universe competition. Roid rash littered his cheeks and shoulders. His T-shirt proclaimed, PAIN IS JUST WEAKNESS LEAVING THE BODY.

"What's the plan?" Esteban asked. "We go in loud or we go in quiet?" He had big sad eyes that made him look softer than his voice and his hands let on. A face begging for a scar.

"Quiet," Guillermo replied. "They may just have a couple of guys at the house. If we can get in and out without them knowing it, all the better."

We agreed to wait until after the bars had closed and the Braceros would likely be asleep. In the meantime, I went out for a sackful of burgers and fries. Guillermo and two of his cousins were playing cards on the floor when I returned. Miguel was still in the corner, now with his legs stretched out in front of him, drawing abstract patterns on Bonita's carpet with the tip of the knife. I made a pot of coffee to keep us awake.

"Not hungry?" Guillermo asked his youngest cousin, seeing him rewrap and set aside two hamburgers.

"Saving 'em," Miguel replied.

I rifled through my suitcase until I came up with a black sweatshirt and a pair of steel-toed Doc Martens I hadn't worn for years. Ready for a night prowl.

At two-thirty, we loaded up. Little Joe took the eight-foot length of chain I'd found and sprawled out in the backseat of Guillermo's Camaro. The other two got back in their black pickup and followed us out of the driveway.

The street we were on was quiet. We circled the house. No lights shown from either the front or the back. Guillermo pulled to the curb alongside the empty lot behind the property and we closed the car doors without a sound. The moon had set a couple of hours before; there were few shadows.

A dog started barking behind the fence on our right. A big dog. Loud. Miguel approached the fence and lobbed over one of his wrapped hamburgers. The dog shut up.

We went single file. Guillermo first, with Little Joe right behind. I was near the back of the line, with Miguel bringing up the rear. I pushed past a bushy creosote, releasing the smell of desert rain as I walked on.

Guillermo and Little Joe cut a four-foot slit through the chain-link fence at the back of the Braceros' property and peeled the mesh up from the bottom. I ducked through and followed Esteban's shadowy form toward the rectangular structure in front of us.

It was the size of a garage, all right, but more shedlike in its upkeep and age. Thin sheets of warped wood over a malnourished frame; tar-paper shingles, grayed with tamarisk needles and debris. Weeds grew knee high in the path from the house. If the driveway had been used recently, it wasn't by a car.

A flashlight came on ahead of me, Guillermo shining the light on the garage door. Whatever he saw there required only a snip from the bolt cutters.

He had started to inch the door open when it smashed back against him. Three shadowy figures rushed out, one cracking Guillermo across the temple with a two-by-four, another swinging wildly at Esteban with a metal pipe. Little Joe went down in a pile with two guys wearing light-colored bandanas like masks across their faces. One of them stayed down when Little Joe rolled away.

"*Puta!*" Grunts. Cursing. But no lights and no gunfire.

I stepped to the left and kept the LadySmith in my hand. I didn't want to be the first one to shoot, but I was ready to.

Guillermo had pushed his assailant back toward me and I sidestepped him. When the guy raised his slab of wood again, I planted my foot right behind his heel, pulled him backward, and sent him sprawling. He grabbed my ankle with his left hand, then slashed at my calf with his right. I felt the pain only after he let go. Cold and searing.

Rage traveled through me like a shot of tequila—rage against knives and strong hands. Against pain-givers everywhere. I kicked him in the head until he lay still.

Lights were on in the main house now, and more Braceros raced—shouting—out the door and toward the garage. Little Joe and Esteban fired toward the silhouetted figures. Three went down.

Guillermo and I rushed into the garage. He flashed the light in a circle—kaleidoscopic images of a rusted mower, four bald tires in a tottering pile, and three lawn chairs where the Braceros had waited. And at the back of the room, a slumped figure roped up against one of the support columns.

"Carlos!" Guillermo dropped the flashlight and ran to his brother.

The smell alone was enough to tell you he was dead. No wonder the Braceros had been wearing bandanas in here while they lay in wait for us.

I picked up the flashlight and followed, training it on the young man's downturned face. His body was bloated and the skin was dark gray. His mouth was neutered by a ball gag. Guillermo scrabbled at the gag, pushing it at last under his brother's chin. I set the flashlight on the floor to shine up and started in on the knot of ropes that held his hands trapped behind the post. The hemp was buried in the swollen, rotting flesh on his wrists.

"Use this," Miguel said, offering me his switchblade. I sliced through the bonds and Carlos's body slumped to the ground.

Guillermo took his brother's face in his hands, his fingers sinking into the loose flesh like it was a Halloween pumpkin in December.

If he was searching for signs of a peaceful death, he would find none. Carlos's face and chest were branded with blisters and cigarette burns. His tongue had been cut out before the gag was put in place. A bib of dried blood covered his chin and chest and the oily stench of decay rose from his body.

Miguel quietly picked up the switchblade from where I had dropped it and returned to the yard. Guillermo bowed his head and wept.

"Let's get out of here," Esteban said from the doorway. Guillermo wriggled his hands under Carlos's body and tried to stand.

"Leave him," I said. "We can't help him now."

"I can't leave him. He's my brother." I don't know that I've ever seen such hollow-eyed emptiness in a man's face.

"The cops are probably on the way. They'll take care of him."

I teetered against the post, the pain of the slash across my calf finally reaching through the adrenaline. There was a six-inch slit in my Levi's where the Bracero's knife had found its target. I couldn't see the cut, but my shoe was filling with blood.

Guillermo let me lead him out of the garage by the hand. Little Joe and Esteban were already at the fence, gesturing us to hurry. The lights were on at the houses on both sides, although with the gunfire no one dared to look out the windows.

Miguel took his time behind us. All but one of the Braceros had limped away into the night. Miguel approached the last fallen man and lifted his chin for a final slice. He wiped his knife off on his jeans.

I led Guillermo back to the car.

CHAPTER TWENTY-TWO

I drove Guillermo's car and followed the cousins back toward town. They pulled to the curb at a small stucco house near the university. "This is Miguel's place," Esteban said. "Let's get Guillermo inside."

"No." Guillermo fought to keep the car door closed. "I can't." His eyes were still glassy with loss. Esteban touched his forehead to Guillermo's for a moment, then turned away. I drove us back to Bonita's house.

"Turn on the lights," Guillermo said. "All the lights." I did as he asked, the little house blazing from back porch to front. It showed every empty corner, every old, faded, forgotten wish. It felt cold, the loss of a brother and innocence, of hope and a future already sadly realized.

I retrieved the first-aid kit from my truck and brought it back in. Shucking my jeans, I could see how lucky I was. The gash across my calf was long but not deep, and it had missed the tendon entirely. Guillermo cleaned the wound for me, then painted the flayed skin together with New-Skin and wrapped my leg in gauze. The injury didn't merit more than a sharp intake of breath with every step, but then again, there's more than one kind of pain.

I wished I had something stronger than beer in the house. Tequila, maybe. Absinthe. Heroin. Something to make time move backward.

"I'm so sorry." I placed my hands on both sides of Guillermo's face and forced him to look at me. The lump above his ear was hidden in his hair. I caressed it gently. The emptiness in his eyes had been replaced by ice.

He knocked my hands away, then streaked out one muscled forearm and grabbed my wrist. He forced me to the floor and jammed his hand into my crotch, then shuddered as if he'd awakened from a nightmare and rolled off me.

"I'm so sorry," he echoed.

I didn't need to reply. I understood that animal desire to prove you're still alive, to drive death away when it had come so close. He'd stopped himself before the final act. He was still in control.

"The police will be looking for you when they identify Carlos's body," I said.

His chin ducked in acknowledgment.

"They have my blood at the scene." I thought of my Doc Martens awash in blood, dripping onto the floor of the garage. "And our fingerprints for sure."

He nodded again, but didn't reply.

"What about your cousins?"

Guillermo rolled over, retrieved the cell phone from his pants pocket, and made a call. He rolled back into position when the call was done, his shoulder under my head.

"Joe may have a broken arm, but the other two are fine."

"Tell them to get rid of their guns." My crime cover-up skills were coming back to me.

"They know better than to keep them. But Miguel would be hard-pressed to lose that knife."

The calm confidence with which Miguel had slit that last Bracero's throat suggested a longtime tryst with the blade.

I marveled at the fact that, for one brief, metallic moment there in that shed, I had thought of calling the police. Let them see that the Braceros—at least one of them now dead—had killed Carlos Ochoa and were probably responsible for the deaths of Darren Markson and Felicia Villalobos as well. Before the thought could become action, however, I had done what any other criminal would have done. I ran.

When had I crossed that weathered threshold that divided the world between citizens and survivors? Between what we could be and what we are in our darkest hours?

I think it was the night that the woman from Children's Services reported back that they couldn't find any evidence to support my claims of Racine's danger to his great-niece. I'd felt like a diver whose air had been cut off. Silent. So scared for Katie.

I'd picked up a fist-sized stone and heaved it through the woman's car window. The glass shattered inward, like my faith in the safe world of citizens. A world where police and counselors and arrest warrants could stop bad things from happening to little girls. A world I could no longer count on.

"I have to tell my mom about Carlos," Guillermo said as the sun finally parted the slatted blinds.

I put my finger across his lips. "Not until the police come by. You have to hear it from them first."

"I can't—"

"It won't be long."

I got up to put on a pot of coffee. It wouldn't take much time for the cops to match the corpse's fingerprints to those of the missing man whose car had been found at the dog track. Would they start the ID right away or wait until they had processed the whole crime scene? How long would it be before they found my fingerprints on the wooden post next to the ropes that had held Carlos or matched my blood to that pooled next to his body?

I handed Guillermo a mug. "Where will you be?"

"At Carlos's house." He still seemed a half step behind the danger.

"We'll need to get our stories straight. The phone records will show the call to your cousin. My neighbors may remember their truck, or hearing their voices here last night."

He nodded but I wasn't sure that he was listening.

"So that's the story. You and your cousins came over here to play cards. We're not sure what time it wrapped up—maybe eleven or twelve. We don't know anything else."

"I'll tell the others." He fingered his car keys like they were a puzzle to him.

I watched him walk to his car, spine stiff and head steady, but with a hesitation in his step, as if his world had gone off plumb and he couldn't quite get his balance.

I had to get rid of my clothes and shoes before the cops showed up. First, I ran my jeans and sweatshirt through a commercial laundry on Campbell, then dropped them into two separate Goodwill bins five miles apart. The bloody Doc Martens got tossed into a pile of burning tires at the city dump.

I was back home by eight o'clock, with a big cardboard cup of coffee and a dozen donut holes in hand. Grief demanded sugar and fat.

The next few hours would be the hard part—acting normal until I heard that things weren't.

Guillermo called at one o'clock.

"They've found Carlos." I wondered who else was in the room with him. I waited.

"They say he's been dead at least three days. They won't know exactly how long for a while." The autopsy would confirm his time of death, but that Brazil nut–colored skin, and that fetid, thick smell of decay made me think he'd been dead a long time.

"I'm so sorry," I said for the benefit of anyone else listening. "Do you want me to come over?"

"Not right now. The police want to search Carlos's house and mine. Just to make sure there's nothing there that can help them."

"Of course." We hung up, each cocooned in our web of misery and lies.

Treadwell and Sabin got to me at three o'clock. Standing side by side in the living room, they looked like a basset hound and a weasel had made friends.

"Sorry I don't have more chairs," I said, seated on the one remaining dining room chair from Bonita's set. Treadwell eyed the beanbag chair with distrust and shifted his weight from foot to foot.

"We found Carlos Ochoa's body this morning," he said.

"His brother called me a couple of hours ago. Where was he?"

"Behind a house on the east side of town. It looks like the Braceros might have been involved."

"Does that mean they killed Markson, too?"

"Maybe, they—"

"Where were you last night, Ms. Dancing?" Sabin interrupted. "From say midnight till six this morning."

"I was here. I had some friends over earlier, but they left by midnight or so."

"We'll need their names and numbers," Sabin said, not giving away the fact that he probably just got the same list from Guillermo. He handed me the search warrant as casually as if it were a cocktail napkin.

"Getting better about getting your paperwork in order, huh, guys? No more forgotten subpoenas?"

Treadwell looked at his hands. "It has to be done, Jessie. Just so we can clear you and move on."

"Right. I'll be out back. Let me know when you're done." The gash across my calf was throbbing and it was all I could do not to groan as I stood up.

Sabin was entering the tiny bedroom by the time I hit the back door. I hoped their search warrant didn't extend to the vehicles out front. Since I hadn't fired the new LadySmith at the Braceros' place, I didn't think I had to get rid of it. But it wasn't licensed, so I still didn't want them to find it. After Guillermo had left this morning, I'd hunkered down next to the honeysuckle vine where I couldn't be seen by the neighbors, and tucked it inside the hub-cap on the right front wheel of the VW.

The wait was excruciating. I wished I were a smoker. A magician. Anything to keep my hands busy. "Hey, Deke, can you bring me a beer?" I called over my shoulder.

"Get it yourself," he said, coming to the screen door. He backed away as I came in, and watched me take out the beer and twist off the cap like he'd never seen such an operation before.

"Sure I'm not screwing up any evidence here, Deke?" I took a long swig from the bottle. This was the guy who was supposed to have believed in my innocence, at least in Walter Racine's death. I guess that courtesy didn't extend to any other unsolved murders in his jurisdiction.

He shut the refrigerator door. "I don't know you anymore, Jessie. Where did this anger come from? You've got this chip on your shoulder that's gonna knock you over if it gets any bigger."

"Being suspected of murder will do that to you." He was right about the rage, but being accused of murder was only part of it. It had started when I couldn't get the cops to help protect Catherine's daughter. It had built when my mother pushed me away. It had taken on boulder-size dimensions now that there seemed to be an-other child in danger out there and no one seemed to care.

I took a deep breath. "Can you arrest the Braceros for killing Carlos?" I asked.

"Arrest who? There were two dead bodies there, Carlos and another Mexican guy. Maybe he was a Bracero, but if he was, who killed him? This may be part of a gang war or it may not."

Sabin came out of the bathroom and shook his head, then moved out to the front yard.

"This truck yours?"

I tried not to limp as I followed him out. "Yes."

"I'll need the keys."

I lobbed them to him underhand. He pawed through the toolbox and the cab of the truck, reaching deep beneath the seats to unearth a McDonald's wrapper and a forgotten packet of tissues. I would have thrown away the length of chain and the bolt cutters, but Guillermo's cousins had taken both with them. I hoped they didn't turn up in any search; the police might find my fingerprints on them, or be able to match the blade of the bolt cutter to the broken chain-link fence.

"The VW's yours, too?" Sabin said, approaching the little car.

"No. That's my sister's."

"It's not part of the warrant," Treadwell offered.

"I don't see why not. The house is her sister's, too, and we can search that." The frustration was clear in his voice.

Treadwell met him at the VW's door, but his voice still carried to me. "The warrant's pretty clear. The house and her car."

"Then let's get it amended to include the other car."

"There's no indication she had anything to do with this, Len." Treadwell looked back over his shoulder at me.

I gave them my best liar's face—no guile, no worry. If they got into the VW, they'd find the LadySmith. I didn't want to lose a second gun or give the cops an excuse to hassle me for buying one illegally.

"Let's see if her DNA matches the blood at the scene," Sabin said, then turned to me. "We'd like you to come down to headquarters with us. Give us a sample of your DNA."

My brain was speed-dialing Raisa.

"Look, guys, I've tried to be cooperative here. I never met Carlos Ochoa and have nothing to do with his death. Anything else you want to know, you can contact my lawyer, Raisa Fortas." I started back into the house. The last thing I needed was a police photo of the gash on my leg and a match of my DNA to the blood in the garage.

"I'm not done with you yet," Sabin warned. "This one's a long, slow dance." He was close enough that I could smell the butterscotch on his breath.

Treadwell shook his head and followed his partner back to their car.

I made it to the kitchen, rested my head against one of the thin wooden cabinets, and threw up into the sink.

CHAPTER TWENTY-THREE

"No, they didn't contact me," Raisa said over a take-out dinner at her house that night. "And they had no business asking for DNA. No probable cause at all."

"They asked Guillermo, too. He gave them a sample." I was sorry he had. It made me look guilty by comparison.

"I would have given him the same advice. You shouldn't even have talked to them, Jessie. Don't answer their questions unless I'm there." She added salsa to the chile relleno in front of her, then put down her fork without taking a bite.

"What's the matter?" I asked.

She pushed her plate aside and lit a cigarette. "It's just too much of the same thing. I've got another defendant, a man crossing the border with his family. He killed the coyote that met them on the U.S. side and the prosecutor is going after him for capital murder. How do you say it? 'Same circus, different clowns'?"

"What can you do for him?"

She shrugged. "I don't know. Maybe get him a plea bargain. I really don't want to take this to trial with the way people are screaming about the border crossers right now. Even if he did have a good reason for killing him."

"What's that?" I could think of one reason that was good enough for me, but she didn't need to know that.

"The coyote had taken their little girl away from them. Said she was part of the price of crossing."

"Just like that other woman you were defending before. Isn't that considered a defense of yourself or your family? Trying to stop a kidnapping?"

She shrugged. "Sometimes juries forget those little details when it's an illegal immigrant on trial. Or they think the defendant's lying, that he killed the guy to get out of paying for the crossing."

"Were they part of a group? Maybe the others can confirm the story."

"Most of them have already been deported. The rest aren't exactly the best character witnesses."

"I'm sorry to get you tangled up in my problems," I said. "You've got enough of your own."

She patted my hand, then lit the tip of a second cigarette from the one she had going. "You're not a problem. You're a challenge."

I packed up the remains of our dinner. "How young a child?"

"Hmmm?" Her mind had already moved on to something else. The public defender's office, while not shorthanded, was notorious for heavy caseloads.

"Your client. How old is his little girl?"

"Four, I think. No, five. Why?"

"No reason." The Braceros had a reputation for bringing illegals across the border. And Carlos, a former Bracero who had some kind of problem with one of their operations, had had an unnecessary child's seat in his car: a car seat that might have weighed sixty pounds if it had a five-year-old child in it. A car seat just like the one Darren Markson had purchased. And now they were both dead. It wasn't ironclad, but the facts didn't dispute a connection.

"Did the dead coyote have any ties to the Braceros?"

She looked up. "He was from Nogales, but I haven't heard about any gang ties."

"Maybe you should look into it."

I told her about my thin chain of logic. "I'm not saying that this specific little girl had anything to do with Carlos Ochoa, just that it seems like part of the same operation."

She nodded, thinking.

"I'd like to talk to him," I said.

"Who?"

"Your client."

"No way, Jessie. The police told you that a young Mexican man was killed along with Carlos, right? And they're asking questions about that. So what do you want to do? Get right in the middle of another killing?"

She was right. Sabin would take that as a sign that our "long, slow dance" had just become a tango.

"Where did your defendant come across?"

She named a stretch of land west of Nogales that was still designated as "wilderness" on most maps.

I'd set my phone to Vibrate, and that's what it was doing now. "Jessie?" Guillermo said. "I'm on my way over. I need to borrow something."

"What is it?"

"I'll tell you when I see you. I'm on my way to see Jorge. Can you meet me at your place in ten minutes?"

Jorge, the guy who'd sent us to that red-tile roofed house. The one who swore that Chaco hadn't put him up to it. The one who had betrayed Guillermo's trust. I knew what he wanted to borrow.

"Make it fifteen."

· · · ·

Guillermo was waiting in the shadows on the porch.

"About last night," he started. "I hope I didn't hurt you. I just . . ." His explanation trailed off in the evening air.

"Don't worry. I understand." In some ways I wished he hadn't stopped himself last night. We both needed the release of fierce, urgent sex to drive back the darkness, to prove that life could go on. But it wouldn't have been lovemaking, and that's what I wanted from Guillermo.

"Jorge knew they'd be waiting for us," he said, changing the subject. "He knew Carlos was already dead."

"We don't know that for sure."

He got up from his squat on the concrete porch. "Well, we're going to find out."

First checking the street for passersby or cops on surveillance, I retrieved the gun from its hiding place in the VW's hubcap.

"Are we going back to the bar?" I asked, buckling myself into Guillermo's car.

"No. He's at his aunt's house tonight. I had my mother make some calls."

"Does she know why you were asking?" I'd never met his mother, but couldn't imagine that she would countenance an attack on her best friend's nephew, even if he did play a role in killing her son.

He shook his head.

I told him about dinner with Raisa, and my hypothesis that the Braceros were involved with taking children from their parents when they crossed the border.

"It's not much of a leap from what they have been doing, muling both drugs and people across the border."

"But if they're taking the kids, either for sale or for ransom, that could be what Carlos and Felicia were trying to stop."

He didn't answer, but only because he had no answer to give. My hypothesis painted Carlos in a good light, but no reason was good enough right now for Guillermo to have lost a brother.

We parked on a narrow side street downtown, just around the corner from the purple and cinnamon–hued buildings of La Placita Village. What had once been a quiet, dark part of town after the sun went down was now home to outdoor movies on the plaza, with hundreds of visitors sitting in plastic chairs or lounging against the stone steps, miming the dialogue to *The Maltese Falcon* or *The Wizard of Oz* in the evening air.

The house looked like one of the original adobes built at the turn of the twentieth century, but was more likely one of the replicas that had taken their places just a decade ago. It was not as passionately colored as its neighbors, but a bright coat of whitewash made it glow like a pearl in the night.

I waited in the car while Guillermo went inside. He came out five minutes later, holding Jorge by the scruff of his neck, herding the teenager toward the car.

"Watch him," he said, handing me the LadySmith. Jorge got in the front seat and I got in the back. Guillermo put the car in gear and glided back into downtown traffic. Moviegoers and downtown diners merged and eddied on the sidewalks. The air smelled of spicy beef.

"I'm telling you, I didn't know about Carlos!" the kid complained. "I never would have sent you there if I knew they were waiting."

"Forget it, *hermano*. I know you didn't mean to do it. But I do want to know who was talking about the house with the red-tile roof."

"I can't—I don't remember."

Guillermo was silent for the rest of the ride, stopping once to buy a bottle of tequila at a liquor store on Speedway. We headed west, toward the darkness of Gates Pass. He parked at the summit and we scrambled around saguaros and over truck-sized boulders to claim a bird's-eye view of the city from the peak.

"Here, Jorge. Take a drink."

The kid, who looked like he hadn't changed clothes from the

baggy black pants and undershirt he'd been wearing when I met him, declined the offer.

"I said drink." Guillermo pulled Jorge's head back by the hair and upended the bottle in his mouth. The teenager sputtered and choked on the burning liquid.

"Now who was it that told you about the house?"

The kid fought him and Guillermo slapped him across the face. He forced more liquor down his throat.

"When they find your body at the bottom, they'll think you were drunk—tripped out here in the dark." He dangled Jorge over the edge by the back of his thin shirt.

"That's enough," I said. "He doesn't know anything."

"Sure he does, don't you, Jorge." He backhanded him, sending Jorge sprawling into a low clump of cholla cactus.

The kid picked a fist-sized blade of cactus from his ear and gave up. "It was Chaco and Ricky Lamas. I don't think they knew I heard them." I'd met Chaco, but Ricky's name was familiar, too, one of those that Felicia's friend had given me that day at the mall.

"Oh, they knew, all right. What day did you hear this conversation?"

"I don't know. . . ." He searched around him for the answer in the sand. "Last weekend. Maybe Saturday."

Guillermo kicked at the sandy soil, then flung the bottle of tequila over the edge of the cliff. It broke like childhood dreams on the rocky terrain below. "Carlos was already dead by then. You helped them set me up."

He was already back in the car with the engine running by the time Jorge and I had picked and stumbled our way off the mountaintop.

The plaza wasn't as busy with pedestrians when we returned. Late diners still strolled and window-shopped, but the cinema crowd was gone. We let Jorge out a block away from his aunt's house.

"You set me up once, Brother, don't do it again," Guillermo warned. "If Chaco finds out about tonight, I'll know."

Jorge ducked his head and tucked his T-shirt back into his pants. "He won't know from me. Hey," he called back over his shoulder. "I really am sorry about Carlos."

Guillermo didn't even turn his head.

"We have to take the battle to them," he said when we were half-way home.

"To the Braceros?"

"Right to their front door."

Guillermo stayed the night and this time I could call it lovemaking. I left the electric fan on high but turned off the light. We rolled into each other's arms as if it were a dance we both knew by heart. Guillermo's wet tongue chilled me as he moved up from my ankle to my groin. I let it wash over me in sweet welcome waves.

"Are you ready for a trip?" he asked as we shared a beer afterward. "We leave in the morning."

CHAPTER TWENTY-FOUR

In the morning, Guillermo said he needed a couple of hours to get ready. While he was gone, I packed for survival, not knowing if I was going to be following him down an alley or across the desert. I loaded a backpack with water, beef jerky, and spare socks, but I left the gun at home. The switchblade I'd bought in Quartzite rested inside my right boot.

We headed south, back to Mexico. Creosote and mesquite blurred into a shoulder-high ribbon of dusty green, speckled by pockets of sandy washes and dry brown desert.

"You think this is going to fly in the face of that 'don't leave town' dictum of Detective Sabin's?"

"Yeah, I'm pretty sure of it."

We paid the attendant and left Guillermo's car in a parking lot on the Arizona side of the border, then crossed over on foot, showed our passports to a bored guard, and traveled south along the railroad tracks.

The beggar children ignored Guillermo after he gave them his spare change, but swarmed me like an incoming tide. I gave them half my beef jerky and all my one-dollar bills.

There are few grand buildings in the Mexican half of Nogales—only shanties, lean-tos, and cinder block–square houses, all encroaching with heavy breath on the cracked sidewalks and potholed streets that fronted them. I followed Guillermo down a narrow lane that dead-ended at a half-domed Quonset hut. A sad road that couldn't even find its own way out of town. Thin, stray dogs nosed at greasy papers that had swirled into heaps at the curb. We were turning to retrace our steps when a door in the Quonset hut opened.

"Can I help you with something?" said an elderly Caucasian priest, with white hair in a tonsure and soft tufts of equally white hair growing from his ears. The hem of his black robe was dusty and ripped.

"Hello, Father," Guillermo said. "I have a friend—a friend with no papers and no money—who needs to cross over. Can you tell me where he should go? Who he should see?" Our plan was to take the same coyote-led route across the desert that Raisa's clients had, to find out for ourselves if the Braceros were involved in stealing children. If we could prove that link, and then prove that Carlos had been trying to stop them, the police would have to listen.

The priest looked us over carefully but not critically, his blue eyes rheumy with age and perpetual dust.

"Let's go into the church."

I didn't see a church anywhere, but then noticed two crossed pieces of wood at shoulder height in front of the metal hut. I'd taken it for the anchor post of a Realtor's FOR SALE sign. Instead, it was a FOR SALVATION sign. We followed the priest inside.

The air was still and hot. A small gray bird battered at the upper reaches of the metal roof, looking for a way out.

"We started this church almost twenty years ago." He gestured to the rows of mismatched folding chairs. The altar was built on a raised platform made of plywood, and the priest's steps bowed the wood as he moved. It bounced when he stopped in the middle to kneel and cross himself. Guillermo did likewise. I'd been absent from any kind of belief in a benevolent deity for too long to move my arms and heart along with them.

"Our flock is not primarily made up of the residents of Nogales, although they have been very supportive. It's the temporary residents—those undocumented migrants on their way across the border, or those who are turned back into Mexico after the Migra pick them up in the desert."

"That's a pretty transient parish, Father," Guillermo said.

"We see some of them year after year. Yet another attempt to cross the border to a better life. And those are the lucky ones—the ones not killed by the sun or the heat or the wild things in the desert."

I had read enough newspaper stories about the deaths to know the old priest was right. Their bodies were found every year. Old men who couldn't take one more step and died less than halfway across the blazing desert. Women and children who died slowly and painfully in locked trucks, abandoned scant miles from the border.

"So you tell them not to go?" I asked.

"How can you tell someone, 'Don't try to better yourself? Don't try to feed your family?' I look for U.S. sponsors for them, or get them work permits when I can. With God's help, I'll minister to the rest and help them make a good life here."

"We need to take that road, Father."

"Oh, it's not 'a friend' anymore?"

Guillermo shook his head. "It never was."

"Don't do it, young man. If you can get papers, go across legally."

"We're trying to help the travelers, too, Father," I said.

He didn't ask for the rest of the story. "There is a man I've heard of. Not an honorable man, but the best of the lot that can get you across. They call him El Vez. You know . . . Elvis," he fingered his jawline, "because of the sideburns."

"Where can we find him?"

He named a bar on the west side of town. "He usually hangs around in front."

We thanked the priest and walked west. Although the street we were looking for had shops bursting with serapes and carved art-work and sidewalks full of tourists, there was no sign of El Vez.

"Border crossing's a nighttime business," Guillermo said. "We're probably too early for him." We found a shaded spot on a restaurant patio to wait for smuggler's time.

By nightfall, we were positioned across the street from the bar, in a shallow alcove that allowed us a good view of the street and the entrance. The sidewalk strollers were no longer the shorts-and-T-shirt-clad tourists looking to refill low-cost prescriptions; now it was a younger and more dangerous crowd. Bands of white men strut-ted down the street on their way to the sex clubs. Teenage Mexican boys offered smokes, pills, and powder in hushed voices laced with the promise of euphoria.

By nine o'clock, we still hadn't spotted El Vez. I watched an en-counter between a teenage girl and three young men on the side-walk in front of the bar. She held tight to her purse as their hands darted, as unwanted as disease, from her breasts to her ass. I moved to cross the street and stop them, but Guillermo grabbed my arm.

"*Cuidado.* If we're supposed to be border crossers, we can't be stopping every injustice in town."

"We can stop this one." I stepped off the curb when the boys pushed her against the wall, but stepped back when she moved sideways and they let her go.

When the boys moved away, I saw him. Starched white shirt with the collar raised in the back, and sleeves rolled up almost to his elbows. Dark slacks tight across his butt. Sideburns that wid-ened into fat legs when they reached his jaw. El Vez.

He leaned against the cinder-block wall with one leg cocked, as at-ease as if he were in his own living room. Two younger boys ran down the street to him, passing wadded bills into his hand in exchange for matchbook-sized paper parcels. It looked like human trafficking wasn't his only crime. He feigned a gut-punch to one of the boys who responded with a mock grunt.

"Do you recognize him?" I whispered. We had to make sure that it wasn't anyone Guillermo knew from his days with the Braceros. If Chaco found out we were here, we were dead.

"No. Let's go." Guillermo checked for any other Bracero lookouts and, seeing none, crossed the street. Guillermo mimicked the coyote's pose against the wall. "I've heard you help people cross."

El Vez gave us both close scrutiny, then bent close to a cupped hand to light a cigarette. "Who told you that?" The Bracero tattoo on the back of his hand confirmed that we were on the right track.

"The whores at Plaza San Carlos."

"This is for both of you?" His chin jerked toward me.

We didn't look like his typical clients. Too soft, too well fed, and I wasn't a Latina.

"She has her own reasons for wanting to cross," Guillermo said. "I have money for both of us."

That was enough for El Vez. "I can get you out tomorrow night. It'll cost you a thousand each."

"Five hundred, and it has to be tonight."

The coyote gave us another once-over. "Why tonight?"

"There's been trouble. We have to get out."

"Got your name on a watch list, huh? Then there's even more reason that your trip's going to cost a thousand. I won't be able to take you the easy way. And you'll be walking."

Guillermo grabbed the guy's neck, squeezing until his words sputtered to a stop. He forced a wad of bills into the man's hand. "Here's half. We leave now."

El Vez nodded.

If he felt that we were high-risk travelers, maybe he'd be taking us that same wilderness route that Raisa's clients had gone.

We followed him down the block and around the corner to a quiet side street where his van was parked. I stepped over a trickle of sewage at the curb and got into the back.

"You, too," El Vez said to Guillermo, gesturing to the rear of the van. Guillermo bent double and joined me. We braced ourselves with heels and hands when the van bucked to life.

There were no windows in back and my view out the front was limited, but it seemed that we were heading out of town to the west. Ten minutes later the road under us was downgraded to hard-packed earth, then to sand. We were climbing; the evening breeze coming in the driver's window was fresh.

El Vez had turned off the headlights once we reached the dirt portion of the road. We bumped slowly and blindly across the desert. It took almost two hours of crawling between the cactus and rocky outcroppings, trying to distinguish between shadow and stone, before he stopped the van. The silence was profound, broken only by the ticking of the engine as it cooled.

The van groaned a metal complaint when El Vez opened the door. Guillermo crawled over the front seat and exited the van on the driver's side. I followed him, carrying both of our backpacks. I put them on the ground and stretched my arms overhead.

There were no lights anywhere, just a brocade of shadows sewn by a full, bright moon.

"Where are we?"

"Pajarito Wilderness. The border's about a half mile straight ahead of you. There are camera towers there and there." He pointed to two spots on the horizon. "But they don't work for shit and they don't cover this area. Just keep walking straight ahead."

The Pajarito Wilderness was federal land on the U.S. side, and was one of the most inhospitable stretches of the Sonoran desert, reaching more than twenty-five miles along the border, with five-thousand-foot mountain peaks, wind-carved canyons, and no roads.

· "And what's on the other side?"

The Mexican grinned. "More Pajarito Wilderness. Hey, just kidding. My amigos will meet you on the other side. Just keep walking due north; they'll find you. But they aren't expecting a shipment until tomorrow night, so you may have to lay low for a day."

"How will we know them?"

"I'll tell them where you are and what you look like. Now, the other half of my money, señor."

Guillermo reached into his backpack and straightened up with a length of rope in his hand. "We'd like a little time before you contact your friends across the border," he said. The man fought against the ropes but was soon hog-tied in the cargo area of the van. Guillermo stuffed a rag in his mouth and knotted a second piece of cloth behind his head to hold it in place.

I knew that he was picturing his brother's bound body as he tightened the knots.

"If a delivery was scheduled for tomorrow then I'm sure that one of your Nogales buddies will come find you by then. We'll leave you some water," he said, "even though you're going to have to free yourself to drink it. But that's more than what you do for your travelers."

Guillermo shrugged into his backpack. "They don't use surveillance planes much at night, but we'd better get as far away from this van as we can, unless we want to get stopped by the Border Patrol before we even find the Braceros on the other side." ·

We moved north into the darkness. Within a few hundred meters, cactus and dirt gave way to limestone and shale. Soon, small oak trees joined the mesquite that dotted the land. We must have been at a four-thousand-foot elevation already, but the dark hills in front of us towered still higher.

We followed a narrow animal trail to the border where it met a barbed-wire fence with a six-foot section missing: a six-foot breach in the war between the "haves" and the "wanna haves." We crossed through. There was a hard-packed path paralleling the other side of the fence. It wasn't wide enough for a car, probably a horse trail for maintenance and security, but it was clear that no one had come this way recently or they would have replaced the missing wire. We followed the path along the fence and then north as it meandered between cactus and bushes, down dry wash ravines and up shallow canyons walls.

It took another half hour to get far enough from the border that we could feel easy about stopping. I spotted a rough shale overhang behind a small, bushy oak and hunkered down.

Digging some beef jerky and a bottle of water out of my pack, I offered them to Guillermo. "Why don't the Braceros post lookouts here?"

"The farther they can stay from the border itself, the less likely is they'll be caught."

"But what about the people they're moving across? They could get lost out here."

"They were already lost before they got here."

CHAPTER TWENTY-FIVE

I woke with a crick in my neck, wishing that I'd had the good sense to add a blanket or a sleeping bag to the supplies I'd packed. We headed north with the first morning light.

It hadn't rained for weeks and the ground was covered by tracks, both recent and old. The hoof marks of unshod horses, the spiky piglike marks of javelina, and a dozen different prints from sneakers, some of them brushed out by a torn mesquite branch that trailed behind the traveler, by the looks of it.

As the path detoured to the east, the land began to fold in on itself, straining toward the peaks in wave after wave of rock. Bear grass and hedgehog cactus gave way to madrone, mountain sage, and cottonwoods. I heard birds for the first time since leaving Nogales.

The canyon narrowed in front of us, split by a dry creek bed that might run only a couple of months of the year. Sheer, vertical walls of rock stepped on the toes of the dry wash, looking to claim more territory. The wind had carved the cliffs into ribboned undulations, as smooth and rounded as blown glass.

I used the creek bed as a path, slinking past the limestone walls and over gravel bars and stepping stones. It was the path of least resistance, and the way any other traveler would have come.

We stopped deep in the canyon, where three small pools of water were trapped in the shadow of the cliffs. Except for manmade Peña Blanca Lake five or six miles away, this was probably the only fresh water within a day's march. There were signs of previous passage through the slippery canyon, but none looked more recent than the pad prints of a large cat that were pressed into the damp earth. A mountain lion? It looked too big for a bobcat.

"Should we wait here for El Vez's northern counterparts?" I asked. We had to be at least four miles from the border. "What's this trip going to prove, anyway? That the Braceros are involved with moving illegals across the border? We already know that."

"I need to see who shows up. What their moves are. If Carlos wanted to put a stop to something, the proof will be here in the desert." Guillermo wiped his face with his shirttail.

We moved north through the canyon. Pajarito Peak and Manzanita Mountain were behind us now, but smaller hills and rolling grasslands filled the horizon. I swatted at a tenacious fly. What path would the Braceros expect the travelers to take? Would they cling to the mountainous terrain in order not to be spotted out in the open? Or would they trek across the more level ground at night to put as much space as possible between themselves and the border?

"What's that?" I said, peering west. It was hazy in the ground-level heat, but it looked like hundreds of white skulls, spaced perfectly equidistant from one another and aligned in a row across the horizon.

Guillermo started to run toward them. The ache and pull of the cut on my leg slowed me down, but I followed as quickly as I could.

The image cleared as we got closer. Not skulls, but white plastic one-gallon water jugs, all empty and all marked with a number in thick black ink.

"What the fuck?" Guillermo muttered.

We followed the line of jugs. Number 134. Number 165. Number 166. The last jug was marked 177. Beside it was a small wooden sign with a paper message tacked to the board. There were bits of paper from previous postings caught in the staples. I bent down to read it. "*Ni Uno Más*. Not One More. One hundred and seventy-seven people have died crossing the desert this year alone. Turn back! Do not become one hundred seventy-eight."

"Might have been better if they'd left the jugs full," I said.

"Might have been better if they'd put up the sign at the border fence—before the travelers got this far."

We continued north. Half a mile farther on, the foot-wide path had broadened to a dusty, four-wheel drive road, cleared but not leveled, with stony outcroppings that would cripple a car if it were moving with any speed. We had descended into a shallow ravine when I heard, softly, a woman's voice on the breeze.

"Amazing Grace, how sweet the sound."

Guillermo motioned me to slow, and we crept up the other side of the wash until just our heads were above the edge. Less than a hundred yards away, a man and a woman were unloading boxes from the bed of an old blue pickup truck. Off to the side, several others squatted in the shade of a thick creosote bush.

The singer was a young woman, with straight blond hair down to the hem of her walking shorts.

The man unloading the truck was equally blond, although his hair only reached his shoulders. He added a wooden case to the cardboard box and six plastic water jugs in the center of the clearing.

"Illegals?" I whispered.

"Maybe the ones sitting down. I don't know about the others. Maybe birders or just some kids camping."

We rose slowly and approached the group with our arms held out to our sides. "*Buenos días*," Guillermo called. The seated figures rose like a flock of doves and began to scatter. "No *se preocupe*! We're travelers, too." They held still as we came near.

"We heard you singing," I said in greeting.

The young woman smiled and pushed her hair back off her forehead. "I pretend that it makes it cooler out here."

"That would be a good trick. My name's Jessie."

"Eldon Dallas," the young man said, offering his hand. "This is my wife, Polly."

"And your friends?" Guillermo asked, nodding at the Mexican family that stood ten feet away. The wife's eyes were wide with fright, the two little girls' with fatigue.

The white couple glanced at each other before replying. "Our church is part of a group called Save A Life," the man said. "We're not doing anything illegal here. Just making sure that people don't die in the desert for no reason."

Guillermo looked at the bundles and boxes they'd unloaded from the truck. "You give them supplies?"

"We leave water, clean socks, bandages—some nonperishable food," Polly said. "We're not helping them cross. Just helping them stay alive."

"Are you going to give these people a ride?" I asked. The supplies would have helped them, but a forty-mile ride to civilization would have helped even more.

Eldon shook his head. "It's illegal to transport anyone we find. Or to help them cross."

"But you're here right now, and these two little girls are tired." The girls peered up at me as if they knew I was talking about them.

"You don't understand," Dallas said. "We're supposed to tell the Border Patrol when we find someone. We could go to jail just for stopping to help these people."

"Have you heard any stories out here about kidnapping? About coyotes taking the children of illegals as payment for crossing?" Guillermo asked.

"There was a woman last month," Polly said. "Her son had been taken from her."

"Do you know who's doing it?"

"Does it matter?" Polly said. "There's always some animal ready to prey on a weaker animal."

"We've got a lot more drops to make before nightfall," Dallas said quietly.

Guillermo had moved off for a private conversation with the family that hovered at the edge of our debate. He turned back to us. "We'll walk north with the Delgados for a while."

We gave the little girls our PowerBars and the parents our remaining beef jerky. Guillermo and the father hoisted two water jugs and the family's bed sheet–wrapped belongings. The mother and I lifted the little girls to our hips as the blue pickup drove away.

"*Como te llamas?*" I asked the little three-year-old clinging to me.

"Magdalena."

"*Me llamo* Jessie." Satisfied with the ride and my response, she poked me in the cheek then tucked her head under my chin.

We moved north across the desert. It was forty more miles to Tucson, with only desert, shadeless sun, coyotes, and Border Patrol agents in between.

A mile farther on, we stopped so that Mrs. Delgado could re-wrap the rags around her thin sandals. At first I'd thought it was to smudge out her footprints, but soon realized that it was protection, however minimal, from the thorns, sharp rocks, and volcanic heat of the trek.

They were headed to southern California, the man said, to work in the strawberry fields in the central valley. It would have been shorter to cross farther west of Nogales, but that would have taken them through Altar Valley and that route was even more dangerous.

"They call it Cocaine Alley," he said.

And OTM Alley: Other Than Mexican. The valley was a primary

route for drug smugglers coming across the border from a dozen different nations.

"You'd be safer traveling at night," Guillermo said. "Maybe it wouldn't be so hard on the children."

"We have many miles to go. We have to sleep a little and walk a lot."

I saw a scorpion tail of dust off to the right, a single dark vehicle, moving fast.

"Border Patrol?" I asked Guillermo.

"I can't tell yet." He put down the water jugs, the bundled bed sheet, and his backpack, and turned to face the oncoming truck. I set down my load and bent to get the knife from my boot.

"Ricky Lamas," he said, when the truck slid to a stop in front of us and three young Latinos got out. "Just the man I wanted to see."

Carlos's supposed friend. The guy who, with Chaco, may have lured us to the place where we'd found Carlos's dead body.

"Hey, *jefe*. What are you doing out here? I never thought of the Ochoas as wetbacks." Lamas strutted toward us, his pointy-toed cowboy boots kicking up dust with every step.

"We're just taking a little stroll with our friends here."

"Let us help you. We'll give these folks a lift. Help them get on their way." The other two Braceros circled around behind us.

"No thanks. It's a nice day for a walk." Guillermo held his knife behind his leg and turned to keep the biggest of the thugs in view.

"At least the little ones," Lamas said. "They'd probably like a ride." He made a swipe at Magdalena's arm. She let out a screech and pulled back to her mother's side.

"Drive away now, Ricky. Write this one off as too much trouble and go get somebody else."

Lamas continued to circle him.

The mustachioed Bracero tackled the Mexican father, sending

them both sprawling to the dirt. Mr. Delgado had no weapons but his hands and he used them, gouging and flailing.

Lamas and his partner went for Guillermo. The big one pinned Guillermo's arms behind him, and Lamas concentrated his fists on Guillermo's face and stomach. I gripped the knife and slashed once across Lamas's bicep to get his attention.

"Over here," I whispered, the death wish clear in my voice.

"You want some of this, *chiquita*?" He didn't seem weakened by the gash in his arm. Unbuckling his belt, he drew it from its loops, held the tongue in his hand, and circled the buckle end overhead. "I can teach you a few things."

The belt struck like a snake and the buckle connected with my cheekbone. It hurt like a son of a bitch and I blinked away tears. I shuffled to the left, looking to draw Lamas away from the mother and little girls who were frozen in place beside me.

He swung again, and this time I ducked under his arm and swiped the blade across his stomach. He jumped back to assess the damage and I turned to check on Guillermo. He must have done something to the big guy's eyes; the Bracero was rolling on the ground with his hands over his face. Guillermo yanked the pistol from the man's waistband and turned to Lamas, spinning him around and shoving the gun between his lips.

"Tell the others to give it up."

Ricky Lamas wasn't brave with a gun barrel in his mouth. "*Bastante*," he said around the hot metal. The Bracero fighting with Mr. Delgado took three steps back and held his hands up. The big guy was still curled in a ball and didn't have to stop anything.

"What do you do with the kids?"

"I was just joking," Lamas tried.

Guillermo shoved the barrel back in his mouth, the trigger guard up against his lips. "I wasn't."

Lamas put his hands up and Guillermo withdrew the gun.

"Okay, Okay. It's something that Chaco's got going with some big shots in Tucson. I don't know what they do with them."

"What big shots? Darren Markson? Paul Willard?"

"I don't know. I swear."

"What did Carlos have to do with it?"

"He wanted to stop it."

"And that's why he was killed?" That was venom, not curiosity, in the question.

Lamas shook his head. "Not just that. He took one of the kids. A girl."

CHAPTER TWENTY-SIX

We put the Delgados' belongings in the Braceros' truck and used the bed sheet they'd been wrapped in to hog-tie the three thugs. Guillermo propped the Braceros up in the shade of a big creosote bush, and taped a cowboy hat he'd found in the truck onto the head of the guy in the most westerly position.

"I'm sure someone will find you by tomorrow."

"You're going to pay for this, *cabrón*," Lamas warned.

"I know."

The Delgado family insisted upon leaving the water with them, too.

The keys were still in the ignition. The family piled into the bed of the Braceros' black truck and Guillermo and I took the cab.

"Are you sure you don't want the girls up front here?" I asked. The mother smiled shyly and waved away my offer. She pulled a heavy tarp over their heads so passing patrol cars couldn't see them easily.

"What should we do with them?" I asked Guillermo when we reached the highway.

"Make sure they're safe tonight. After that . . ." He shrugged and turned south toward Nogales and his parked Camaro. Guillermo planned to stay with the Delgados and I would drive his car back to Tucson. Now that we were back in an area with a strong wireless signal, I retrieved my cell phone from the backpack and turned it on. Six messages.

"They could stay with me at Bonita's house until they're ready to move on," I said, waiting for the first message to play. I'd have to tell Deke about the Braceros trying to take the Delgados' little girl. It may tie in with the killings and with that child's seat in Carlos's car. But I wasn't going to call him until the Delgados were well away and couldn't be threatened with deportation.

Guillermo stayed quiet while I listened to the recordings. Four were from Raisa, each asking me to contact her. Another was from Detective Treadwell that was more formal in speech pattern than I'd ever heard him before. He wanted me to call, too.

The sixth message was from Raisa again. I listened to it twice and then held the phone to Guillermo's ear. "Jessie? Where are you? Call me immediately." There was a pause before she continued. "Detective Sabin got the search warrant amended to include Bonita's car. They say they found a map. A map where you marked the crime scene. That was enough to get them a subpoena for a DNA sample."

There was another pause in the message.

"Jessie, they're talking about an arrest warrant."

"Looks like we'll be taking our new friends to my house instead," Guillermo said.

We got the Delgado family settled in at Guillermo's apartment. It was the first time I'd been there and the permanency of the place surprised me. There were shelves of hardbound books in hand-crafted wooden cases, framed posters on the walls, and a set of plates and glasses for eight in the cupboard.

"How long have you lived here?"

"A year or so." He saw me eyeing the matched set of silverware. Not expensive stuff, but modern and sleek. "I brought most of the stuff up from Nogales. I was . . . with somebody down there."

"She didn't want it?"

He started a sentence but didn't get more than "she" out when he changed his mind.

"No."

We made chorizo and scrambled eggs for the exhausted travelers. Little Magdalena helped me spoon sliced peaches into bowls for dessert. After dinner, while the family bathed and Guillermo cleaned up the kitchen, I made a run to Target. Lightweight cotton pants for Mrs. Delgado and the girls, canvas sneakers for all four, plus long-sleeved shirts and hats to protect them from the sun. I added two sturdy backpacks to replace the wrapped bed sheets, and a professional-looking first-aid kit.

The girls were already asleep when I got back. Guillermo and Mr. Delgado were making plans.

"I can take them over to the central valley," I offered.

"Not smart. The police are probably already looking for you."

He was right. We agreed that he would give the Delgado family a lift in the morning. The parents yawned and joined their daughters in the second bedroom's double bed.

Guillermo and I headed out for the last errand of the day: getting rid of the Braceros' truck.

"Where shall we leave it?" I asked.

"How about South Fourth? If we leave the keys in it, it should be gone in no time."

I agreed and followed his car. We took side streets and I obeyed the speed limit. This was not a night to give a policeman a reason to ask for my ID. I parked the truck on a quiet block, wiped the areas I had touched, and returned to his car.

"It should be gone within the hour."

Traffic was light on the way back to his house. We made as little noise as possible coming in, but Mr. Delgado still stuck his head out of the bedroom door to make sure everything was okay.

"Can I spend the night, too?" I asked. "I don't think my place would be a good idea right now."

Guillermo took my hand and led me into the bedroom. The sheets were cool and smelled like him. I rolled against his back and draped an arm across his chest.

"I have friends in Phoenix, so I'm going to start there with the Delgados," he said, changing the subject. "But if I take them all the way to California's central valley, I won't be home until late."

"Carlos took one of the children," I said to his back. "We've got to find out what happened to her." My heart broke thinking about her terror.

"We'll find out. Carlos would have made sure she was safe."

Unless the Braceros got to him first, I thought.

Guillermo and the Delgado family were gone by sunrise. I waited until eight o'clock to call Raisa on her cell phone. She'd either be on her way in to work, or already there and desperate for a cigarette on the sidewalk.

"Where are you?" she said. "No, wait, don't tell me. If I don't know, I can't tell the police."

"I got your messages. What did Detective Sabin say?"

"He's got you in his sights. You were with Carlos's girlfriend when she got blown up. Your fingerprints were found on the post next to his dead body. You had the place marked on a map."

"I didn't kill him, Raisa."

"I don't care," she exhaled deeply. I was right about the smoke break. "Just tell me, is the DNA test something I have to worry about?"

"Maybe." I paced from the front door to the kitchen.

"Good Kind Christ, Jessie. We can explain away the map. They don't know who made that marking, it was found in your sister's car, yada yada. But the fingerprints? And DNA? You're in deep shit this time."

"Hypothetically, if my DNA matches something in the garage—like the blood on the floor, for example—can't they tell how long it had been there? We can prove that Carlos was dead days before that blood got there." I retraced my steps to the living room, and grabbed a loose cushion from the couch.

"Maybe. But all that's for after they test the DNA and match it. You're going to have to give them a sample."

I wadded up the pillow and threw it back on the couch. "I will." Just not quite yet. I needed time to show the cops that there was another way of looking at this.

"Is there a warrant out for my arrest?"

"Not yet. But as your attorney, I'm telling you to turn yourself in for this test."

"And as my friend?"

She paused. "I'll buy you as much time as I can."

I needed a car that wasn't associated with me, so I called my brother at the fire station. "Can I use your car while you're on duty today? Mine's in the shop."

"Why don't you use Bonita's?"

"Battery's dead."

"Do you want a jump?"

Martin wasn't making this easy. "No, it won't hold a charge. I'll stop and pick up a new battery while I'm out."

He agreed.

I smoothed out the pillow I'd crushed during my conversation with Raisa and locked the front door behind me, then hoofed it a half mile to the nearest bus stop. When I arrived at the fire station, Martin was just sitting down to breakfast.

"Don't get up! I've got some errands to run. I'll get the car back as soon as I can."

"I don't get off till tomorrow night. Do you need it that long?"

"I don't think so, but thanks for the offer."

I turned the key and the old Subaru bucked and shimmied to life. It was nice to know it was available for the next two days. I might need it. I headed to Guillermo's cousin's house.

The university neighborhood was coming alive with both pedestrian and car traffic. Miguel's tiny stucco house didn't have a driveway or a carport and I had to drive around the block twice before I found a place to park.

There were two steps up from the sidewalk and then another two to the front porch. I knocked on the screen door and it rattled in response. Miguel opened the wooden door behind it a crack, letting just one eye check out his visitor. His shoulder and chest were bare. Without a word, he opened the door and allowed me in.

"I've come to trade," I said, offering him the knife I'd bought in Quartzite.

"That thing's a piece of shit." He reached for a wrinkled blue T-shirt on the floor and pulled it over his head.

"Yeah, but it can't be traced." And as far as I knew, the only blood it had on it was from my fight with Ricky Lamas in the desert.

"I can take care of myself." He fingered the handle of the blade in the hard leather pouch on his belt.

"I need your knife."

"What for?"

"I can't tell you."

"Then I can't give it to you." He turned away. I noticed a stack of thick textbooks on the linoleum table. Locke. Bacon. Descartes.

"You're studying philosophy?" It was the last thing I would have expected from a man who had so implacably slit the throat of another. But then again, it was pretty unlikely training for the killer I'd become, too.

He managed to blush through brown skin. "Yeah."

"You want to be a teacher someday? A professor at some fancy college? That's not going to happen if you get picked up with that knife."

"It's over, Jessie. They killed one of ours. We killed one of theirs. We're even now."

"You think Chaco's going to take it that way? You think Guillermo's satisfied now?"

He turned, picked up the book on Francis Bacon, and thumbed it open. "'A man that studies revenge keeps his own wounds green.'" He still had a taste of the barrio in his accent.

"'Revenge is sweet and not fattening.' Alfred Hitchcock," I countered.

He smiled but didn't move to hand over the knife.

I reached for his arm and he stiffened. "Miguel, it's for Carlos. You've got to trust me. It won't come back to you."

He finally gave in. "All right. Take it. But I'm not taking that butter knife of yours. I'll get another one." He drew the knife from its sheath and handed it to me.

I tucked it into a pocket in my purse.

Back in the car, I took Miguel's knife and depressed the lever near my thumb. A black blade shot out of the front, razor sharp on both sides, with a wavy line of serrations on one edge. It was shorter than the knife I'd tried to give him but looked twice as deadly. He'd made a good attempt at cleaning it, but there—under the cross guard and inside that hidden channel—was what looked like a spot of dried blood. It would have been enough to hang him. I hoped it was enough to hang somebody else.

I wiped any prints off both the blade and the handle, then used a Kleenex over my thumb to depress the lever one more time and retract the blade.

There were a couple of ways I could plant this knife on the Braceros. Maybe I could get it inside the black truck we'd stolen yesterday, and then get the cops to tow the truck in for some violation. If the truck was still there, of course. I wished that I'd come up with this idea before we'd abandoned the damn thing on South Fourth.

I circled the block four times, hoping that I'd misremembered a landmark or a cross street. The truck was gone. Damn, our open-door policy had worked too well.

There was another, more difficult option, and for that I needed Guillermo. He wouldn't be back for hours, but there was something else I could do in the meantime.

Felicia's notebook had listed the details for six day-care centers funded by Darren Markson in Tucson and Nogales. I no longer believed that Markson was a saint who was paying for the day-care centers out of the goodness of his heart. And if the Braceros were tied in with him in stealing or selling children, I'd bet those facilities were somehow involved.

The oldest of the facilities was out by the airport. I parked the Subaru next to a blue Taurus in the lot. The day-care center looked like an elementary school that was short on classrooms and long on recess. Sandboxes, swings, and slides dotted one corner of the dusty yard like Christmas gifts in the Sahara. There was a blacktop basketball court and a soccer field with chalked sidelines drawn into the dirt. Two picnic tables with umbrellas were the only places to rest rather than run.

All the kids in the yard looked like Latinos, but the massive woman watching them was black.

"I'm interested in enrolling my little one," I called to her. "Is there someone here I could talk to?"

She fanned herself with a *People* magazine. "I don't know if we have any more space, but Mrs. Pogue is inside. You can ask her."

I followed the sidewalk to a metal door in the dun-colored building. There were bathrooms marked BOYS and GIRLS on the right, and two window-walled offices on the left, then the hallway opened into a big gathering room/play area. The first of the offices was dark, with the blinds pulled down, but light and voices came from the second.

"You're going to have to keep them a little longer," a woman said.

"That's not possible. The children—" Another woman's voice sputtered to a stop when she turned in my direction. "May I help you?"

"What are you doing here?" Emily Markson said.

Emily occupied one of the two guest chairs in the office. I couldn't see past her to see the other person.

"You know her?" the older woman on the other side of the desk asked. She was middle-aged, with thin lips, gray-rooted blond hair, and the posture of a dictator. She tapped her forefinger on the desk with impatience. The nutritionist I'd worked out with at a gym in Phoenix would have diagnosed those white lines across her nails as a liver problem. My mother would have said that each white line indicated a lie.

"She works for that car navigation company—HandsFree or something," Markson said. She didn't seem particularly unhappy to see me, just surprised.

"No she doesn't," the third woman said. "She's the journalist who came to interview me. Remember, Em? I told you all about it."

Damn. What was Aloma Willard doing here, too? And how could I be both a journalist from Tucson and a HandsOn operator from Phoenix?

"Hi, Mrs. Markson. Mrs. Willard. What a coincidence. I was just following up on your husbands' charitable work building these day-care centers—for a magazine article."

"You're a journalist? But I thought—" Mrs. Markson started.

"I left HandsOn. This is a new job. Sorry to interrupt you. I'll come back when it's more convenient." I backed out faster than I'd come in.

"Make an appointment next time," the woman I assumed was Mrs. Pogue called after me.

I raced back outside and ducked around the corner of the building, still keeping an eye on the Taurus in the lot. They didn't know my brother's car; hopefully they would assume I'd gone.

Emily Markson and Aloma Willard came out ten minutes later, their voices low but urgent. Markson shrugged off Willard's grip on her elbow, spinning her away. The fight continued after they got in the car, first with pointed fingers and steely glances, then finally reconciliation of a kind I hadn't expected. Aloma Willard reached across the front seat and took Markson's face in her hands. She spoke directly and softly to her, brushing Markson's cheekbones and eyebrows with a gentle finger. Then she leaned forward and kissed her slowly on the lips.

Guillermo had a bench and a full set of weights under the ramada at the back of his house and I made good use of them, although I still couldn't do anything like a squat with the tear across my calf.

Had I totally misread the adultery I'd imagined when I saw Paul

Willard leave the Marksons' house at dawn? Who was Emily Mark-son having an affair with? The husband? The wife? Both?

I was still feeling the burn in my biceps when Guillermo pulled into the driveway.

"Where did you leave the Delgados?"

"There's a church in Phoenix associated with the same group Eldon and Polly Dallas belong to. As long as the church members can say they didn't help anyone get across the border, and they don't know for sure that they're here illegally, they can help them."

"Are the Delgados still going to try for the San Fernando Val-ley?"

He shrugged. "Maybe. They'll stay in Phoenix a few days, then make a decision." I hoped they'd find someplace safe. The life of an undocumented worker wasn't easy, whether it was in the fields or in the back room of a restaurant.

"Do you know where Chaco lives?" I asked, changing the sub-ject. I knew where the Bracero leader's uncle's house was, and where he drank, but not where he slept.

"I think Esteban does. Chaco moved up here to Tucson about six months ago, but still hangs out in Nogales most of the time. Why?"

"I need to get into his house."

"Are you nuts? We killed one of his men, Jessie." He opened the refrigerator then shut the door, not finding what he wanted. I handed him my half-full bottle of cold water and he drained it in one gulp.

"I've got a way to put Chaco right in the cops' crosshairs, but I'll need that address."

He shook his head. "Too dangerous."

"Not if he's not there."

"Then I'll go."

"Look, the cops are already after me. There's nothing I can do

224 | Louise Ure

about that except turn their attention to someone else. I don't want that someone to be you, to have them thinking you had something to do with Carlos's death. Go see your mother. She needs you right now. I'll be fine."

He sighed. "Let me make a call."

A few muttered moments later he had the answer. "He's got a place in the Tucson Mountains."

"But he's probably down in Nogales right now, right?"

"Friday afternoon? I guarantee it. He's drinking and getting ready for Friday-night business."

I hoped he was right.

CHAPTER TWENTY-SEVEN

If I had a lot of money and lived in Tucson, the Tucson Mountains west of the city is where I'd live. Just as tony as the residential areas in the Catalinas, but far more private, with houses a half mile apart and backing up to the protected Saguaro National Park lands. Dark volcanic rock ripped through the dirt into saw-toothed ridges. It was a world of brown and gray and merciless sun.

Chaco's house was a good indication of his arrogance. Single story, mortar-washed burnt adobe, with no perimeter fence, no cameras, and no guard dogs that I could see. It sat alone on the far side of a dry gully that looked as if it had last seen water during the Middle Ages. The house bespoke a man with nothing to hide and that was probably true on this side of the border. I didn't think Chaco would keep anything here that would incriminate him in a U.S. courtroom, and I wasn't going to change that. I wasn't here to leave something; I was here to take it.

I pulled into the U-shaped driveway, parked by the front door, and rang the bell. A hollow echo from inside was the only response.

There was no other house within sight, but just in case somebody with binoculars could see me, I pretended to check the time on my watch and tap my foot impatiently for a moment, before "remembering" that I was supposed to go around back. I scuffed my way around the side of the house, obscuring my footprints as much as I could. A scorpion, looking like a tiny lobster with a cramp in his tail, scuttled sideways out of my path. I let out a breath I hadn't known I was holding.

There was no easy entrance on the north side, nor the back of the house, although the sliding glass door back there was tempting. Too obvious. I'd have to leave broken glass everywhere.

I was in luck on the south side of the building. Someone had left a bathroom window cracked open two inches with only a screwed-on screen for protection. A little jimmying with my Swiss Army knife and a slit along the edge of the screen was enough to get my hand in and on the window crank.

Once it was open, I hauled myself up and in. The house was so quiet you could hear the refrigerator hum. I tiptoed down a dark hallway and into the living room. Chaco had a taste for modern furnishings, all black leather and sharp angles against a concrete floor dyed bloodred. Bright woven throw rugs were the only nod to his Mexican ancestry.

I tried the kitchen first, using sleeve-covered fingers to open cupboards and drawers. Everybody has a spare set of car keys. Where would Chaco keep his? The kitchen drawer that I would have used as a catchall held only coins—both American and Mexican—and menus from take-out restaurants downtown. The cupboards had four of everything—mugs, glasses, plates—but there were no fancy pots and pans or exotic appliances. It looked like he did most of his dining as take-out. There were no drawers in the sleek modern tables in the living room.

The bedroom was more reflective of the gangbanger I'd met in that Nogales bar: a furry tiger-stripe bedspread on an unmade bed, a set of weights including an Olympic barbell with a hundred pounds of plates fastened on it, and a velvet painting of an Aztec warrior with his shield and arm raised in a victory cry. I skirted a metal footlocker at the end of the bed and headed to the small table on the far side of the room.

I'd found Chaco's catchall drawer. I pulled my shirtsleeve down over my hand again and opened the drawer. A fifty pack of banana-flavored Durex condoms. The receipt for a car stereo with a ten-inch subwoofer. Two comic books about Araña Verde—the Green Spider. And there, tucked under the paper and magazines, two sets of keys.

One set were house keys, maybe to his uncle's place or a storage unit, but the other was what I was looking for: the spare keys to his Cadillac.

I shoved the keys into my pocket and backtracked through the hallway and out the bathroom window, winding it almost shut just like I'd found it.

I stopped for a cold drink at a convenience store on Stone, making sure that my brother's car was outside the range of the store's camera, but that I was caught on their video, to give myself time-stamped proof of being in Tucson. Then I headed south.

As much as I wanted the car near me for a quick getaway, I couldn't afford to have any record of the trip to Nogales this afternoon. I parked in the same lot where we'd left Guillermo's car before.

I'd been concerned about an ID check at the border. Our last visit to Nogales would have been shown as an entry, but no return to the U.S. since we'd walked through the desert to get north. When a scan of my passport on the U.S. side didn't result in any alarms going off, I breathed a sigh of relief and hurried through the Mexican security area.

I stuck to the side streets to get to the Braceros' hangout. A block away, I hunkered down in an alley with a narrow view of the bar's parking lot and front door. The smell of rotting tomatoes and moldy beans rose from the dumpster at my side and I sweated in the still air, almost screaming when a fat brown rat crawled over my shoe. Nobody went in or out of the bar, but there, in the second row of parked cars, sat a midnight blue Cadillac like the one I was looking for.

With no traffic from either direction, I ran across the street, then hugged the buildings to stay out of sight of the bar. Getting down in a duck-walk made my calf scream, but it was the only way to reach the Cadillac unseen. I inched my way down the row. Yep, the same key scratch ran down the side of the car.

I pushed the unlock button on the Cadillac key and the lock released. Opening the passenger-side door just wide enough to get my shoulders through, I made a small slit in the carpeting on the floor and tucked Miguel's knife up tight against the car's frame. Then I closed the door as quietly as I could and clicked the lock shut again.

Mad Cow, my buddy at HandsOn up in Phoenix, would never have believed my story if I had called and asked her to do a remote unlock on a car I didn't have the title to. And even if I could have convinced her, there would have been a record of it. This was better all the way around.

I'd thought about leaving the knife in Chaco's Tucson house, but that would have made the cops' job more difficult. Chaco would have gone to great pains not to keep anything there that could be associated with his Bracero life. And it probably would have been tough for the cops to get a search warrant for the house, based solely on the anonymous tip I planned to phone in.

But I could make it easier for them. I picked up a fist-sized rock and tapped gently on the Cadillac's right taillight until the bottom of the red plastic covering shattered and the bulb inside was visible. Now they had a reason to stop him, and once they ran his name and license information, Chaco's Bracero affiliation would be enough to make them look a little more closely at his car. I crabbed back to the safety of the wall, then joined a group of tourists whose arms were loaded with the baskets, glassware, and serapes they'd bought as souvenirs.

At the border, we passed single-file through the U.S. Customs and Immigration area. The tiny, gray-haired woman in front of me groaned when the line slowed to inspect a package.

"Damn tourists."

"You're not just visiting Nogales?" I asked.

"I'm not that kind of tourist. I come down once a month to get my prescriptions filled," she said, holding up a paper bag that rattled with a half dozen plastic bottles. "I call it Arizona Medicare."

Neither of us got much scrutiny when it was our turn. As day visitors walking across, we didn't need visas and didn't have to go through the more rigorous screening given those folks who were traveling from farther south in Mexico, beyond the border tourist zone.

I headed back to the parking lot where I'd left the car.

It was after four o'clock when I got back to Tucson. I crawled through the window at Chaco's house one more time and put the keys back in the bedside drawer where I'd found them, then dropped Martin's car off with him at the firehouse. From there, I took the bus back to Guillermo's place, stopping to get cash at a Wells Fargo ATM so that I'd have another time stamp to offer the cops if they got curious.

Good thing, too, because Detective Sabin was waiting for me at the curb.

"I still don't understand why I had to come downtown for this," I said once the forensic technician had taken a mouth swab to test my DNA. "Couldn't you have done it right there?"

"Why should I inconvenience our forensic team on a Friday afternoon when I can inconvenience you?" Sabin replied. "And this way we get a chance to talk."

"I'd like to call my lawyer now."

"Raisa Fortas? She's up at a legal seminar in Phoenix for the weekend. What a shame."

"You asshole. You did this on purpose."

He ignored my characterization of him. "Did what? Pick up a murder suspect?"

"We're ready for her," a female officer said, sticking her head through the door.

Sabin took my elbow and escorted me into another room down the hall. Four other women about my age were already there, lined up against the height chart on the back wall. I glanced down the row. We all came in just under the five-foot eight marker, except the woman in the first position who looked to be more like five-six. All blondes, too, although only one had the spikes I did. Sabin handed me a long-sleeved white shirt and gestured for me to roll the sleeves down so my tattoos didn't show.

A few moments later a disembodied voice came from the mirror in front of me. "Turn to your right. Now face forward."

I stared straight ahead, holding my breath, willing the eyewitness behind the glass to develop myopia on the spot. A long two minutes later we were let out of the lineup area and Sabin took me back to the first interview room.

"Where's Deke?"

He ignored my question and flipped through his notes. "We've got a witness who saw your sister's car in front of the house where Carlos Ochoa and Reuben Sanchez were killed."

I folded my arms again, tighter this time. Holy shit. Had the witness identified me? And had he seen Guillermo, too? Reuben Sanchez must be the Bracero whose throat Miguel had cut as we left.

"What's in it for you, Jessie?" Sabin cocked his head like a curious predatory bird. "You moving drugs for the Braceros? Maybe using the HandsOn network to pass on messages and drops?"

Let him talk. I turned sideways and gave him my profile.

"We know you didn't kill Markson, but you could have been involved with him. We've got that call from you to his cell phone that night."

"That was after he was attacked, you idiot! I was trying to find out if he was okay!"

"Maybe." He didn't look convinced. "Or maybe you already knew what was going on. You sure hooked up with Felicia Villalobos quick, and look what happened to her. Did she tell you about a deal between Markson and the Braceros? Did your Bracero friends think she was going to rat them out? And then you're spotted where her boyfriend gets killed, and you'd marked that house on your map."

He leaned back in the chair and hooked his hands behind his head. The picture of comfort and ease. "That DNA sample comes back as a match? I've got you, girl."

"That's it!" I slammed my hands on the desk. "No more questions without my lawyer. You either arrest me or I'm walking out."

"If that's the way you want it." He reached to the back of his waistband where his handcuffs rested. "Jessica Dancing Gammage, you're under arrest for the murder of Carlos Ochoa and Reuben Sanchez." He wasn't even waiting for DNA results.

Sabin called a female officer in to take me to booking. I already knew the way. It hadn't changed much in three years.

CHAPTER TWENTY-EIGHT

I made my one phone call.

"Mom, can I talk to Dad, please?"

"I don't think that's a good idea, Jessica."

I recoiled with the thought of being locked up—for the weekend, at least—without anyone knowing where I was. My vision swam and dark circles narrowed my line of sight. I put my head down to keep from passing out.

"Please, please. It's the last time—Mom, I'm calling from jail."

"My God, what have you done?" At last, confirmation that her worst fears were real. There was a heavy clunk and I thought she'd hung up.

I breathed into the silence. Then, "Jessie, is that you?" My father's voice, gentle, with an undertone of panic. "Your mother says you're calling from jail."

"Detective Sabin just arrested me for murder. I think Raisa might be gone for the weekend. I need . . ." I couldn't bring myself to say help. Save me. Make everything okay again.

"Hush, hush. It's okay." I could almost feel him rocking me. "I'll try Raisa and if I can't get her I'll find someone else."

"I don't think Deke knows about this, Daddy. Maybe he can help."

"Time's up," the female cop said behind me. I raised one hand for a moment's patience.

". . . nothing till Monday," my father said. "But I'll see what we can do about bail." My heart broke, remembering what the last murder trial had cost him.

"I didn't do it."

"I know, I know." I heard the change in his voice: steel where only soft silk had been. He'd convinced himself once before that I hadn't killed anyone. He could do it again.

"Don't worry, honey, I'll take care of—" he started to say.

The female officer reached past me and depressed the button on the phone, severing the connection in mid-sentence.

Two hours later, I was the newest resident of the Pima County Female Detention Center. The booking photos were still unflattering, the jumpsuits were still orange, and the strip search was still an act of purposeful degradation.

But there had been a few positive changes since my last visit. The big general population ward that had held over a hundred detainees was now broken up into eight-woman dormitory cells with bunk beds and TVs. And based on the *What Not to Wear* program that my roommates were watching, it looked like there were more channels now.

No way I'd be arraigned before Monday. Sabin had made sure of that, the asshole. And then what? Did they even offer bail for multiple murder? This might be the beginning of another yearlong wait for a trial. And then? And then? My vision dimmed again.

A bell rang and a voice called "Lights out!" Like a city in a brownout, the shadows raced grid by grid toward our dorm. When the TV went off and the only light left was on the other side of the bars, I kicked off the plastic jailhouse sandals and stretched out on the thin mattress. One woman near the door was praying in Spanish and another in the bunk just opposite me cried in gulping sobs.

Unlike my neighbor, I cried silently.

Welcome home, Jessie.

"You have a visitor," the guard said. I had taken advantage of the less-than-ninety-degree October temperatures to do sit-ups and push-ups out in the quad. Many of the women had family show up for Saturday visiting hours; I didn't want to be reminded that I would probably have none.

"Who is it?"

The woman shrugged, her badge and pinned-on nametag ("Delta Bragg") rising with the gesture. I followed her inside. She gave me a cursory pat-down then unlocked the metal door that led to the visiting room. My father was seated on a plastic chair on the other side of the glass in the second booth from the end.

"I got in touch with the public defender's office," he said when I sat down in the facing chair, his palm pressed flat against the Plexiglas. "They said there's nothing they can do before Monday when you're arraigned, and Raisa Fortas will be back by then."

I'd thought as much. "That's okay, Dad. Thanks."

"We can get a real lawyer if you want."

I knew he couldn't afford that.

"Raisa's good. She'll be fine."

He hesitated, fingering the scratched initials in the laminated desk in front of him. *P.K.*, it said in sawtooth letters. "Can I bring you anything?"

I shook my head, then reconsidered. "Maybe some pin money."

Any money you had on you got credited to your account when you were booked, and you could use it for things like snacks, socks, and underwear. Visitors could add to it. I didn't know how long I'd be in here, but the twenty-seven dollars I'd had on me wouldn't go far.

"Your mother," he started. "She's pretty shaken up by this."

I nodded. If there had ever been any hope of reconciliation, it was gone now.

I needed to get a message out to Guillermo. Or even better, to someone who had no ties to me. Tell somebody to place an anonymous call to the Tucson PD, and get them to search Chaco's car. But I couldn't involve my father in that. I'd have to find another way.

"I'll put some money in," he said, drawing a well-creased twenty from his wallet.

I returned to the yard, and was halfway through the next hundred sit-ups when a shadow fell over me.

"Didn't think I'd see you back here."

"Lisa!" I jumped up and hugged her. Lisa Goodrich was the old cellmate who had given me that jittery jacks tattoo. She hadn't changed much—still stocky with a Jay Leno jaw and heavy upper body. Back then she'd been up on charges of domestic abuse. "I'd say the same about you. What's up?"

"Corey again. I love him, but when I get mad, I just can't stop myself from whaling on him."

"Jesus, girl. What did you do?"

"Nothing, Officer." She held her hands up in mock surrender. "But he's still in the hospital. Damn. I really didn't mean to hurt him."

Lisa must have had forty pounds on her bantam-weight husband, Corey. And he never fought back.

"How did you make out last time?"

"I did nine months of a three year. I'm headed back up to Perryville on Monday." She wouldn't even have to wait for a trial this time. She'd busted her parole.

"My ex–sister-in-law's up there. Paula Chatham. You'll have to look her up." I couldn't really picture my Bible-spouting ex–sister-in-law cozying up to fight-ready Lisa, but you never know. Maybe Lisa would be good protection for her.

"Have you got any visitors coming in?" Lisa might be the conduit I needed to get the cops sicced on Chaco.

"My mom's coming by tomorrow. Want her to bring you something?" Lisa swung her arms forward and back, almost simian in her gesture.

"No. But here's what I want you to tell her."

Raisa showed up on Monday morning. The same guard who'd taken me to see my father led me to the interview room where detainees met with their lawyers. It was a small space with three metal-legged chairs and a plastic laminated table. Mesh-covered fluorescent lights buzzed overhead.

I wrapped my arms around Raisa in greeting, her head mashed squarely into my chest. She smelled like freedom.

"How was your weekend?" I asked to be polite.

"Better than yours, I'm sure." She separated papers into two stacks in front of her and opened a notebook with a lined yellow pad in it. "We don't have much time. The bus to the courthouse leaves in a half hour."

"What's going to happen?"

She tapped her pencil hup-two-three on the table. "Even with a rush on it, they can't possibly have DNA results back yet. But the judge will most likely say there was probable cause for an arrest. You'll plead not guilty and they'll set a trial date."

"And if there's any new evidence that comes in that exonerates me?" I didn't know how fast the anonymous call from Lisa's mom would be acted on. Hell, I didn't know if the police would follow up on it at all. And even if they searched Chaco's car and found the knife, they still had to test the blood on it and make sure that Chaco had no alibi for the time that Reuben was killed. Shit, I wish I knew where he'd been that night we raided his uncle's place.

"What kind of new evidence?" Raisa asked, sucking the pencil like she was ready to light it.

I told her about our trek across the border and the story Ricky Lamas told about the children.

"You've got to get Deke in here. Carlos had one of the kids with him and now he's dead."

She nodded. "I'll set up a meeting with Deke, but you're going to tell an abridged story. Nothing about sneaking across the border or the knife fight with the Braceros. Just what you heard Lamas say. And I'll make sure Guillermo Ochoa knows what we're doing."

After a minute's silence, she slammed the notebook shut. "Okay. They probably won't set bail, but we'll try. Can your family come up with anything?"

"Talk to my dad. He's been working on it all weekend."

I stood up when she did, but we parted ways at the interview room door. Raisa was headed for the sunshine. I was on my way to the Corrections Center bus.

We pulled up to the back entrance of the courthouse. The men were let off first, then the four of us women in the back. Shackled at the ankles, waist, and wrists, we danced in a short conga line with clanking metal instrumentation.

The holding pen felt subterranean, cavelike in the Arizona heat.

The eleven o'clock timing of the arraignment must have been just a suggestion. I was still waiting when they brought a cheese-on-white bread sandwich at one o'clock.

At one-thirty, a guard at the end of the corridor called my name and I approached the bars. He let me out and I walked ahead of him down the hallway to the courtroom.

A woman judge today. The Honorable Rose Griffiths, the name plaque said. She had hawk eyes and a beak to go with them. Raisa stood when I came in, leaning to pat my father's hand in the first row behind her. I tried to give him a smile, but it came out like a grimace. His eyes were wide with concern.

The bailiff read the charges. First-degree murder.

Raisa did her best, saying that the state's case was purely circumstantial, that I had family in the city, and that I'd never been convicted of a crime.

Judge Griffiths seemed to have heard of me before. She dismissed that "no previous convictions" comment with the wave of a turquoise-jeweled hand.

"The defendant has no job and no permanent residence here, your honor. We ask for remand."

I spun around, gutted by the sound of that voice. It was Ted Dresden, the county attorney who had prosecuted me for Walter Racine's murder. The man who'd already tried to send me to prison for the rest of my life. The man who'd said I was "a card-carrying member of Liars Anonymous."

And now he was going to prove it.

CHAPTER TWENTY-NINE

Dresden's curly black hair was trimmed shorter now than it had been during my first trial, but he still had the raisin-sized wart below his eye. A lesser man might have had it removed just for vanity, but I'd heard Dresden tell an associate in the courtroom once that the mark was his own version of the prison-inked teardrop denoting a kill. "I'm tougher than any of these bastards," he'd said. "My ink is three-D."

"I see your point, Mr. Dresden," the judge said, bringing me back to my current dilemma. "The defendant is remanded to the custody of the Pima County Sheriff's Office." The gavel rang down. "The trial is set for"—she flipped through a poster-sized calendar—"December thirteenth."

It was over that quick, and the bailiff shooed me back toward the prisoner's door.

"Nice to see you again, Miss Gammage," Dresden whispered as I passed by. He wiped at the spot where the wart met his eye. "Second time's the charm."

· · ·

Deke and Raisa were both in the small interview room at the Detention Center the next morning as promised, but so was Detective Sabin.

"What's he doing here?"

"We're working this together," Deke said. "If you know anything pertinent about these killings, we both need to hear it."

I rolled my eyes. Sabin had never been open-minded to anything I had to say.

"I'm not going to let her testify against herself here, gentlemen," Raisa said, then nodded to me. "Go ahead, Jessie."

I swallowed hard and took the last remaining chair. "I saw Ricky Lamas and two other Braceros in the desert south of town. They were trying to take a small child from a family that had just crossed illegally—"

"What family?" Sabin asked. "Where are they?"

I ignored him. "He said the Braceros were taking children from illegals when they cross, and that Carlos Ochoa had taken a little girl that they were holding. He said some big shots in Tucson were involved."

"And you believe him because Ochoa had a child's seat in his car?" Sabin said, as if that belief stretched credulity.

I replied to Deke instead. "Children are being stolen."

"Do you know any other specifics?" he asked. "Any names, or where they take them?"

I shook my head.

Deke and Raisa both gave me a hug on the way out. Sabin was the last to leave, and he turned back to me at the conference-room door.

"I'm never going to be on your side, Ms. Gammage. I know you've killed before, and this time I'm not going to let some jury let you get away with it. But what you did here—coming forward with this—thank you. If it helps us get that child back even one hour faster . . . well, it was the right thing to do."

I took the offered butterscotch from his hand.

. . .

I settled back into jail life as if I'd never left. Up at six to stand in line for powdered eggs and cereal. Work in the laundry until twelve-thirty, then back in line for bologna on white bread. One hour outside, trying to counteract the carb-and-calorie-heavy diet. Six p.m., pressed turkey with skin-colored gravy and mashed potatoes.

The nights were long without my old friend Lisa to talk to. I became an expert on Tyra Banks and *American Idol*. No visitors. No calls. No hope. Maybe Raisa had told Guillermo and my father there was no need to come. It was more likely that Guillermo stayed away for fear of bringing police attention to himself, and my father didn't come back out of respect for my mother's wrath.

I'd become so used to other names being called during visiting hours that I didn't hear my own when it was announced.

"Gammage? You want to see this visitor?" Delta asked for a second time.

"Who is it?" Like I was going to turn down anybody at this point.

"A woman named Racine."

Catherine's aunt, Elizabeth Racine, waited in the same visitor's chair my father had taken. A pastel pantsuit, hair coiffed into that nonstyle favored by plain women in their sixties, knuckles swollen to the size of shooter marbles.

I remained standing behind the chair on my side of the glass. "I have nothing to say to you."

We glared in a mutual standoff.

"That's okay. I don't want to hear anything from you." She fingered a half-inch-thick stack of papers in front of her. "I came across this last year, in a trunk with Catherine's things." She waited a beat and then answered her own unspoken question. "I couldn't go through it before. It was . . . it hurt too much."

I waited her out.

"But then I read about your arrest in the papers. You always think you're right, don't you? Think that God gave you the right to decide who lives and dies?"

"You didn't protect Catherine. And you weren't going to protect Katie." What kind of woman would put her own flesh and blood in the way of a monster, and then defend that monster after he'd acted?

Elizabeth raised her glance to the guard leaning against the wall behind me and held up the stack of papers in her hand. "May I give her these?"

The guard reached over the glass barrier to take the papers. He thumbed through them and shrugged, placing them on the table in front of me. It was a stack of Xeroxes, in a handwriting I knew as well as my own. I kept my hands at my sides.

"They're notes from Catherine. Kind of a diary, I guess, that she was keeping for her therapist. Read it."

"If you expect me to say I'm sorry, I'm not." The killing was lodged in my heart like a stone, but I'd had to do it, no matter what the price to me. "I'm glad your husband is dead."

"I'm not." She turned and walked away.

I took the papers out to the yard and squatted down next to the post at an unused basketball court. Catherine's notebook had been small, maybe five-by-eight, with a spiral bind on the side. It was lined paper that showed up in the Xerox as a pearl gray; it might have been pink or eggshell in the original.

Elizabeth Racine could have trusted me with the real notebook. I would have protected and cherished anything of Catherine's. I wondered if it still smelled like her. I raised the loose papers to my nose. Nothing, of course. Too many degrees of separation. Too many copies of copies of heartbreak.

I slid off the rubber band.

Day one: September 19, it said. *Cambria says that it's important to tell the truth someplace, even if I can't say it out loud. It won't go any further. I don't even have to show it to her.*

Catherine had been seeing this therapist, Cambria Styles, since the beginning of the year, but that September date would have been only three weeks before she died, and three weeks after that, Walter Racine would be dead, too.

I'd been glad Catherine was getting help, at first because the divorce had taken such a toll on her, then those last weeks because I thought the therapist could help her come to terms with the abuse I now knew about.

I flipped to the next page. *I always wanted the middle name Eloise. Maybe be if I just start using it, it will become real. Catherine Eloise Chandliss.*

At first, Catherine had been quiet after a visit to Cambria. Later she came back from her appointments giddy with strength and fortitude. I thought the therapy was helping.

The next entry said: *I have mother's nipples. Not MY mother's nipples, just breasts that announce I've had a child. Huge. Brown. Thumb shaped. A baby's chew toy. Not that I'd trade Katie for anything. But it would be nice to have the body I had ten years ago. The body Glen fell in love with. Now, if I meet someone new, I can't lie about who I am. My breasts betray me.*

I'd never understood why Glen had left her. I'd heard three different versions from Catherine—all of them blaming him—and was sure there were many more that both sides could have come up with.

As I finished each page, I turned it facedown on the asphalt beside me. The air was still and heavy, no breeze to disturb the pile.

Later pages were a tirade against her aunt and uncle for having taken Glen's side in the divorce. At least that's the way she saw it. I hadn't thought the rest of the family was siding with him as much as they were telling her to learn to get along with him from a distance, for Katie's sake.

Uncle Walter said that I brought it on myself, she wrote. *That I wished Glen away. I'll show him. I'll show them all.*

Three pages on, I tripped over my own name. *Have to tell Jessie,* it said. *I've imagined it for so long that it seems real to me now. All the details. The fear. The anger. Well, the anger was real enough, although not quite the way I told her.*

What was not quite the way she'd told me? Did she think that somehow she'd seduced her Uncle Walter, coerced him into molestation? The therapist could have helped her with that. There was no way that Walter Racine would have been able to blame the victim for his crime.

I flipped through more pages. She'd used the diary for any kind of note taking: to-do lists (*brownies for Katie's playdate*), appointments (*Jessie/12:30 at El Charro*) and short bad poems. The last entry was two days before Catherine's car had plunged into the flooded arroyo.

It's gone too far. I have to stop it. Jessica, dear friend who believes in me, has taken my cause in hand. She's stronger than I am. I know she'll succeed. And then what? I'll have to live with this lie for the rest of my life. I'm going to show this to Cambria. She's right. I can't stop lying to the rest of the world until I stop lying to myself.

Poor Catherine. She had felt somehow responsible for her abuse. What might she have done, if that wall of water in a normally dry arroyo hadn't taken her life that night? Tell me to back off my campaign against her uncle? Leave town with Katie? The diary made it sound like she'd come to some decision.

I wiped away a tear, and returned to the last page. It was dated the day before Catherine died, and said simply, *"I'm going to do it*

right this time. No more stories. No more lies. I'm going to live in the
real world starting now. I wanted to get Uncle Walter in trouble be-
cause of how mean he was about Glen. I hope he can forgive me."

I jumped to my feet—every nerve end on fire, the breath frozen
in my chest—and charged the razor-wire fence in front of me. A
siren shrieked, angry voices sputtered and cawed through a loudspeaker, but I climbed, fingers clawing at the diamond grids in the
wire, higher, higher, to reach enough air so that I could breathe.
My vision dimmed until there was just a pinprick of light ahead
of me. Suddenly, strong hands grabbed my legs and I was thrown
backward to the ground, then tackled—face pressed into the
asphalt—and handcuffed.

Dear God, what had I done? I'd killed a man for no good reason
at all. And then, God help me, I'd set about getting away with it.

My legs wouldn't hold me, so four Corrections Officers dragged
me across the yard by my manacled arms. I watched, struck dumb
with regret and shame, as a fifth officer gathered the loose pages of
the diary and tamped them back into a pile.

My sin, written out in longhand.

CHAPTER THIRTY

Eight days passed in a cloud of recriminations and gut-shredding loss. Realizing that the image in the mirror is the monster and not the savior you've built yourself up to be. Recognizing that you truly belong in that jail cell for the rest of your life.

They weren't calling my run at the fence an escape attempt, but I spent the next week first in the medical ward, then in an isolation cell so they could watch me. Every breath caused pain. They said I'd cracked a rib, but I knew it to be my newly burdened conscience, sparking to life every time I inhaled.

Raisa came by and expected a smile when she said, "I may be able to get you out of here."

I toyed with the ragged sleeve of my jailhouse scrubs. "How?"

"The DNA results came in. You matched the pool of blood in the garage, but the cops also proved that Carlos had been dead almost a week by then. That, plus no witness ID, means they can't hold you for Carlos's murder."

"No witness ID?" Sabin had been so confident after that lineup. Raisa shook her head. "The neighbor didn't ID you. Said she couldn't be sure. She recognized the car but said she only got a look at the back of the driver's head."

"They'll still hold me for the other guy—Reuben whatever."

"Maybe not. They can prove you were there, but not that it was the same time Reuben Sanchez was killed. The time of death is too big a window."

I nodded distractedly. Why hadn't the cops followed up on the tip to check on the knife in Chaco's car? That would have given them another suspect they could tie to Reuben's death. Maybe Lisa's mom never made the call.

"Sabin will probably stall," Raisa said. "Use the arrest warrant as a lever to get you to talk about who else was there that night. You could be out of here today if you told him."

I shook my head.

"Okay. Hold tight. He doesn't have much of a case left. I'll see if I can get a judge to dismiss."

I shrugged, remembering the revelations in Catherine's diary. If her words were true, I didn't deserve to be set free.

It took another week for the dismissal to come though. When Corrections Officer Delta came to get me at two o'clock the next Friday afternoon, I handed over the scrubs and plastic shoes and they gave me back Catherine's diary and twenty-nine dollars from my account. Damn. More money than when they booked me. But I had more crimes to my credit now, too.

I walked out to the road and waited for a bus back into town; back to join the living. First thing on the agenda was some real food. The kind that makes you chew before you swallow. Second, find Catherine's therapist and get the truth.

My truck was still in front of Bonita's house. I gathered up the flyers and junk mail that had arrived during my three weeks in jail, tossed them in the trash, then took a long, hot shower, trying to wash away my recriminations as well as the jailhouse funk.

I stopped at a hole-in-the-wall Mexican restaurant for a plate of tongue tacos, then headed east toward Cambria Styles's office.

The building was one of three small bungalows on a cul-de-sac behind the Tucson Mall. Oleanders bloomed head high against the windows. It was close to five o'clock; I didn't know if the therapist would still be there.

I crunched up the gravel drive and had raised my hand to knock when I read the sign on the door. PLEASE COME IN AND REMAIN IN THE WAITING ROOM. I'LL COME GET YOU WHEN I'M FREE. I let myself into a pleasant, quiet waiting area that contained a small secretary's desk, three upholstered armchairs, and a glass-topped coffee table. *Sierra Club*, *Arizona Highways*, and *Field & Stream* magazines fanned out across the glass. Nothing there to stir a patient's frantic mind.

I didn't have to wait long. At ten minutes to five I heard a door open and footsteps across the front gravel. I peeked through the blinds and oleander leaves to see a walrus-shaped man trudging toward a black car at the curb. The interior door to the office opened and Cambria Styles caught me peering out.

"Did we have an appointment?"

Styles hadn't changed much in the three years since I'd seen her—she still had dishwater-blond hair, poker-straight almost to her waist, and sallow skin like she was an underwater creature. I reintroduced myself.

"I was a friend of Catherine Chandliss's. We met when I dropped her off here a couple of months before she died."

Her eyes widened as she remembered the other associations with my name. Catherine's friend, accused of killing her uncle. There would be no handshake.

"How can I help you?" she said, taking a step back. Clearly the woman thought I needed therapeutic help of one kind or another.

"Have you ever seen this before?" I held out the banded stack of pages from Catherine's diary.

"What is it?" She stripped off the rubber band and flipped through it.

"Catherine's notes. The ones you told her to write to tell herself the truth."

"I didn't think she'd even . . ." Her voice faded as she continued to read. She seemed fascinated by the pages. If she'd ever seen them before, she was putting on a good act.

"I want to know if what she wrote is the truth."

"I don't understand."

"Is this the truth—or is it some kind of therapy game? That's all I want to know."

"I couldn't possibly . . . without studying it . . . Catherine was—"

"Read it."

Styles looked at her watch, then tapped the pages back into a stack on the desk. "It will take some time. Why don't you make an appointment for next week and then we can—".

"I'll wait." I settled myself into one of the upholstered chairs.

She sighed and took the swivel chair behind the desk. She read a few pages, then stopped at one of the sections I'd marked with two dark vertical lines in the margin. "Excuse me a moment. I want to check something." She retreated to her private office and came back a moment later with a file in her hand, then continued reading.

I studied photos of the Grand Canyon and trout. An unseen clock ticked like a loud, slow metronome.

After twenty minutes, she slapped her own file shut and restacked Catherine's loose pages.

"You were tried for the murder of Catherine's uncle."

"Yes." No need to go into the equivocation about being found not guilty.

"And you want to know if she was ever really molested, is that it?"

I nodded. I wasn't breathing. Once again waiting for the verdict.

"What difference would that make? Either you killed a man or you didn't. Either he was guilty or he was innocent. What are you going to do with the information?"

I tried to shrug, but the tension kept my shoulders tight up around my ears. "I have to know. Was Catherine molested? Was her daughter in danger?"

She put down the pencil she'd been chewing on and steepled her fingers.

"I'll tell you what I told the police back then, when they were following up on your accusation about Mr. Racine. In all our months of therapy, Catherine never gave me any indication that her uncle had abused her. She never mentioned it."

"Maybe it takes more than a few months of therapy to get around to it."

"Sometimes. After you were arrested, I actually wondered if you'd seen something I hadn't."

"Had I?" I'd heard Catherine's accusations in the weeks before she died. And I had seen Walter Racine with Katie in the playground. Wasn't that proof of abuse?

She tapped the diary with a forefinger. "Not according to Catherine."

I shut the front door quietly behind me. I'd forgotten to take Catherine's notes, but that didn't matter. I'd memorized all the important parts. They were words I'd never forget. A death sentence.

I got back to Bonita's house and plugged in my cell phone. The battery had gone dead in the Corrections Center property closet and it wasn't until it started charging that I heard the beeps for waiting messages.

No one had called during my early days in jail. Guillermo had called twice today. The last message, listed at 2:30 p.m., was from my father. "Jessie, Raisa told us you're getting out today. Do you need a ride home? Deke's here at the house with me. Call me when you get this message."

My fingers traced the familiar pattern of the buttons.

"I'm back at Bonita's house, Dad."

"We'll be right over."

I wasn't sure if I could keep up a happy façade around him. And Deke hadn't done me any favors. He'd stood by and watched Len Sabin railroad me into an arrest with insufficient evidence.

"No need. Everything's okay."

"Ten minutes."

It was actually fifteen, but by the time they got there I hadn't had a chance to do much more than throw out the spoiled food in the refrigerator and wipe the worst of the dust and grime from the few remaining pieces of furniture.

"I'm glad they dropped the charges," my father said, enveloping me in a bear hug.

"I'm glad to see you home," Deke said over my father's shoulder.

No thanks to you, I wanted to say. Where were you when Len Sabin was filling out that arrest warrant? "Do you know any more about the kids?" I asked instead.

"Not yet." Deke ducked his head and addressed his comments to the floor. "We picked up Ricky Lamas but he's not talking."

"It's got something to do with Darren Markson and those day-care centers. I know it does. Have you checked them out? And did you test that car seat?"

"We got DNA from the seat, but we've got nothing to match it to. Jesus, Jessie. Don't you know when to butt out? Didn't three weeks in jail teach you anything?"

I didn't have any evidence I hadn't told him about except a wet kiss between two women in a parking lot, and that was hardly proof of murder. "Those day-care centers are the only things that tie everything—Markson, Felicia, Carlos Ochoa, Reuben Sanchez— together."

"How do we know Reuben Sanchez had anything to do with the day-care centers?"

"We don't," I admitted.

"Maybe the whole thing is drug related, and Darren Markson was just in the wrong place at the wrong time," Deke suggested.

"But Felicia worked for his attorney. That's not just a coincidence."

"Enough already!" my father interrupted. "We came by to see if you were okay, Jessie. Maybe go get some dinner."

"I'm okay, Dad. Thanks. I just want to be alone tonight."

I spotted a ballerina and a tiny skeleton through the open doorway, faces covered with masks and makeup, open bags in their arms. "Trick or treat!"

My heart caught in my throat. Jesus, it was Halloween. The third anniversary of my crime. But the first day that I truly knew to call it such a thing. Three years ago, I, too, had been a masked reveler on the street, but in my case, a killer hiding in a white sheet.

"I'm sorry, kids. I forgot. I don't have any candy."

Their shoulders slumped, losers at this new game their first time out. They were turning back toward their mother at the curb when my dad called out, "Here, I've got something for you!" He dropped two quarters into each bag.

"Thanks, Dad." He saw the smile, but also the sadness in my eyes.

"I know this is a hard time of year for you, Jessie. Catherine's accident . . . having to deal with the police. But you've got to put it all behind you." Unwavering in his support, he misunderstood the reason for my grief.

"Does Mom have the altar done yet?" Although she wouldn't

light the Day of the Dead candles until tomorrow, I was sure she'd be populating the shrine by now.

"Almost."

Would I ever have a place on my mother's table of remembrance? Maybe she'd find my old adoption papers, fold them small, and tuck them between two candles at the back of the table. Maybe a bullet casing to memorialize the killer I'd become.

I walked my father out to the front porch and this time allowed Deke a hug as well. They got in the car and left it idling at the curb until a flock of small Halloween superheroes ran past them and reached the sidewalk safely.

Sighing, I stooped to pick up a palm-sized rock at my feet. It was a broken shard of agate, the dull brown exterior belying the shiny gray swirls inside. There was a notch on one side just big enough for my thumb and a razor-sharp ribboned edge, like lethal taffy, on the other. If I held it there, thumb cradled into the depression, I could be a cave woman, hollow out the trunk of a tree for a canoe, scrape the skin of a vanquished animal. Or I could rake that edge across my own flesh—a slow, purposeful stripe of pain—and make all the regret disappear.

It would be easy. Quiet. My blood would sink into the gravel and refresh some shallow-rooted desert plant. I'd get rid of the pain. I'd never hurt anyone or disappoint anyone again.

I caressed the dark edge with my thumb, identifying my own ridges and whorls with the stony blade, then turned to go back into the house.

Not yet. The blade would still be here tomorrow. I could wait.

CHAPTER THIRTY-ONE

I pulled the sheet up over my eyes, ignoring the sun flooding into the bedroom.

Three years ago my meddling had cost Walter Racine his life. How much more damage had I done this time? Had Felicia died because someone saw her talking to me? I wouldn't shoulder the burden of Carlos's and Reuben's deaths—they brought that on themselves. And Markson had been killed without any help from me at all.

The air-conditioning was off and I sweated through the sheets like a purification ceremony, but it was a ritual with no release. My cell phone rang every half hour or so. I ignored it.

By afternoon, I'd made it to the living room, a hand of solitaire arrayed on the carpet between my outstretched legs. I couldn't win a hand even when I cheated.

I heard hammering at the front door.

"Go away," I said from my seat on the floor.

Guillermo peeked through the window, then let himself in.

"Raisa told me you got out and I've been calling since yesterday. I've been worried."

I dealt myself another card, a queen. No place to put it. I threw the cards across the room.

"What about the kids? What about that little girl in the car seat?" Was she still alive? And an even more gut-twisting question: Was she safe?

"We've done everything we could," he said.

"Maybe not everything." I told him about Willard's and Markson's kiss in the day-care parking lot.

"So you think the Willards killed Markson to keep their love life a secret? And then killed Felicia and Carlos?"

Guillermo was right. It didn't seem like a secret worth killing over. However, maybe threatening to make it public would get the lawyer to open up about other things.

"Let's go ask the man."

The offices of Willard, Levin and Pratt were in a converted adobe house, right at the twisty bit of Pima near the Arizona Inn. The circular drive was anchored by a hundred-year-old palo verde in the center of the yard. We parked on the east side of the building and went in. A thin older woman with cat's-eye glasses rose from the chair at the reception desk as we entered.

"I was just closing up," she said, indicating the blank computer screen at her side. "Did you have an appointment?"

"We're here to see Paul Willard. Tell him it's Jessie Dancing from HandsOn." If he was part of the attack on Darren Markson, my name alone might be enough to spook him.

She nodded and left the waiting area through an arched doorway on the right. She was back a moment later with a smile. "Mr. Willard only has a few minutes, but you're welcome to come in." She showed us down the hallway and into an oversized room with a kiva fireplace in the corner.

"Would you like me to stay, Mr. Willard?" she asked.

"That's okay, Serena. I won't be more than a couple of minutes myself. You can head home."

She backed out and shut the heavy wooden door behind her. I sat down in the guest chair and Guillermo took up a position near the door.

"Serena?" I asked him. "She must be the one that Felicia Villalobos was reporting to here for her internship." Serena McDowell had been the starred name in Felicia's notebook.

Willard did a double take, probably associating my name with the day we met at Emily Markson's house and nothing else. "I believe she was, but I didn't know much about what Ms. Villalobos was doing."

"Right. Like you don't know that Emily Markson never talked to her husband in New Mexico. Like you don't know what your wife and next-door neighbor are doing."

"What are you insinuating, Ms. Dancing?"

"No insinuations. Just facts. There's no way Emily Markson could have talked to her husband in New Mexico. He was attacked, beaten up, and killed in Tucson. And she and your wife are having an affair. All I want to know is whether it's just the two of them, or are you part of this as well? You like threesomes, do you?"

"Who are you? What do you want?" he said, belatedly realizing that a HandsOn operator had no business asking these questions. I stayed seated.

"Was Darren Markson part of this sex show, or did you three keep it all to yourselves? All those bruises on Emily's arms. And an e-mail to her about meeting at the riverbed. It was signed 'A.' 'A' as in Aloma. Was your wife involved in Markson's death, too?"

"That's enough! Aloma had nothing at all to do with Darren."

"Then what were your wife and Mrs. Markson doing at the day-care center together? Are they part of this child abduction ring, too?" I didn't have any facts to back up the assertion, but maybe the jab would cause a counterpunch on his part.

He jumped to his feet and slammed his palms on the desk. "Get out! Now!"

"We can always ask the cops the same questions. Or the newspapers," Guillermo said.

"Get a clue, you two. My client Darren Markson is dead, and we're going to have to sell the management contract for the day-care centers. I'm just trying to shut them down gradually so nobody gets left in the lurch. Aloma was there helping her friend. End of story."

"It looked like a whole different kind of help, with her lips locked around her neighbor in the car," I said.

He raised both hands in a "what am I going to do?" gesture. "That's private. We're consenting adults. . . ."

It looked like the tryst I'd witnessed that morning at the Markson house was a three-way affair.

The door banged open, pinning Guillermo against the wall.

"Robert, thank God. Get these people out of here."

Robert Levin. Heavy eyebrows. Dark hair retreating in an ox-bow shape. I recognized his face from the newspaper photo of the groundbreaking ceremony for the day-care center. What I didn't recognize was the gun in his hand.

Guillermo slid out from behind the door and grabbed at Levin's gun arm. Levin spun away from him and backed toward Willard.

"Down on the floor, both of you."

"Just get them out of here, Robert," his partner said.

"I heard them ask about the day-care centers." Levin's gaze pinballed from Willard to the two of us on the floor.

"I was just saying that I proposed Emily Markson shut them down—"

"I can't let that happen. It would ruin what's taken a long time to set up."

"I don't—"

"Get over there on the floor with them, Paul." It looked like I'd picked the wrong attorney as the bad guy.

Levin opened a tall cabinet behind Willard's desk and rummaged through it until he found a roll of duct tape, and tossed it to Willard. "Tie their hands behind them."

"Robert, I don't understand."

"Oh, I understand, all right," I said, rolling toward Willard. "Your partner has been working with Darren Markson and the Bracero gang to set up a smooth-running child-abduction ring. They kidnap children coming across the border illegally, stash them at the day-care centers, and then sell them. Isn't that right, Mr. Levin? The parents can't get anybody to pay attention because they're illegals, and they've either scattered or been deported after you've taken their children." In some cases, they were probably in jail, like Raisa's two clients, twisting in nightmares about the day their child was ripped from their arms.

I wondered why they hadn't left the legal side of the day-care business to Levin. That way they wouldn't have had to deal with Willard at all. But maybe this kind of legal work was Willard's specialty and it would have looked weird to have another lawyer in the firm take it over. Above all, they would have wanted everything to look normal.

"Shut up or I'll tape your mouth, too," Levin said.

"You're lying," Willard said to me as he wrapped the tape tightly around my wrists. "Darren Markson would never have been party to that kind of scheme. Nor would my partner."

Willard was wrong. Darren Markson must have grown a conscience, and he convinced Carlos and Felicia to help him. That signed their death warrants.

"On your feet," Levin said. Willard helped us up, then followed

Levin's pointed gun out to the hall and toward the back of the office. Levin looked both ways out the back door and hustled us to a minivan in the back lot. The rear seats were pushed flat and he shoved us into the cargo area. I skidded across the rubber flooring on my chin.

Paul Willard got into the driver's seat and Levin rode shotgun, his gun aimed at his partner's gut.

"Robert, this is insane," Willard tried. "We've got to let them go."

"Shut up and drive."

He pointed west. I hoped the lawyer would be strong enough to resist, to crash the car or drive it straight to a police station, but he followed Levin's instructions to a T. Maybe he wasn't a brave man or maybe he had another plan. In all likelihood, he probably still thought he could talk his way out of it.

Guillermo and I scooted closer to each other and I began clawing the tape off his hands. Levin spotted us and smashed the gun butt down on Guillermo's head.

"You—over there." He motioned me to the far side of the van with the gun barrel. I inched over to the side panel and leaned back against it. A ray of setting sun lanced through the back window. It was already the Day of the Dead.

It was only twenty minutes before Levin directed Willard to turn into a driveway. The minivan door slid open. No blindfolds. He wasn't worried about us telling anyone where we were.

Levin pulled me out of the cargo area by my hair, and my eyes filled with tears from the pain. When my vision cleared I recognized the rambling adobe: Chaco's house. Levin prodded the three of us up the path.

Unlike the first two times I'd been here, there were already cars in the driveway: Chaco's dark Cadillac, a green Jaguar, and a low-rider that looked remarkably similar to the one that had followed me around town.

"What are you doing here?" the young man at the door said, the XI tattoo on his arm clearly visible as he leaned against the jamb.

"Let us in, Bobby."

Not Bob Eleven, after all. Bobby Levin. Robert Jr.

Fuck. They should have just shot me for being stupid.

CHAPTER THIRTY-TWO

Bobby stepped back into the room and ushered us in. The remains of a beer and pizza dinner spilled across the counter in the kitchen, abandoned where it had first been torn into after being carried in. Chaco himself sprawled in one of the black leather chairs, TV remote in one hand and a slice of pizza in the other.

I tried to keep the shakes out of my voice. "You killed Carlos, didn't you, Bobby?" Bobby Levin with the dreadlocks beard and dark, wild eyes. He was the real threat in the Bracero gang. "And Felicia, too," I continued.

"Last fucking time I use a bomb," the kid said. "Almost blew myself up putting it in."

Chaco giggled, more amused by us than by the football game on the flat-screen TV. Robert Senior busied himself checking messages on his BlackBerry and Paul Willard stood as stiff as the Tin Man in the middle of the room.

"So what happened that night by the riverbed?" I slumped to the red-stained concrete floor and kept working at the tape behind me. "Markson and Ochoa had taken a child from the day-care center, right? Were they going to shut you down or turn you in?" My guess was that they were going to rescue as many kids as they could. If they had gone to the cops, they'd be in trouble for their involvement, too.

"Darren wanted to shut it down," a female voice said behind me.

I spun around. Of course. The Jaguar out front. Emily Markson crossed the room, picked a slice of pepperoni off the pizza, and ate it.

"You told Chaco and Bobby where your husband would be that night, didn't you?" I'd wondered how they'd known to be at the arroyo; both Markson and Carlos Ochoa would have noticed if they were being followed.

She shrugged. "The kids are worth a hell of a lot more than he was bringing home from that damn real estate business."

"But, Em," Paul Willard said. "You always told me—"

She didn't even glance at him. "Shut up. I only put up with you and your wife's stupid games in case we needed to keep you in line."

The elder Levin popped the tab on a Tecate and took a swig. He tipped the can in Willard's direction. "We'll need to get rid of him now, too."

"Okay." His son grabbed the gun from his waistband and—no hesitation, no reflection—shot Paul Willard in the forehead. Willard fell like a stringless puppet, brain and blood and bone scattered behind his crumpled form.

"You idiot!" Emily Markson said. "You should have made it look like an accident!"

The kid shrugged again. "Then he should have said that."

My vision dimmed. I tried to take regular breaths. A little in. A little out. If they could kill the lawyer that easily, then disposing of Guillermo and me would be no problem at all.

I flashed back to the night of the phone call from Markson. He'd been waiting there at the cottonwood tree for Carlos to come take the little girl from him. Maybe Carlos came in too fast, and hadn't intended to rear-end him. Markson had covered it well enough with me on the phone. He hadn't sounded scared. Not until that third voice showed up. That third voice. Bobby Levin. A boy who could kill without even raising his blood pressure. Had Emily Markson been there, too? Maybe that's why she'd wanted to hear the HandsOn tape; to make sure her own voice wasn't recorded.

I glanced over at Guillermo, who had managed to uncurl a good eight inches of duct tape from his hands. The senior Levin seemed fascinated by the blood pool seeping from Paul Willard's head. The two Braceros had returned their attention to the football game and Emily had gone back into the bedroom, none of them troubled by the dead man or the spreading pool of blood on the floor.

Had Emily also watched them kill her husband two days later? He might have died right here in this house. Maybe Chaco's red floor had been colored that way on purpose, to hide the blood he knew might be there someday.

I stood slowly, my partially unwrapped hands behind me, and leaned against the dining room table. With one final tug, I broke free of the duct tape, grabbed the car keys off the table, and pushed the alarm button. The Cadillac out front responded with a shriek. I tossed the keys in the only place I knew they'd be difficult to retrieve: under the refrigerator. Guillermo moved, lunging for Bobby Levin and crashing to the floor. Hands gouging, they rolled against Chaco's seat, pinning his legs against the chair. I grabbed a full beer can and hurled it at the lawyer. He didn't see it coming, and it smacked his temple with a thud. He went down.

Emily Markson ran back into the room, this time with a gun in her hand. She raised her arm in Guillermo's direction.

I let out a roar and ran toward her, lowering my head below the level of the raised gun and crashing into her. She staggered back into the bedroom and the gun flew from her hand. We followed it to the floor, each kicking and clawing with one hand, the other blindly groping under the bed in a desperate race to reach the weapon.

Emily got to the gun first, but before she could pull it from under the bed, I rolled off her and ran to the barbell in the corner. It was almost a hundred and fifty pounds—more than I'd ever lifted before. Could I do it? One exhalation, bend the knees and lift with every ounce of energy and adrenaline I'd ever known. Up.

The movement caught me unbalanced and I spun around, a hundred and fifty pounds of lead weight careening like a windmill. Emily rolled over on her back and aimed the gun at my face.

I let the bar drop straight across her throat.

I kicked the gun across the room. She was pinned by a weight she couldn't move, but the plates were tall enough that the bar hadn't crushed her neck. I panted, hands on my thighs, for the space of three heartbeats, then ran back to help Guillermo.

I took hold of Bobby's long, tangled beard and yanked. He howled as the strands pulled away in my hand, but didn't loosen his grip on the gun. Guillermo had both hands around Bobby's gun wrist, forcing the barrel away from his face.

Chaco kicked at the tangle of men at his feet and dug in the seat cushion for his own weapon. I grabbed a floor lamp and swung it hard at his face. It didn't make a solid connection, but at least it distracted him.

A child's muted wail came from the next room and my heart caught in my throat. Where? I hadn't seen a child in the bedroom.

Then a gunshot split the air and Chaco's chest blossomed with a new red rose. A stray shot from Guillermo's battle with Bobby had found a different target.

Guillermo bucked hard and rolled on top of the last Bracero. They could have been statues, frozen nose to nose with only their panting breath to give away the pantomime. Four hands gripped the gun between them.

Another shot. I held my breath, then watched Guillermo close his eyes and slip sideways as the young Bracero squirmed out from under him.

Bobby gave me just a moment's glance, then turned and ran out the sliding glass door in the back and zigzagged from cactus to cactus up the sloped hill and into the darkening night.

I knelt at Guillermo's side. The bullet had grazed his temple and blood oozed down his face and neck. His eyes blinked slowly. He was still alive.

"I need help!" I screamed into the phone I found in the kitchen. "Ambulance! Police! Three people shot. One on the loose! And call Deke Treadwell!" I gave them Chaco's address then turned back to Guillermo. "Stay with me. You're going to be okay."

"The wife?" he asked.

"She'll live."

I glanced over at Robert Levin. He was still unconscious, but I made sure he wasn't going anywhere by tying his hands and feet with the cord from the floor lamp. I picked up the gun he'd threatened us with and placed it in Guillermo's lap.

A cry from the bedroom set me in motion again. In taking care of Guillermo and getting help, I'd forgotten all about that previous wail.

On the floor, Emily Markson squirmed to rid herself of the weights, but the bar across her neck kept her down.

Where was the little girl?

The sound was coming from the metal footlocker at the end of the bed. Two air holes had been drilled in the side. I unhooked the latches and pulled the lid open. A brown-haired three-year-old girl blinked away tears and recoiled into the far corner of the trunk.

"Hush, hush, it's going to be okay." My God, had she been here all along? Imprisoned in that trunk the day I was here raiding the car keys but too afraid to make a noise?

I lifted her from the metal tomb, singing soft nonsense syllables to quiet her, repeating them in a slow cadence until they sounded like two pieces of silk rubbing together.

I returned to the living room, cradling her like an overgrown doll. Chaco and Paul Willard's blood had mingled into a work of macabre art on the floor. Guillermo had managed to prop himself up against the black couch and held a wad of paper napkins to his temple. His face was pale, but his eyes tracked me as I moved.

After Guillermo tucked Levin's gun under his thigh, I set the little girl down next to him on the floor. He cradled her face against his chest, blocking much of her view of death and gore. She seemed to settle there, giving soft mewling sounds and rocking softly against him.

I stooped to pick up Bobby's gun from the corner. A little triangular piece of hard rubber was missing from the grip. I'd been right about who ransacked my house. It was Catherine's gun, used in a homicide the police could no longer try me for. But now it had new deaths to its credit.

The car alarm continued to scream from the front yard. I pushed aside the pizza box on the table. There, shoved under a flyer for free brake inspections, was a box of .38s. I loaded the gun.

"The cops are on their way," Guillermo said, watching me spin the cylinder and click it into place.

"Make sure she gets back to her parents."

"You don't have to do this. They'll catch him."

"I know. So will I." I didn't have time to explain, but I was surer now than I'd ever been. I knew what I had to do.

I followed the first three zigzags I'd seen Bobby Levin make as he ran. Saguaro to cholla and back to duck behind a saguaro again. It looked like he'd slid at that point, leaving boot-heel gashes in the dirt. Twilight was deepening, I wouldn't be able to see the tracks much longer.

A steep rocky hillside rose only a couple hundred yards from Chaco's back door. I looked up. He was up there somewhere.

I climbed about a hundred feet, using only one hand to scramble up so I could keep the LadySmith out of the dirt. No sounds until the wail of an approaching siren echoed off the dark rock. I turned to look back at the house; a small army of police and fire trucks were turning into Chaco's driveway, lights spinning like a carnival ride.

A cascade of dirt and pebbles to my left told me that Bobby Levin had heard the same thing and was on the move. I kept climbing; the old gash in my calf now no more than a goad, spurring me on. Another fifty feet up, the mountain ran out of dirt and reverted to its primitive volcanic self. Black spires of craggy rock offered few footholds but lots of places to hide.

"Come on down, Bobby! The cops are right behind me. You won't get away!" No response. As far as I could tell, I was the only one of us with a gun, but that didn't make me feel any better.

I scanned the shadowed hillside and settled on what looked like a javelina track between the largest outcroppings. The wind was light. No sound but the garbled radio transmissions from the cops below echoed around the canyon.

I moved cautiously around a barrel cactus in the narrow path and heard a groan. Bobby Levin slumped against a stony ledge, both hands holding his right knee.

"Hurt yourself?"

"Fuck you."

I held the gun steady. Only eight feet away, I couldn't miss.

"Give it up, Bobby." I gestured with the gun for him to precede me down the hillside.

He panted, head hung down. I watched, transfixed, as his hand dropped from his knee to his boot. He came up snarling and clicked open the long, dark knife in his hand. He lunged at me, swiping right to left at waist level.

I pulled the trigger.

.

I told myself that I would have killed him anyway—that's why I had chased him up the mountainside—but I wondered if I really could have done it without provocation. Bobby had saved me from finding out.

I scooped up the knife that had dropped from his fingers and flung it as far as I could to the west. Deke would have no reason to look for it there.

I was sitting cross-legged on the ground next to Bobby's body when Deke and two uniformed officers reached me.

"What happened, Jessie? Are you all right?" Deke's voice was ragged with exertion and anxiety.

"I killed him."

"In self-defense?"

I shook my head.

"Don't say anything else," he cautioned, turning to look at the two cops behind him. "We'll get you a good lawyer."

"Don't need one, Deke. I'm pleading guilty."

"I'm so sorry about this," he said, cuffing my hands in front for the trip down the steep hill.

Poor Deke. He'd tried so hard and for so long to believe in my innocence, but this time there was no way he could ignore my criminality. Sabin would have no trouble with my guilt. Neither would I.

But I did have one condition as part of my guilty plea: I wanted to make a Day of the Dead altar before going to jail. Deke was the first to agree. Len Sabin and the prosecutor, Ted Dresden, soon followed suit.

We made quite a crowd there at the cottonwood tree by the arroyo the next day. It was November 2, the last day of the Day of the Dead celebration.

Guillermo's head wound had been wrapped and the doctors had cleared him to come with us. He'd brought pictures of Carlos and Felicia. I looped thin pieces of string through pinprick holes and hung them on the highest branches I could reach.

My dad brought a picture of Catherine, and had clipped a newspaper photo of Paul Willard and—my own private shame—Walter Racine. I gave Catherine and Walter pride of place, tucked into the strongest crook of the tree at eye level.

Darren Markson, Reuben Sanchez, Chaco, and Bobby Levin were on their own. They had been masters of their own destinies and had no business being remembered on my Day of the Dead altar.

I wondered if Aloma Willard ever put together an altar, and whether she would now yearn for the day that she could add Emily Markson to the list of the dead. I'd heard that Emily had hired my old pal Buckley Thurber to defend her. If he did his usual stellar job, she'd be growing old in prison. Unless Emily and I got assigned to the same facility, that is.

I placed a dozen votive candles around the base of the tree and lit them, although it was still too bright out for the candlelight to be seen. Just like the ghosts of all those children taken by the Braceros, the Marksons, and Robert Levin; young lives whose flames had not had a chance to blaze brightly enough.

A lavender smudge, in honor of the birth mother I'd never met, curled wispy gray smoke toward the group. I added a long pink satin ribbon for Catherine's child and the unclaimed three-year-old from the trunk. Deke told me that her first name was Baila—Dance—but they hadn't found her parents yet. As it should be,

I thought. One Dancing ends her old life and another girl named Dance starts a new one.

I strung another card to the tree. That optical illusion drawing of a vase—or was it two faces in profile?—that was what I'd been doing the last three years. Looking at one image but not recognizing the truth of the other. I'd only seen the hard lines of the vase—Catherine's story about the abuse—and not the faces, the truth. I'd even misinterpreted Racine's actions that day he pushed Katie on the swing. It had been a proud, loving great-uncle's gaze, not that of a predator. My guilty plea now was the only way I could, even in part, pay my dues to Walter Racine and his family.

Guillermo was lost to me now, and he, too, had to be remembered on the altar. Giving him up, saying good-bye to whatever possibilities we might have had, would be one of the hardest parts of my incarceration. I lit an orange candle to signal a change of plans and to open new roads for him.

Mad Cow had taken the day off and driven down from Phoenix. She was the only one with tears in her eyes. The rest of us were already too steeped in pain to cry.

"Can I come visit you?" she asked.

I laughed and hugged her. "Yes. And you just won the Dumb Question contest."

Finally, I knelt between the tree trunk and the orange candle and tucked away the broken shard of agate that I'd fingered, contemplating my own suicide. I'd built up a hard shell of anger these last three years, but could feel it melting away, leaving me strangely calm and at peace there in the clearing.

Deke gave me a few minutes, then stepped behind me and gently held my wrists in place for the handcuffs.

"I don't understand, Jessie. You could have said it was self-defense. Nobody could prove you wrong."

The wind came up, twirling the cards and photos and threatening the tiny flames.

"But it wasn't."

The undisputed queen of Liars Anonymous was back.